IF WE SURVIVE THE NIGHT

IF WE SURVIVE THE NIGHT

JO SALAZAR

sourcebooks
fire

Published by Sourcebooks Fire, an imprint of Sourcebooks
1935 Brookdale Rd, Naperville, IL 60563-2773
(630) 961-3900
sourcebooks.com

Originally self-published as *The Dead Weight* in 2024 by Jo Salazar.

Cataloging-in-Publication Data is on file with the Library of Congress.

Printed and bound in the United States of America.
PAH 10 9 8 7 6 5 4 3 2 1

For the girls

CHAPTER 1

I can hear footsteps slapping the linoleum a few feet outside my open doorway. The morning shift is here.

I roll myself out of bed before Ms. Michelle can tell me to wake up. It's a small and probably futile act of rebellion, but I hate the look on her face when she tells me what to do. I won't give her the satisfaction today. By the time she gets to my door I'll be in my bathroom brushing my teeth. She might even give me a compliance point for it.

I already hear January screaming from the door closest to the staff's workstation. I'm pretty sure they put her there on purpose so they don't need to walk so far when they have to deal with her tantrums, which is just lazy, if you ask me.

"Shut the fuck up, Jan!" Tracy yells groggily from her room across the hall. It's times like these I wish they let us have doors.

"Two demerits for swearing, Tracy. Please try to have a little more compassion for January today," Ms. Michelle chirps. I imagine her pausing to make note of Tracy's two demerits on her clipboard and roll my eyes. Her footsteps continue.

When Ms. Michelle gets to my doorway, she peers in and smiles with a twinkle of pride in her eye. She actually thinks she's responsible for my "*marked decrease of defiant episodes.*"

"Wow! Up already and getting an early start on personal hygiene without prompting! If you keep this up all day, you'll earn a compliance point," Ms. Michelle chirps. Ms. Michelle is always chirping. I force a smile, and toothpaste drips down my chin. Her smile falters. Her eyes shift to the left uncomfortably, and she keeps walking. *Goddammit.* I make a mental note not to show so many of my teeth next time.

Down the hall, January is still screaming her head off about being too tired to go to school. She's just making it worse for herself, but she's only been here for three months, so you can't really blame her. She doesn't know that if you just play along, they leave you alone. Or maybe she's too stupid to figure it out. I haven't read her chart yet, so I'm not sure.

Ginger adds to the chaos, demanding loudly to use the phone to call home. It's not even her phone day today, and I don't know why she bothers. Her mom barely tolerates those calls anyway.

I spit in the sink, wipe my face, and then peer across the hall toward Keisha's room to see if she's awake. She is. I can tell she's been waiting for me. She stands in her doorway, casually examining the ends of her braids, and doesn't say a word. She just locks her gaze on me, lifts her eyebrows, and then glances over to the staff's workstation. That's all the communication I need. I look down the hall and see Mr. Josh making notes in an electronic chart. I look back at Keisha and make just enough eye contact so she knows that *I* know. Today is the day.

I dress quickly and make sure to put on my white running sneakers with the red laces. Those laces are a prize that took me six months to earn. I can be trusted in my room alone with shoelaces. It's a status symbol.

As I walk into the hall, Keisha casually leaves her room a couple of beats behind me and we head toward the meds line. Octavia, Diamond, and Tracy wait in the line in front of us. They stand there looking like those dolls that stack up and fit inside each other. Hollow, identical copies of each other in various sizes. Their charts are just as boring as they are. Tracy looks me and Keisha up and down, and the other two follow suit, but neither of us acknowledges their dumb attempt at intimidation.

Ginger joins behind us, crestfallen, having finally accepted that her phone call isn't happening. Tall and lanky with Coke-bottle glasses, she confidently sports a frizzy hairdo complete with puffy bangs like an eighties mom headed to a Jazzercise class. Tracy eyes her and whispers something to Diamond. Ginger's hair is exceptionally messy today, and I silently hope that Tracy doesn't taunt her about it. I don't think I can handle two tantrums at once.

Across the hall, January lets out a gurgling scream, a little louder than before, and we all turn to stare into her room. She's flopping on the floor, red-faced in her too-small pajamas. Sweat and tears glue chunks of auburn hair to her round cheeks. Ms. Michelle speaks calmly, trying to reason with her, as if that has ever worked in the history of January's tantrums. Nurse Patrick is close by though, armed with a syringe full of diazepam. I guess January isn't going to be of much help today. That's okay. We don't need her.

Mr. Josh keeps an eye on the tray of undelivered meds while he writes in January's chart. Documentation is important here. God forbid these people aren't aware of every single moment of our existence.

January starts screaming even harder as Nurse Patrick enters her room with the syringe, and I lean in closer to get a better look. No turning back now. Nurse Patrick whispers something in January's ear, then sticks her with the needle. The meds go in; the lights go out. Jan's body deflates, and the cacophony shrinks to a whimper. *Finally. Jesus.*

Once Jan ensures we'll all be late to breakfast, Nurse Patrick comes back to the meds line to distribute the goods. When it's my turn, I take my paper cup. Just one pill now, one beige oval. They're not sedating me anymore, and thank god they gave up on the one that gave me headaches and made me sleep twenty hours a day. It took me weeks to bounce back from that little experiment. My chart says my diagnosis is difficult to medicate, and I'm pretty sure they just quit trying. I'm told the beige pill is to help me focus in school. Whatever. I take it, swallow, and open my mouth for Nurse Patrick to check. He gives me a warm smile, and his blue eyes crinkle.

"Thanks, kid! Have fun at school!" he singsongs. Nurse Patrick is corny as hell, but he's not a bad guy.

At six foot two, his size and solid build should make him intimidating, but his dopey smile instantly gives him away. He's a marshmallow. He holds out his elbow, and I raise my own to give his elbow a tap. A sanitary high five. He really does try.

Keisha is next, and I watch her palm her meds and slip them into her hoodie's front pocket. She's really gotten good at that. Nurse Patrick seems none the wiser, gives her an elbow tap, and calls Cat forward with a smile.

Keisha and I leave the meds line together and join the rest of the girls. We lean against the wall in the north hall, waiting to be escorted downstairs to breakfast. We're all quiet, tired from another long night of hearing Diamond screaming in her sleep. As we wait, I can smell Mr. Josh approaching, and my gut twists. His cologne smells like arrogance and asshole, and it takes everything I have to calm the muscles in my face, release my fists, and conjure a look of indifference as he walks up behind me, just a little too close. His shirt sleeve brushes my bare arm. Goose bumps.

"All right, ladies, we're heading downstairs," he says, strutting in front of us. "I want an orderly line. Absolutely no talking until we reach the cafeteria, and I hope I don't need to remind you—you are not allowed to talk to the boys. Sit only at your designated table. Any deviation from these rules will result in a demerit and a demotion in your level. Have I made myself clear?" he asks, smiling falsely.

"Yes, Mr. Josh," we say in chorus.

He leads us down the stairs, single file, toward the cafeteria. When we come to the locked door standing between us and our breakfast, he tells us to turn around. We do. I hear him punch in a six-digit code followed by a soft *click*.

Mr. Josh steps into the doorway and holds the door open, blocking half of the entrance. I hate this part.

"Let's go, ladies!" He leans his back against the doorjamb and waits. Everyone cringes. One by one, we move through the doorway, each of us trying to make ourselves impossibly small. Inevitably, we brush up against Mr. Josh. He smirks. My skin crawls. I keep walking.

Mr. Josh is more than a jerk on a power trip. I've kept my eye on him since I got here, and it wasn't hard to figure out his game. I've met dozens of men just like him. The creep hiding in plain sight. Places like this are full of them. Nobody questions a do-gooder who helps troubled kids. But we all know better.

When we enter the cafeteria, the boys all look up. Of course, they beat us here and took all the good cereal. One more reason to hate January and her useless tantrums. I grab a box of plain Cheerios and sit across from Keisha. Now we can finally talk.

"So today, then?" I say casually, glancing toward Mr. Josh to make sure he's not paying attention to us.

"Today. Right after lights out. Mr. Josh is working a double, so he'll be exhausted. He'll be working on evening charts, so he won't even notice if we do it right at shift change at nine," Keisha says, carefully controlling the excitement I know she's feeling.

"You realize if this goes sideways, we lose everything, right? We'll be in our rooms without privileges for weeks."

"We're not going to get caught," she promises.

"Are you sure you have the right code?" I press.

"Jesus, Quinn, for the thousandth time, I have the right code. I watched Mr. Josh use it again yesterday, and I'm not an idiot. Do you think I'm an idiot?" Keisha says, challenging me with an arched eyebrow and wry smile. I roll my eyes but crack a smile of my own to answer hers.

"Of course I don't think you're an idiot. If you say we're good, we're good." But truthfully, I'm not one hundred percent sure. Keisha's one of the smartest people I've met, but I've been doing things like this long enough to know you can't predict everything.

I sigh and let my eyes wander across the room to where the boys sit. I do a quick headcount, just to be sure I know who's in the room with us. An old nervous habit from my last group home. All twelve are here. Same as us girls. We only see the boys at mealtimes and during school, but even then we barely interact. Half of them are too high on their meds to even bother trying to talk to us. I already read their charts, but even if I didn't know their histories, symptoms, meds, and the reasons they're in this place,

I wouldn't interact with these boys on purpose. Sometimes you can just look at someone and know.

I let my attention come back to Keisha. "So, obviously, January isn't going to be any good to us tonight. Those meds will have her knocked out until breakfast tomorrow. I can probably get Ginger to go off the rails and give us a good distraction, though."

"What did you have in mind?" Keisha asks, a smile playing on her lips.

"At dinner I'll tell Tracy I heard that Ginger's mom called this morning. Tracy won't be able to resist a good rumor, and it'll get back to Ginger within the hour for sure. Ginger will lose her mind in twenty minutes or less trying to get phone privileges. Boom. Instant distraction. They won't even bother to trace the rumor back to me."

"And if that doesn't work?" Keisha asks skeptically. She always demands a plan B.

"It will. But if all else fails, I'll just tell Ginger I heard Ms. Michelle call her a brat behind her back. She'll spend all night crying about it." Again, it's simple. Ms. Michelle won't even give me demerits for lying, because it's the truth and she knows it.

"Jeez, Quinn. That's kinda messed up," Keisha says, but I catch her smiling.

I shrug. "People are predictable."

Keisha knows just about everything about me by now, but she doesn't know I read everyone's charts, and she definitely doesn't know I've read some of hers.

Her chart is very long. Like a lot of our parents, her mom and stepdad were addicts. She was placed in foster care when she was eight years old. She spent the next eight years failing out of every foster placement and group home until she ended up here a year ago, barely escaping a juvenile detention sentence. It's not like her history is special. We're all walking around with some version of the same old story. Bad childhoods and parents who were terrible, dead, or both. Keisha's only different in that she turns eighteen in a month and will be moving into transitional living. She's not being considered for placement in a locked adult facility, as she loves to remind us. But what makes people feel special is also their weakness. If I ever needed to mess with Keisha, I'd start there. I wouldn't do that to her though. I hate just about everyone, but not Keisha.

I'm sixteen, so I have about a year and a half to go before I get to leave. The best I can hope for is transitional living like Keisha. They give you your own apartment, a job, and tuition for community college or a trades program if you want it. That's the goal. That's why I'm usually on my very best behavior. I can't go to an adult facility. I just *can't*. And I'm definitely not going back home. There's no home to go back to. Meredith and Daniel Wallace adopted me when I was two. I don't really have any memories of life before them. Anyway, they surrendered me back to the state four years later. No hard feelings. Not everyone is cut out to be a parent, especially to a kid like me.

I entered foster care after that and bounced from home to

home. After the last foster family dumped me, a judge ordered a residential treatment center. I've been at the Pegasus Center since then. It could be worse. They could have easily sent me to juvenile detention for the things I did. Instead, they sent me for treatment. The system has a weakness for girls who look like me. Blond hair, white skin, sweet face, small build. I'm not saying it's fair, but it's true.

I've learned all kinds of things in therapy too. My therapist tells me when I've hurt someone's feelings and when my facial expressions don't match the situation.

She explains how other people think and feel and why. I pay attention as if my life depends on it, because it probably does. If I can read people, understand what makes them tick, and match their energy, I can usually go unnoticed. I think I'm blending in pretty well now.

After breakfast Mr. Josh escorts us to the elevator and down two floors to the classrooms. We're split into small groups according to age and ability level. Only a few of us are smart enough to qualify for regular high school classes. It could be worse. As long as you put in a little effort, you pass your classes, and your teachers can go home to their families and feel better about themselves because they saved a crazy child today. It's best to keep them feeling optimistic about you. They'll let a lot of things slide if they feel like you're making progress.

I raise my hand to let my teacher know I'm done with my work early. Without a sound, she smiles and points to the tablet cart. I grab one, find an empty corner, and settle in. These things aren't supposed to connect to the internet, of course. In fact, the only things we're allowed to do on them is read books, play math games, and draw. It wasn't hard to unlock the good stuff, though. I can't get on the internet, but I figured out how to get into the internal server if I have a staff member's password, and I do.

Mr. Josh charts on us so often that nobody notices the extra log-in records. His password is his own birthday, which I learned while watching him show pictures of the big day to Ms. Rose, trying to impress her. When she asked how old he turned, I did the math. It was too easy.

I open the electronic charts and start reading where I left off. As always, I check my own notes first.

> Quinn Wallace woke and initiated her hygiene routine on schedule without prompting. Her cooperation continues to improve per her behavior plan. She showed patience toward a struggling peer during the morning routine. However, she did not show empathy or attempt to console her peer. She avoided eye contact and maintained a flat affect throughout the duration of her peer's tantrum. Empathy and compassion remain underdeveloped for her age and developmental level.

"Dammit," I mumble under my breath. I make a mental note to remember to try to talk to January during her next tantrum or at least act concerned.

I back out of my own record and scroll until I get to January's chart. It's about time I read her file. Her daily notes are just a timeline of her tantrums. Boring. I check her psychological test scores. That explains it. She's fourteen, but it says here she's functioning like a kid less than half her age. I guess she can't really help it. I scroll back to the beginning to read her family history. Both her parents still have legal custody of her. That's different. Why would someone with two functioning parents get sent to a residential treatment center? I skim past her developmental milestone records and behavioral testing. I just about choke on my own spit when I see the answer. "Jesus Christ, Jan," I sigh quietly. Who knew she had it in her? It's right there in her chart, though. About a month before she arrived here, she started a small fire in her family's garage. From the notes, it looks like they believed it to be an accident.

Then, a few paragraphs down, there's a note about her using a lighter to set the family dog's tail on fire because he was getting more attention than her. Then I read what must have been the final straw. In a blind rage over her bedtime, January used a nearby candle to set her parents' bed on fire. I guess they lived to tell the tale and then sent her here. Wow.

I don't get spooked easily, but something about this rattles me. And I thought *I* had a colorful record. I log out of the tablet quickly, erase my history, and ask to visit the library. My teacher smiles and nods, and I walk to the back of the room, my heart slowing as I go.

Our library has a pretty decent selection. We get a lot of donations from local businesses and charities. We also get castoffs from local high schools and the public library. There's enough here to keep your mind occupied for years. The shelves in the back of the room are ancient, made of carved hardwood, rising all the way up to the high ceilings. It feels like another world, not like the sterile hospital-like environment on the sixth floor where we spend most of our time.

My first stop is the fiction section. I scan the shelves for anything written about teenagers. I've missed out on a lot living here, and the foster care system and group homes aren't exactly normal either. If I want to blend in with other people my age, I need to know what they know. I need to behave like they behave and speak like they speak. I choose two thick novels, and then I move on to biographies, specifically autobiographies. Reading people's stories about themselves gives me a lot of information about what people think about and how they feel. I usually end up learning something about history or politics while I'm at it. Win-win, I guess. I tuck a memoir into the growing stack in my arms.

My last stop is the nature and travel section. We see almost nothing but white walls in this place. What few glimpses we get of the outside world are usually from the inside of a transport van. I like to know about what's out there. I choose a picture book on birds of the Midwest, which I've checked out multiple times already, a book on state parks, and a United States road atlas.

Satisfied, I bring my stack to the teacher's desk. She notes my choices in my chart to be analyzed by my therapist later, and then she logs the books into the library system. When she's done, she smiles stiffly and shifts her eyes away from mine uncomfortably as she hands them back to me.

"Enjoy!" she says a little too sweetly.

Three o'clock finally hits, and I line up by the door with everyone else and wait for our escort. They're always escorting us everywhere, like it matters. Even if one of us managed to make a break for the door and run outside, there's really nowhere to go. Peoria, Illinois, isn't that bad, but once you get outside of the city, you're basically in the middle of nowhere. If you want to go anywhere worth going, you'll need a train ticket, and train tickets cost money. I heard that a few years ago one girl made it to the station, did a few "favors," and got all the way to Chicago by the next morning. Whatever it takes, I guess. The elevator stops on the third floor, and Ms. J pushes her cleaning cart into the tiny space next to us. She's just clocked in for her shift. The sharp smell of cleaning solution fills the elevator, burning my nose. Ms. J gives us a small wave and a smile. She avoids making eye contact with me though.

As adults go, Ms. J isn't the worst. When she cleans our unit, she's supposed to search our rooms for contraband, but she never narcs on anybody for their candy stash and leaves Jan alone when she hides extra art supplies under her bed.

The elevator dings. Ms. J pushes her cart toward the

fifth-floor bathrooms as we continue up to the sixth floor. When we get back to our unit, I drop my books in my room and join the rest of the girls in the dayroom for free time. I usually skip this part. Given a choice, I'd always rather read in bed. Lately, though, I've been trying to force myself to be social once in a while. Ms. Michelle started writing notes in my chart about isolation, and my therapist started contemplating adding another personality disorder to my diagnosis. This week I've socialized almost every day in hopes that today's meeting with Keisha wouldn't seem suspicious.

I scan the dayroom and find Keisha by the game table, saving a seat for me. Without a word, she deals a hand of Go Fish. Here we go.

"So, we're still good for nine then?" Keisha asks quietly, her eyes on her cards.

"Give or take," I say with a wave of my hand. "The timing depends on how well I can plan out the distraction. It'll be close to the shift change, right after Mr. Josh does his last round of bed checks before he leaves for the night. Do you have any fives?" I ask to keep up the optics.

"Go fish," Keisha says.

"What about the alarm on the south door?" I ask as I pick up another card.

Keisha gives me a little smirk and rolls her eyes. "I already told you. I have the staff code. Do you have any twos?" she says a little louder. "All we need to do is make sure no one sees us leave.

Once you set Ginger off, all eyes will be on her. I've got the rest covered."

"Already on top of it," I whisper. "Got any sevens?"

"I can't wait to watch the master work."

Behind us, the word "riot" catches my attention. The news plays quietly on a boxy television hanging from the ceiling, and I crane my neck to see it. On the screen, a middle-aged man in a crumpled suit addresses the camera confidently, though he looks like he's been up all night.

"Riots continue to break out throughout the city of Chicago and its surrounding suburbs, resulting in multiple police-involved shootings and at least forty-three deaths. The riots began earlier this month and appear to be growing in size and frequency throughout the area. The mayor of Chicago is advising citizens to avoid large crowds and adhere to a strict curfew in hopes of containing the disturbances. At this time, Police Chief James Roberts reports that the group responsible remains unknown at this time. Police have been unable to identify a pattern in—"

Mr. Josh unceremoniously flips the channel to a nature documentary, leaving me hanging on the anchor's words. It's not the first time I've heard the news talking about these riots, but it *is* the first time I've heard them talk about them spreading to the suburbs.

"I was watching that," I grumble at no one.

Mr. Josh struts over to our table, leans low, and whispers in my ear.

"I bet you were, psycho." He chuffs, stands upright, and moves toward the center of the room, where Ginger and Diamond flip through magazines.

My skin rips into flames, and my heart beats faster. I'm on the edge of losing control, but years of therapy kick in. I close my eyes and take three deep breaths. Count my fingers. Remind myself how much I have to lose if I react. My heart slows, and a trickle of sweat drips down my spine. I open my eyes, calm again.

"Nice work," Keisha says, impressed.

"Do you have any tens?" I ask.

CHAPTER 2

At six thirty we're escorted downstairs for dinner, and I get ready to set my plan in motion.

I carry my tray to my usual spot, where I sit alone with Keisha. We eat and keep an eye on the staff, who are gossiping in the corners of the cafeteria. They're fully occupied. Now we wait for the perfect moment.

Finally, Tracy stands up and saunters toward the kitchen to drop off her tray. Keisha and I get up and follow closely behind her, talking just above a stage whisper. Tracy slows her pace and turns her head just slightly. She's listening. This is my favorite part. It's showtime. "So, then Ms. Michelle told Mr. Josh that Ginger's mom called, and you're not going to believe what he said," I say to Keisha.

"What did he say?" Keisha asks, with just enough surprise and shock. She's putting her best acting skills to work.

"He said Ginger would have to wait until her phone day to call her mom back." I shake my head as I drop my tray onto the pile. Tracy has paused next to us and picks at her nails, desperate to hear what comes next.

"But her phone day is three days from now! What if it was an emergency?" Keisha says.

"All I know is, if I were Ginger, I'd want to know. But it's none of my business." I shrug.

Back in our seats, I can see Tracy's little wheels turning. She gets that twinkle in her eye when she thinks she knows something special. I watch as she scans the room for someone to tell. To Tracy, information is a prize and a status symbol. She won't tell Ginger first. No, she'll tell her little girl squad, trying to impress them with her gossip. She finds Diamond across the cafeteria and skitters over to start spilling. It's exactly what I was counting on.

We sit in the dayroom, watching reruns of *I Love Lucy*, but I'm watching the clock, waiting for it to happen. Just before eight, it does.

Ginger marches out of the dayroom and into the hall. It starts with a soft, obnoxious whine. "She needs to talk to me! She has news! She's probably coming to get me! Please! I need the phone."

"Ginger, I don't have any record of a call from your mother today, yesterday, or any time this week. Tonight's not your night to make calls. You can call her on Thursday," Ms. Jackie says calmly. We gather in the doorway of the dayroom to watch the fireworks, and then we slowly spill out into the hallway.

"You're lying! This is a crime!" Ginger screams. God, it's like knives on a chalkboard. But it's working. Impatiently, Ms. Jackie orders us to go to our rooms, but we drag our feet to try to catch as much of the drama as possible.

"Ginger, let's remember your coping skills. Take a deep breath with me, and then let's count to ten," Ms. Jackie says.

"You're violating my civil rights, and you're going to have to kill me if you think I'm going to sit here and take it!" Ginger bellows, red-faced. "I know *all* my rights!"

Jesus, the dramatics. We filter into our rooms, but we all lean out of our doorways to watch. Every eye is on Ginger. Nurse Patrick starts rummaging through the locked cabinets for the diazepam, right on cue.

Just then, the elevator dings and the night shift starts clocking in. The chaos of it all is a thing of beauty. The lobby is buzzing, and Ginger is screaming, and all the girls are getting a free show. It's a little early, but it'll do. I lock eyes with Keisha from my doorway and lift my chin toward the south door. I leave behind a girl-shaped mass of carefully arranged clothes and pillows in my bed.

With all the chaos, they won't check beds for another two hours at least. We have time.

I follow a few steps behind Keisha until we get to the south doors. She peers behind us, and I catch the smallest twitch of her mouth. She's nervous, and she's not hiding it very well. She punches in the stolen code slowly. My heart hitches in my chest as we stare at the little red light in the corner of the keypad for what seems like an eternity. Finally, it chirps. Turns green. Keisha doesn't hesitate. She grabs the handle, turns it quietly, and pushes it forward.

We move into the dim stairwell as the door clicks behind us. Keisha's chest deflates as she pushes out a breath she must have been holding the entire time.

"No going back now," she says evenly.

I swallow louder than I mean to and start up the stairs. Two flights feel like forever when you're trying to move silently. When we get to the top, I can just make out the writing on a red door. ROOF ACCESS. AUTHORIZED PERSONNEL ONLY I can barely find Keisha's eyes in the dark. For a moment, I worry about the door having an alarm. I'm pretty sure some of the staff come up here to smoke on their breaks. Now I'm definitely sure. The smell of stale cigarette smoke hangs in the air. If they come up here, then there shouldn't be an alarm on the door, but it's a risky bet. I hold my breath again and push the bar in the center of the door. Only the sound of summer crickets greets us.

I step out onto the roof and breathe in the hot, soggy air. Keisha flies past me, jogs to the edge of the roof, and looks down. She leans over. She lifts her arms. I almost call out to her to stop, but before I can say a word, she spins around, arms wide, with the biggest smile I've ever seen spread across her face.

"We made it, Quinn!"

"We made it."

"Look at the stars!" Keisha beams, throwing her arms above her head.

"They're really bright," I say lamely.

"Oh my god, Quinn. Why did you even bother breaking out if you don't care about what's outside?" Keisha twirls as she emphasizes the last word. God, I've never seen her like this. She's actually joyful.

"I just wanted the quiet," I say, listening to the crickets. I'm lying, though. I just wanted to see if I could get away with it. Plus hanging out with Keisha alone is a nice bonus.

"This is how it's supposed to be," Keisha says, touching my shoulder tentatively. Her touch sends a ripple of energy through me.

She's right. This is how it's supposed to be. The stars, the crickets, the calm. It's something we don't get to experience very often. The cold floors, the sterile air, the constant supervision—I had almost forgotten how stifling it is until now. In this moment, I decide this feeling is worth the risk of getting caught.

We've pulled a lot of tricks over the last year, but this is by far the biggest risk we've taken. My heart slows as I wonder when we can do this again. How often could we get away with escaping out here, just the two of us? How many ways could I find to manipulate the other girls and the staff to distract them?

Then I start to think of other possibilities. I look over the edge of the building and imagine what it would be like to go for a walk out on these streets. I breathe in the humid summer air and the smell of fresh-cut grass and picture myself walking in a straight line for miles. I almost do it. I almost step onto the fire escape and take my chances. But the rust covering its bars changes my mind. That thing looks like a deathtrap.

Behind me, Keisha has lain down on the roof. She pats the spot next to her, so I lie down too. Even a foot apart, I swear I can feel the heat of her, burning the bare skin of my arm. We stay like that, staring up at the sky, just breathing in the summer air. Soon, my eyes grow heavy, and I can feel myself drifting off to sleep. The sound of plate glass shattering makes me jump.

My head whips toward the noise, but I can't pinpoint exactly where the sound came from.

"What was that?" Keisha whispers, wide-eyed, scrambling up on her elbows.

We don't waste time wondering. We run to the edge of the roof, duck low, and peer over just as a man pushes through the hole in the window leading into the Pegasus Center's lobby.

"What *was* that?" Keisha repeats, more urgently.

"Somebody broke into the center."

"No shit, Quinn. It's probably one of those terrorists from the news," Keisha says, panicking.

"What does a terrorist want with a residential treatment center, Keisha? There's nothing here," I say, trying to convince us both.

Breathless, we watch the empty hole in the lobby, but nothing happens. It's oddly quiet now. I look around expecting the cops to fly around the corner any second, but instead we just stand there in silence. Then I notice the coffee shop across the street.

The glass from the storefront window has shattered onto the sidewalk, glinting under the streetlight and... Is that... Is that blood?

"Keisha, look."

She startles out of a thousand-mile stare.

"I think there's blood in the glass down there at the coffee shop," I say, pointing. "I think whoever just broke into the Pegasus Center was there first."

"This is crazy, Quinn. We need to go back inside before the cops come."

A scream rises to the roof from below. It's coming from the front lobby. My spine tingles, and I feel a jolt of energy.

"Keisha, I think that was Ms. J. She always cleans the lobby before she leaves for the night."

We hear a muffled cough, then silence.

"Oh god, what do you think happened to her?" Keisha says, panic rising in her voice.

"Stabbed maybe?" I wonder aloud.

"*Stabbed*? We have to go back inside. Now. The cops will be here any second. Nobody can know we were here for this," Keisha says, speaking faster.

I sigh. I know she's right, but everything in me wants to climb down the rusty fire escape and see what really happened. Safety be damned. But as much as I want to see what happened, I know our time is up.

"You're right. Let's go," I say, resolved.

I turn back to the red door, but Keisha is shaking and wide-eyed. She looks terrified.

"Get your shit together! When we walk back through that door, you need to forget this ever happened. I'm not losing my privileges because you can't keep a straight face," I say, trying to shake some sense into her. It seems to work. It only takes seconds for her to slip into a well-practiced mask. Her eyes clear, and the wrinkle in her forehead smooths out.

"I'm fine. Let's just go," she says.

We move quietly down the two flights of stairs back to our locked unit. Keisha punches in the code, and the red light flips to green. She pulls the door open and listens.

The floor has quieted down. I can hear the night shift chatting at the staff's workstation on the opposite end of the hall. The girls are in their rooms, listening to quiet music, reading, or snoring softly. It's like nothing ever happened just six floors down. When the coast is clear, I slip off my shoes and run as quickly and silently as I can into my dark room.

When I'm safely inside, I peer out of my door into Keisha's room. She's looking back at me. I give her a meaningful look and a sharp gesture that says, once again, *"Keep your shit together,"* and move back into the darkness.

I undress, climb into bed, and stare up at the ceiling. The blood in my veins is on fire. I can't stand not knowing exactly what happened in the lobby. I want to see it. I play back the scream, the muffled cough. Who did that? Will they get away with it? I decide to do everything I can to find out more tomorrow. I close my eyes and wait for morning.

CHAPTER 3

The next morning my eyes fly open and the memories of last night come pouring back.

My heart pounds as if I'm back on that roof. I thought maybe an alarm would go off or the cops would show up on our floor and start asking questions, but if I hadn't known better, last night would have been just like any other night at the Pegasus Center.

I get out of bed and start my routine as quickly as possible. I need to be first in the meds line this morning. The staff are always standing around talking to each other near the front desk, and I wonder if they'll reveal some details about what happened last night.

My teeth are brushed, and I'm fully dressed in record time. I walk out of my room as casually as I can, keeping an eye on Keisha's door just a few feet ahead of me as I move. Her room is still dark.

I'm halfway down the hall when I see Ms. Michelle step off the elevator. I look at the clock above the staff's workstation. She's late for the morning shift. And she looks like shit. I make a mental note to take advantage of that later. When the staff aren't feeling well, you can always get away with more. I wonder if she'll let me put on the local news in the dayroom before school.

I get closer to the front desk and say good morning to Nurse Patrick, giving him a careful, no-teeth grin, making sure to raise my eyebrows slightly. Apparently the most convincing smiles are all in the eyebrow raise. He gives me a warm smile and a little wave, and then he goes back to preparing the morning meds. When Ms. Michelle is within earshot, I call out to January.

"Jan. Hey, Jan."

She appears in her doorway right on cue, with the kind of energy only Jan can muster at seven thirty in the morning.

"Quinn, hi! You're awake! Look at the bracelet I made when I didn't go to school yesterday. The beads are clear. Did you know we have clear beads now? My favorite color is yellow, though," Jan prattles on at lightning speed.

I instantly regret this.

"Yeah, Jan. That's pretty. Hey, I know you had a hard day yesterday. Are you feeling better?" I say with as much concern as I can muster. I flit my eyes toward Ms. Michelle to see if she's listening to me.

"I'm on track today, Quinn. Mr. Josh said I can earn back my privileges in a week if I can stay rel-a-gated and keep going to school every day."

"Regulated. If you can stay *regulated*," I correct her.

"Yeah. That's what I said. If I can stay regulated and keep going to school every day, I can get on level thirteen, and I can go to the movies, and I can take another level thirteen with me, and if you're still a level thirteen, you can come with me," she continues.

Oh god. Why did I do this?

"Cool, Jan. That would be fun," I say, but my attention is already elsewhere. Ms. Michelle is whispering to Nurse Patrick. I don't even think she heard my attempt at "*developmentally appropriate empathy*." What a waste.

I watch as Ms. Michelle pulls back her sleeve to reveal a white bandage, stained brown. Nurse Patrick snaps on a fresh set of gloves and unravels the gauze. I lean forward to get a closer look. *HA! A bite.* She must have worked overtime on the little kids' psych unit on the fifth floor. Vicious little buggers. The oozing wound looks disgusting and is probably infected. I bet Nurse Patrick will send her home for the day.

I shift my eyes to the computer bank at the staff desk. Sure enough, someone has googled the news. The headlines describe more riots, this time in smaller towns downstate. I guess that would explain the broken glass last night. But I would hardly call what we saw a riot. Plus, it's not like we're in a big city. What's there to riot over in Peoria, Illinois?

"Good morning, Quinn. Please back away from the staff workstation and go wait for your medication," Mr. Josh says, barely looking up from his morning charting. I stifle a sigh and take three steps back until I'm behind the white line surrounding the workstation. "Mr. Josh, I'm ready to go down to breakfast."

"I can see that, Quinn," he says, still not looking up.

"Can I go in the dayroom and watch TV?"

That gets his attention. I can see him thinking. His eyes shift to the window, then to Ms. Michelle. He's not sure how to answer.

TV is a limited privilege given to level tens and above only. We can watch pre-approved movies and TV shows with no violence, no drugs, no sex, no tragedies, and no triggers. Every once in a while, we're allowed to watch the local morning news show. It's boring as hell with the most obnoxiously fake hosts, but it's better than listening to January talk about her arts and crafts for the next twenty minutes.

I wait for Mr. Josh to come up with an answer, but his pager starts beeping. He looks down and checks the message. Looks back at me. Looks over to the dayroom TV.

"Sure, yeah. But only channel seven, Quinn. You know the rules. If I come back and you're watching *anything* but the nature channel, I'm taking you all the way down to level nine," he says sternly.

I wait for him to turn away before rolling my eyes. I walk slowly toward the dayroom past Ms. Michelle and Nurse Patrick as Mr. Josh shows them the message on his pager. They look wide-eyed and worried. Mr. Josh punches in his staff code for the elevator and heads downstairs. The psych unit must be having quite a day. Good. That means fewer staff up here.

The dayroom is still. The sun is just barely coming through the barred windows, and nobody seems to care what I'm doing, so I take the risk and flip to the channel nine news and... Oh my god.

"Breaking News" flashes across the bottom of the screen as I watch a city in absolute chaos. I cough, choking on air. This has to be a movie. I check the channel again. Nine. I check the clock. Seven forty-three. The local morning show should be on right now. Instead, cameras show helicopter footage from downtown Chicago. There's not a pane of glass left on the bottom floors of the tall buildings. Cars litter the sidewalks and streets at odd angles. People are fighting one another. No, not just fighting. They're tearing each other apart.

My heart is pounding, and I can't take my eyes off the screen. I'm hypnotized by the chaos. I don't even hear Ms. Michelle come up behind me, so when she puts her hand on my shoulder I jump. The staff are *not* supposed to touch us. She pulls her hand back like she touched a hot stove.

"I'm so sorry. I—" Ms. Michelle stutters, her face the color of ashes, as she looks at the TV screen.

"Are these terrorists?" I ask, trying to get as much information as quickly as possible. The other girls could walk by any second, and Ms. Michelle is notoriously difficult to get information from.

"Turn that off," she says, defeated.

"But I want to..."

"Turn it off, Quinn." She's serious now.

I reach for the power button just as one of the people on screen takes a bite out of someone's neck. The screen goes dark.

"Chicago is almost two hundred miles north of here," I say.

"Yes," Ms. Michelle responds.

"But it's not just Chicago, is it?" I ask, but I already know.

"It started there," she replies, looking out the window.

"Why are people rioting?"

"They're not sure."

"Is it happening here?"

She almost answers me, but before she can speak, Ginger and Diamond pass the dayroom door and get in the line for meds. Time's up. That's all I'll get.

"Quinn, we're safe here. Do not scare the other girls. Please," she begs in a whisper, but she doesn't wait for an answer. She turns and walks away to tend to a whining call from an impatient January.

Something is seriously wrong. I'm trying to decide whether being in a locked facility during something like this is a good thing. Whoever broke into the lobby last night didn't make it upstairs, so that's promising. But what if they did? Where could I go?

Our bedrooms don't have doors. Our furniture is bolted to the ground so we can't barricade ourselves in our rooms. The only places with doors are the dayroom, a few closets, and a lounge reserved for staff. Aside from that, there's no hiding from whatever is happening out there. As weapons go, nobody has anything sharper than a crayon. If someone comes up to our unit and actually gets in, the only option is to hide in a closet or under the bed. These are shit options.

I leave the dayroom and get in line behind Ginger and Diamond. I study Nurse Patrick's face for any hint he might know about what happened in the lobby last night, but he gives nothing away. He just passes out meds like it's any old day. Keisha joins me in line and gives me a questioning look. She wants to know if I learned anything.

I show no emotion and shake my head slightly. We'll talk at breakfast. We get our meds. I take mine; Keisha palms hers. Then we wait by the stairs to be escorted to breakfast.

"Please go back to your rooms. We're staying on the unit today," Ms. Michelle says, looking grayer and grayer.

I whip my head around, unable to hide my reaction. "What? Why?"

"Maintenance is doing some work near the cafeteria. They've asked us to stay upstairs today," Ms. Michelle chirps unconvincingly. She's lying.

"What about school?" asks Tracy.

"We're doing school upstairs today. It'll be like an adventure!"

That's when January storms toward Ms. Michelle.

Oh boy, here come the fireworks.

"I have to go to school! If I can't go to school, I can't earn my points back! Mr. Josh said I could earn my points back if I go to school! This isn't fair!" January whines, getting louder and higher pitched with each syllable.

"January, you can still earn your points for compliance if you follow today's routine with the rest of the group. Even if it's not our normal routine, you can still…"

January screams the most obnoxious scream I've ever heard and falls to the ground, bawling and red-faced. Here we go again. She kicks her legs wildly, taking out the med cart. Empty paper cups and a half-full pitcher of water scatter across the floor. Nurse Patrick moves toward the meds closet for the diazepam, but he pulls up short when Ms. Michelle hurls into a nearby garbage can. Everyone freezes in horror. Even Jan.

Watching someone vomit is not a rare event here. I've been living with at least a dozen kids at a time for most of my life. I've seen a lot of puke. This is different. I've never seen anything like the putrid black mess spilling out of Ms. Michelle.

I look at Nurse Patrick, and I don't think nurses are supposed to look this scared in situations like these. I scan the hall to see Keisha's reaction but can't find her. Down the south hall, I see just the ends of her braids as she ducks into her room. The rest of the girls cover their noses and stare, waiting for it to end, but it doesn't. Ms. Michelle isn't a big person. Ten minutes ago, I would not have guessed there was enough room inside her to fill that entire wastebasket with ooze. I would have been wrong.

When she finally stands upright, her eyes are bloodshot and

streaming tears. She wobbles. Nurse Patrick finally recovers his wits and leads her to the dayroom couch to lie down. Ten anxious faces turn and look at one another. No one knows what to do next. With Mr. Josh off on an emergency call and Ms. Michelle sick, the only staff member left on the floor is Nurse Patrick. The therapists don't come in until two in the afternoon. I've never seen the unit this vulnerable. January, still lying on the floor fresh off her tantrum, looks up at me, of all people.

"How are we going to get breakfast now?" she whines.

I ignore her.

"Everybody go back to your rooms. When Mr. Josh comes back I'm sure he'll pass out cereal," I tell the girls.

All ten girls walk back to their rooms in stunned silence.

Before I turn to leave, I grab a roll of paper towels from the desk. I know I'm not supposed to touch staff supplies, but I throw a few towels over the mess around the wastebasket anyway. Maybe it will keep the smell from wafting down the hallway.

On my way back to my room, I stop at Keisha's doorway and tap on the frame.

"Keisha? Keisha, we need to—" I call quietly.

"I went back outside last night," she interrupts, meeting me in the doorway with a whisper.

"You *what*? When? What did you see?" I ask frantically.

"I went out after everyone was asleep. The night shift guy passed out in his chair around one, and I decided to risk it," she explains.

"I can't believe you went without me," I say accusingly. Resentment flares in my belly, but the need to know more has me forgiving her before her apology leaves her lips.

"I'm sorry. It was too risky to come get you. Listen, something is happening."

"Yeah, I'm putting that together. What did you see? Did whoever broke in get Ms. J? Did the cops come?"

"Yes." She pauses as if she's afraid to tell me more.

Her eyes flash down the hall toward the stinking garbage can before she continues. "I watched them carry Ms. J out of the building last night. She was dead, Quinn."

"Oh wow. Could you tell what happened to her? Did they—"

"That's not the craziest thing," she says, waving her hand, cutting me off. "She got back up, Quinn."

"Wait, slow down. I don't understand. I thought you said Ms. J was dead."

"Listen to me. She *was* dead. They carried her out, strapped to a stretcher and covered by a sheet like in the movies," she explains, her words pouring out faster and faster. "Before they loaded her in the ambulance, the paramedics were just standing there talking to the cops like assholes, laughing and carrying on. Then Ms. J started trying to sit up! For a second, I thought maybe she was okay. Then the sheet fell off, and I saw her neck. It was *shredded*. There's no way she could have survived that. Then somehow she snapped the straps and rolled off the stretcher. I'm telling you she woke up! But she didn't look like herself, and she moved so fast! Then she went after the paramedics, Quinn. Do you understand what I'm saying?"

I've read a lot of patient charts. I've seen some seriously disturbed kids come through the Pegasus Center. Keisha isn't one of those kids. But she has conned a lot of people. In fact, I've never seen anyone lie so smoothly in my life, but she's not lying now. And unless something has changed very recently, she's not the type to hallucinate or have delusions. I'm tongue-tied trying to come up with a third reason why she's telling me absolute nonsense. Maybe she just wasn't close enough to see it all clearly? I go with that.

"It sounds like Ms. J wasn't dead after all, Keisha. You were all the way up on the roof. Maybe you didn't..."

"No! You're not listening to me! Ms. J attacked them. The paramedics. She bit one guy in the neck! She wouldn't stop! They tried to pull her off, and then she bit the next one. Quinn, it was a bloodbath!"

She's still talking a mile a minute. I interrupt her. "You're not making any sense, Keisha. First of all, Ms. J is a tiny old lady. How could she possibly...and why would she be one of the rioters?" I ask.

"Rioters?"

"They've been mentioning it on the news all week, and then I saw it on TV this morning. There are groups of people rioting in Chicago. Ms. Michelle seemed to think maybe the riots are spreading into smaller cities too," I explain.

"Oh my god," Keisha says, then goes silent, staring off into nothing.

"Keisha. Keisha? Keisha!" I urge, trying to bring her back to me. "What happened to Ms. J and the paramedics? What did the cops do?"

"That's just it, Quinn. It turned into a brawl. Nobody came to help. They tried to fight back, but Ms. J bit every single one of them and didn't stop until they were all lying on the ground. She just kept biting and biting and biting, even after they all went still. Just when I thought she had killed everyone, I heard gunshots coming from the park over on Jamison Street. That's when they all stood up. It was like they heard an alarm clock. They just stood up and ran away toward the sound of the gunshots. All of them," she says.

I still can't accept what she's saying. I scan her face again, looking for the lie. Keisha has a way of convincing people to believe what they already know is ridiculous, but I know all her tells. I know that when she lies, she takes lots of deep, slow breaths to appear calm. I know she keeps her voice even. I know she blinks more frequently. And I know Keisha isn't lying to me right now. She really saw something out there, and it lines up perfectly with what I saw on the news this morning.

"Okay. Okay," I say, pacing just outside her doorway. "So you're saying Ms. J was dead."

"Yes."

"And then she woke up and bit a bunch of paramedics and police officers to death."

"Four of them," she says, nodding.

"Four of them. Okay. Then after they died, you heard gunshots in the park, and they ran toward it?"

"That's what I saw."

"You realize you're describing zombies, right, Keisha?"

She looks down at her feet. "Quinn, I'm not lying this time," she says, slowly looking up to meet my eye.

"I know."

CHAPTER 4

"Quinn, to your room, please!" Nurse Patrick shouts from the dayroom doorway. He's bobbing in and out of the dayroom, trying to keep one eye on the unit and one eye on Ms. Michelle. He jets back into the dayroom, not even bothering to see if I comply, so I stay with Keisha.

"Ms. Michelle has a bite on her arm," I say. "Do you think she was bitten by one of the…" I hesitate. What are they? "…rioters, or whatever?" I ask quickly. I can't bring myself to say *zombie*. It's too crazy.

"Quinn, you saw her. What do you think? Have you ever seen someone get sick like that?"

"She's going to turn into one of them. In here. With us," I say, but I don't need to. Keisha figured this out ten minutes ago.

"Quinn, I said get in your room, now!" Nurse Patrick yells.

It's a strange thing to be yelled at here. Not only can they not touch us unless it's for safety reasons, but also the staff are not allowed to yell at us. They're firm; they threaten in a sickly-sweet tone, but they do not yell. Especially Nurse Patrick. He's never yelled at any of us. It startles me enough that I turn and go back to my room. Ten wide-eyed faces pop out of their doorways to watch me go.

My mind is racing. My heart is a steady thump in my chest. If Keisha is right, Ms. Michelle is going to start attacking people soon, and Nurse Patrick is the only thing standing in her way. I exhale and make a promise to myself. I'm not dying in this place.

Frantically, I start looking for a weapon, but I quickly realize I have nothing. If only I had something heavy to swing like a bat. But anything big enough to make an impact is securely bolted to the floor. Which also means there's nothing I can use to barricade the doorway. This place was designed to prevent any sort of violence. They've made any kind of uprising impossible. I sit down on my bed and rack my brain.

"Think, Quinn!" I scold myself aloud.

The bed. I study the frame, and hope fills my chest. I run to my dresser and snatch a small cup of coins I've been saving for a coveted trip to the lobby's vending machine. I spill the cup on the floor and frantically sift through the coins until I find what I'm looking for. A shiny half-dollar coin that one of my foster dads gave me for Christmas one year. I don't know why I kept it. At the time it seemed like such a dumb gift, but now I'm glad I have it. It feels heavy in my fist, and I hold it tight like a lifeline. I dive onto the floor, wiggle under my bed, and get to work.

Just like I knew it would, the coin fits perfectly into the large bolt securing my bedframe to the floor. The coin is just large enough to give me the leverage to move the bolt to the left. I force the coin to turn again and again.

The ding of the elevator interrupts me. I scramble to my doorway to see who it could be. It's Mr. Josh, back from his emergency page. I can hear his voice, a little too loud and high-pitched, coming from the workstation, but I can't make out the words. I want to move closer but push myself to stay disciplined. I need protection more than I need information, so I get back to work, and I strain my ears to listen for danger.

Ten minutes and one bloody fingernail later, I have liberated two three-foot lengths of bedpost. They're heavy, solid pieces of wood, thin enough to wrap my fingers around if I use two hands and light enough for me to swing but still do some damage. I feel safer already.

My bed leans awkwardly. There's no hiding this. If Keisha is wrong about this, I'm getting sent to the acute psychiatric floor for sure, but it feels worth the risk.

I cough, cough, then sneeze loud enough for Keisha to hear me, and her head pops out of her door at the signal we made up for emergencies. I check the hallway for onlookers but see no one. I flash her my new weapons, then show her my coin. She squints at the coin and the bedpost in my hands, and then I can practically see a lightbulb turn on above her head. She nods, understanding. I kneel down and aim carefully, sliding the coin across the hall and slightly to the left. Keisha grabs the coin and disappears into her room.

I can still hear frantic whispers coming from the dayroom. I lean my weapons just out of view near my doorframe and tiptoe down the hall. As I get closer, the voices become clearer.

"People don't die from a bite! She was fine two seconds ago!" Nurse Patrick whispers harshly.

"Well, she's dead, Pat. I don't know what else to tell you," Mr. Josh says coldly.

"I couldn't call out! The phones! I tried, but there was nothing I could..."

"Everything is fucked, Pat. A sick doctor just went nuts on a bunch of the psych patients downstairs on the fourth floor for no goddamn reason. We got him under control, and they're treating him now. We're just going to have to wait for help. But these kids can't see her like this. They can't see *us* like this. We need to stay calm. Cover her with that blanket and close the door. We'll move her after the girls have gone to sleep," Mr. Josh says in a daze.

"But..." Nurse Patrick starts.

"I can't deal with this right now. We'll figure it out," Mr. Josh says firmly.

Dead. Ms. Michelle is dead. My heart thuds in my ears. According to what Keisha saw, Ms. Michelle should be waking up soon. But how soon?

They leave the dayroom, closing the door softly, and see me standing in exactly the spot where I'm not supposed to be. Crap. I need to think fast. Do I tell Mr. Josh and Nurse Patrick what I know? That Ms. Michelle is about to turn feral? That we're all screwed? Or do I play along like everything's fine?

"Quinn, what are you doing out of your room?" Mr. Josh asks, seething.

I channel Keisha. I breathe evenly, let my face relax, and prepare to lie.

"I was just wondering if you need help handing out breakfast," I say sweetly.

"That's very kind of you, Quinn. Yes, you can help me," he says, relaxing a bit.

I should tell him what I know. I'm not sure why I don't. Maybe it's sixteen years of getting my head knocked off every time I'm caught doing something I shouldn't. For some reason I'm still afraid for him to know Keisha and I snuck out. Besides, maybe Keisha was wrong and we're all overreacting. I keep my mouth shut.

I walk with Mr. Josh up the north hall toward the snack pantry to help with breakfast. Then January's head pops out of her door.

"I want to help too," January whines softly at Mr. Josh.

"Thank you for offering. Not today, January," he replies.

"But I want to help!"

"Here we go," Mr. Josh says, sighing discreetly. "January, I appreciate your offer, but I already have a helper. Please stay in your room," he says with more patience than I could ever muster.

"I. WANT. TO. HELP!" January wails.

Her scream is the kind that stings your ears and blurs the edges of your vision. The hallway practically vibrates from the sound.

I know someone once loved January. Someone loved her enough to give her a unique and beautiful name. I'm sure they looked forward to her birthdays. Maybe they even thought she was cute at some point. But right now, in this moment, I can't fathom a world where anyone could stand to exist in the vicinity of this child.

Only a dose of diazepam from Nurse Patrick can fix this. My eyes dart down the hall to find him, but he's distracted.

Nurse Patrick's eyes are locked on the dayroom door. Over the piercing noise that is January, I can see the door shake and hear the low thud of it trying to escape its jamb.

Mr. Josh stares at it wide-eyed. That's when I realize it didn't matter if I told him what Keisha and I figured out. He already knows.

Nine faces peer out of their doorways to watch the drama.

"Who is in the dayroom?" Ginger asks from her doorway over Jan's screams.

"Go back in your room, please, Ginger," Nurse Patrick says.

"I *am* in my room. And you're not allowed to lock people behind closed doors. It's against our rights," Ginger says firmly, her eyebrows pinching in the center of her face.

"Ginger, Ms. Michelle is sick. She needs to stay in the dayroom," Mr. Josh says quickly, knowing exactly where this is going.

"You're violating her rights! She has rights! Let her out! Let her out now!"

January continues kicking and screaming red-faced on the linoleum floor, but Ginger is giving her a run for her money, working hard to be heard over her. The door is quaking behind Nurse Patrick. Just when I think things can't get any more chaotic, Tracy comes out of her room, unable to miss a chance to get in the drama, and she joins Ginger, demanding rights for Ms. Michelle.

It's a complete mutiny. On any other day I would absolutely live for a moment like this. In fact, it probably would have been me who orchestrated the whole thing, just to sit back and watch the show, but now I'm desperate for it to stop.

"Pat, get the meds, now!" Mr. Josh shouts frantically as he runs toward the dayroom door to help block it.

As Nurse Patrick moves for the meds closet, Ginger and Tracy move on Mr. Josh. Tasha and Diamond rush out of their rooms to join them. The four girls easily push Mr. Josh aside.

"STOP!" I yell just as Tracy rips open the dayroom door. But it's too late.

The sixth floor falls eerily silent. Even January has stopped screaming to stare wide-eyed at the thing that just leaped out of the dayroom and into the hallway.

Ms. Michelle is a snarling shell of herself. Her empty eyes

scan the hallway, black saliva drips from her chin, and a low growl rattles in her chest.

"Ms. Michelle?" Tracy squeaks.

An inhuman screech fills the hallway as Ms. Michelle lunges at Tracy's throat, silencing her. The momentum flings Tracy backward. It's like slow motion as her skull hits the linoleum with a low thwack. Ms. Michelle goes with her, tearing at her throat on the way down.

My heart has never beat like this—fast, steady, hot. I don't feel fear. I feel excitement. I feel ready. I run.

When I reach my room, I grab the two liberated bedposts, comforted by the weight of them in my hands. I turn to go back down the hall and see Keisha standing paralyzed in the corner of her room, clutching her own bedpost out in front of her.

"Keisha, come on!" I call to her, but I don't stop moving until I reach the chaos.

As I run, I can see Tracy's lifeless body lying in a pool of blood off to the side of the mass of girls in front of me. I look back and forth, trying to understand what I've missed. Just as I'm approaching the group, two of the girls turn toward me, leaving a small opening in their circle, and I see it. Ms. Michelle has her newest victim. Diamond is pinned to the floor.

Ms. Michelle tears at her bubbling throat with her teeth as Mr. Josh tries to pull her off, but Ms. Michelle is determined. I scan the hallway, looking for Nurse Patrick, and see him staring, standing dumbly holding a syringe full of meds.

"Nurse Patrick! Heads up!" I yell, tossing him a bedpost. He snaps back to life, swiftly grabbing the weapon mid-air, letting the syringe fall at his feet.

"Stand back!" I shout at the girls still watching the bloodbath. Somehow, they listen, and I have a clear path toward Ms. Michelle. I widen my stance, grip the bedpost, pull it backward, and swing with everything I've got. The upward arc of the bedpost meets Ms. Michelle right under her chin. The momentum sends her and Mr. Josh tumbling to the floor on their backs. They both lie there, stunned for a moment, until Ms. Michelle's empty eyes lock onto mine. Her newly broken teeth have made her mouth a snarling, empty pit, allowing even more black bile to escape onto the floor. I step backward and nearly lose my balance, but that thrill of readiness settles in my chest again as Ms. Michelle begins to push herself off the floor. She's found her next target, and it's me. Her hands, slick with blood, slip on the wet tiles, giving me the precious seconds I need to find my footing.

I square up again. This time I raise the bedpost over my head and swing it downward like an axe. The bedpost connects with her left shoulder. *Dammit.* Another screech rips from Ms. Michelle's throat, and I'm desperate to slap my hands over my ears. Fear prickles my spine, and I ready myself for another swing. This time I can't miss. I reel back and let the momentum of my body bring the bedpost around until it meets her skull. I feel the bone give way as her head ricochets off the floor. She falls at my feet, motionless. I breathe a sigh of relief and feel the edges of my mouth start to rise into a satisfied smile. Something in me stirs, and I feel what I can only describe as peace. The moment is fleeting, though. When I look up, every wide eye is on me. I see horror on their faces and quickly rearrange my face to match theirs.

The air smells like copper and rot. Three bodies lie in front of us: Ms. Michelle, Tracy, and Diamond. Nurse Patrick vomits into the wastebasket near the dayroom. Some help he was. Before I can dodge him, Mr. Josh scrambles to his feet and snatches the bedpost out of my hand.

"Quinn, what have you done!" he shouts.

"I just..."

"What the hell, Quinn! Where did you even get this?" he says, shaking the bedpost in his hand.

I brush him off. "Listen, she wasn't going to stop. I had to—"

He cuts me off with a growl, pointing the bedpost at the group of girls gaping at the mess in front of them. "Every single one of you, go to your rooms right now!"

The girls listen, stunned into silence. Even January is quiet, her tears half-dry on her red face. I look for Keisha, but I guess she never left her room. As the girls walk back down the hall, I see a small group of them sneak into Tasha's room even though we're not allowed to go into each other's rooms. Mr. Josh doesn't even bother to remind them of the rules or threaten them with demerits.

I move down the hallway, putting some distance between myself and the fresh bodies. We need to do something about

Tracy and Diamond, fast. I wave for Mr. Josh and Nurse Patrick to follow me toward my room.

"Mr. Josh, Nurse Patrick, we need to—"

"*We* don't need to do anything. You need to stay in your room until the police get here," Mr. Josh snaps. "And don't you dare take apart any more of your furniture!"

"Aren't the cops a little busy with the *riots*?" I say, rolling my eyes, putting "riots" in air quotes.

"Look, what if these people are just sick, Quinn? What if they need a doctor and not a bedpost to the skull! What were you thinking?" he says.

"I was thinking that Ms. Michelle needed to die before she bit anyone else," I snap back at him.

"You had no right! You had no—" He cuts himself off, punching the wall in front of him. His fist flies easily through the thin drywall, making his childish display look a lot more impressive than it really was. I roll my eyes.

"We don't have time for the what-ifs! The same thing that happened to Ms. Michelle is about to happen to Tracy and Diamond. If we don't act fast, this entire unit will turn into a bloodbath. We need to contain them."

"This can't be happening." Nurse Patrick sighs, scrubbing at his face with his hands.

"Ms. Michelle was dead! You saw it yourself. I heard you talking about it. She woke up and killed two people, and she wasn't going to stop! Did you not see the riots on the news? If we don't take care of this right now, Tracy and Diamond are going to wake up and take out the rest of us."

"She's right, Josh," Nurse Patrick says.

"Duh," I say, throwing my hands in the air.

"This is insane! You both sound insane!" Mr. Josh says, pacing frantically. "They must've been sick. You must have missed her pulse. She must not have been dead after all. There is a logical reason for this if you both just calm down."

"How long did it take?" I ask Nurse Patrick. Clearly he's the only rational adult left.

"How long did what take?" he asks.

"How long between the moment Ms. Michelle died and when she got back up?"

"I don't know... I guess twenty minutes or so?" Shit. I jog down the hall toward Keisha's room, leaving them behind. I need more information.

"Keisha, I need to ask you something," I say from her doorway.

In the corner of her room, Keisha stares into space with a death grip on her bedpost. She doesn't even seem to know I'm here. I walk into her room, rules be damned. I put my hand on her shoulder.

"Keisha? Keisha, come on. Get it together."

"I'm fine," she says, snapping back to life.

"I need to know more about what you saw last night. After the cops and the paramedics died, how long did it take for them to get back up?" I ask.

"It happened really fast. They got up all at once. Together," she says.

"How much time did it take?" I repeat.

"Less than ten minutes."

I leap up and look down the hallway. Tracy and Diamond are still lying in a pool of themselves next to Ms. Michelle. I have no idea how much time we have left, but I don't intend to wait.

I make my way back down the hallway in front of my room, where Nurse Patrick and Mr. Josh still stand arguing quietly. When I reach them, I break down and confess to the outdoor adventure Keisha and I had last night. I tell them everything as fast as I can. There's no point in keeping it to myself now. Nurse Patrick takes in the new information seriously. Mr. Josh just looks pissed, but the facts seem to be sinking in, finally.

"So, we don't know how much time we have. They could get up any second, or we could have ten more minutes. Or more, I guess," I say, finishing my story with a shrug.

The three of us turn to stare down the hall at the bodies, looking for any twitch. It's Ginger who diverts our attention. Two doors south of the massacre, she steps out of her room, tears and snot dripping down her pink face. "I need to call my mom to pick me up. I want to go home," she sniffles.

"Ginger, the phones are dead in the whole building. I'm sorry, but none of us can make any calls right now," Mr. Josh explains, mustering as much fake sympathy as he can. Boldly, Ginger walks past the bodies and over to the staff workstation and picks up the desk phone. I guess we're done with *all* the rules now. She drops the receiver and lets it bounce by its cord, useless. Nurse Patrick and Mr. Josh walk down the hall toward the workstation to try to coax Ginger back to her room. I follow them.

"You could let me use your cell phone. I know you have one," she accuses Nurse Patrick.

"Ginger, I tried calling an ambulance for Ms. Michelle an hour ago; there's no signal. Too many people are trying to use the phones right now. People are getting sick just like Ms. Michelle, and people are all trying to make calls at the same time," Nurse Patrick attempts to explain patiently.

"But you have to let me try! At least let me try! I have human rights!" Ginger whines.

This is just how Ginger is. She latches on to a topic and can't seem to let it go. Human rights aren't the only thing she's obsessed with. She'll also go on and on about the phases of the moon and the life of Abraham Lincoln. It's odd, but you get used to it. Her obsessive demands for her rights almost always end in disappointment, but not this time. To my surprise, Nurse Patrick actually hands Ginger his cell phone. *What kind of alternate universe is this?*

Ginger snatches the cell phone from his hand, hardly believing that her whining actually worked. She punches in the numbers quickly, and I watch her face fall. Silence on the other end. She begins breathing heavily, short and fast. She slams the cell phone into the unforgiving floor, shattering the screen. This is why we have rules.

She isn't finished though. Ginger storms toward the discarded bedpost I had tossed to Nurse Patrick. She grabs it and stomps behind the staff's station, and I brace myself for the noise as she takes a heavy swing at a line of computer monitors, making an awful crash with each swing.

Mr. Josh moves toward Ginger with his hands up in an attempt to de-escalate her. But my eyes flash toward the pile of bodies near the dayroom. Diamond's arm twitches. Did I imagine it? Tracy's eyes fly open. I'm not imagining it.

As if they were brought to life by the sound of the shattering computer monitors, Tracy and Diamond stand up. Fresh black foam froths from their mouths and noses, dripping down their chins. Their empty eyes scan the hallway. I hear a tiny scream escape from someone behind me, and then eight horrified faces duck back into their rooms.

I sweep the area, looking for the other bedpost. I find it right where Mr. Josh carelessly left it, leaning against the meds cart, and I make a note to keep it in my hands at all times from now on. I run toward my weapon with everything I have, slide across the linoleum, and snatch it just as Tracy begins moving toward Ginger and Mr. Josh. Tracy lets out a bubbling screech that sends chills down my back, and then she lunges at Ginger.

I plant my feet and intercept her, swinging my bedpost and catching her in the jaw. She bounces off the nearby wall with a thud, then snaps her head toward me, her loose jaw swinging sickly a moment behind. I have her attention. She takes two steps toward me, and I use the bedpost to sweep her legs. What used to be Tracy clumsily tumbles to the floor, never taking her milky eyes off me. With her head at my feet, I swing the post like a golf club, connecting with the side of her face, and I feel her cheekbone give way, but it's not enough. She keeps coming, crawling on her belly, reaching out for me, spilling black bile as she pulls herself forward by her fingernails, making a hair-raising scraping sound.

I step back and take a deep breath in. I let the bedpost rise over my right shoulder and use the momentum of my entire body as I swing, this time aiming for the back of her head. It's enough. With a sharp crack, her body goes still.

I feel absolutely giddy, but this time I quickly swallow the giggle before it reaches my lips. I wait for Mr. Josh to lay into me, but there's no one near the staff workstation. Where are they? It only takes a second to find out. I just have to follow their screams.

I run toward Tasha's room and arrive to find Mr. Josh and Nurse Patrick grunting as they try frantically to pull Diamond off Tasha, but it's easy to see their efforts are too little too late. Tasha is no longer putting up a fight. Her throat is an open pit. Her eyes stare blankly at the ceiling. She's long gone. Olivia, Octavia, and Haley lie nearby with similar wounds and matching empty expressions. Cat, the sole survivor, cries helplessly in the corner, cradling her bleeding arm. Five. Diamond got five girls, and these idiots haven't even managed to stop her. It seems impossible, but Diamond keeps a vise grip on Tasha and appears completely unbothered as Mr. Josh uses my spare bedpost to swing hopelessly at Diamond's back while Nurse Patrick pulls at her legs. She can't weigh more than a hundred and fifty pounds, but they still seem to struggle. I make a mental note of it. These things are impossibly strong. "Get back!" I yell.

Thankfully, Mr. Josh and Nurse Patrick listen. I step up, get as close to Diamond as I dare, and bring my bedpost down on the back of her skull with a satisfying crack. She goes still. I exhale sharply, and then I look up from the mess and lock eyes with Nurse Patrick and Mr. Josh.

"You have to go for the head."

Behind us, Cat's cries are more persistent, and we all turn our attention to her. She's as good as dead, but none of us acknowledge it. Nurse Patrick leads her away, offering to bandage her up.

Diamond, Tasha, Octavia, Olivia, and Haley lie still. With Ms. Michelle and Tracy, that's seven dead in less than an hour. Add Cat's imminent death, and it's eight. More than half of the girls and a third of the staff.

"It was the noise," Mr. Josh whispers numbly, interrupting my mental math.

"The what?"

He grabs my arm and pulls me into the hall away from the bodies before continuing. "The noise! You told me Keisha heard a gunshot in the park last night. January's screams. The computer monitors shattering. Loud noises are waking them up."

It makes sense. Maybe he's not as dumb as I thought. "We

need to get everybody out of here," I whisper. "This is getting out of control."

"It's no better outside. The news isn't even scratching the surface of what's really happening. I saw one of those carriers on my way to work today," Nurse Patrick says.

"Carriers?"

"Yeah, like disease carriers," he answers. "That's what they're calling them on the news. Look, I hate to say it, but I think we should stay here until they get this under control. We're safer here than out on the streets."

I almost argue, but the fear in his eyes is enough. If he'd rather be in here with five ticking time bombs, he must know something I don't. "Then we need to stay away from these bodies. Let's get the girls into the dayroom, close the door, be quiet, and hope help comes," I say.

"Right. Quinn, get Keisha and Lucia. I'll get Ginger and January from the north hall. Cat, you come with me. Pat, get some supplies from the pantry. We could be in there all day," Mr. Josh whispers, annoyingly handing out orders like this was his idea.

I nod anyway. Gripping my bedpost at my side, I quietly make my way down the hall to Keisha's room. She's still in the corner, cradling her bedpost.

"Keisha, come on. We're all going to the dayroom to make a plan."

"What happened?" she asks.

"I'll explain later. We need to be quiet. Come on."

Keisha takes a reluctant step but follows me down the hall to Lucia's room. Out of habit, I stand in her doorway and knock softly.

"Lucia?" I wait. "Lucia?" No response.

I walk into her room, but she's nowhere to be found. I look under her bed. Nothing. I move around the corner and see a pair of shoes peeking out from the bottom of her shower curtain.

Lucia is the youngest of us. At thirteen years old, she barely qualified to live here. She almost never speaks. For the first month she was here, we thought she was completely mute. Eventually she spoke up, but only when it was absolutely necessary. To be honest, I would have completely forgotten she was here if Mr. Josh hadn't just reminded me.

Gently, I pull back the curtain. She stands stiffly, her tiny frame curved in on itself. Her big brown eyes hide behind a mess of soft brown curls. In her tight fist, she grips a large Phillips head screwdriver. How the hell did she get one of those?

"Lucia, come with us. It's not safe here. We're going to the dayroom."

She shakes her head, her curls bouncing back and forth. I sigh impatiently and turn to leave. We're on thin ice, and I don't have time to argue with a child. "Fine, have it your way," I say with a shrug, but Keisha grabs my arm before I can take another step.

"Lucia, I'm scared too," Keisha says empathetically. "We'll be safer if we're all together. Come with me," she says, holding out her hand with a warm smile.

Somehow, that's all it takes. Lucia locks her brown eyes onto Keisha's and grabs her hand like a lifeline, gripping it tightly, holding her screwdriver in the other. Keisha's always been able to get people to trust her quickly. I envy that. People look at her and see someone caring and gentle. People look at me and feel instantly uneasy.

I hold a finger to my lips and gesture toward the dayroom. We creep down the hall, and after a few steps, we're nearing Tasha's room and the bodies inside it. I grip my bedpost a little tighter, but as we pass by I can see no one has moved from their places on the floor. More than ever, I wish they let us have doors. We keep moving.

As we enter the dayroom, I do a quick headcount. Mr. Josh, Nurse Patrick, Ginger, January, Lucia, Keisha, and a bandaged-up Cat sit on the couches lining the wall. Only eight of us left. I close the dayroom door quietly and choose a seat near it. I let my bedpost fall into my lap, but I don't let my guard down. Across the room, I eye Cat cautiously. She cradles her bandaged arm, but she doesn't look sick yet.

Nurse Patrick has wheeled in the water cooler from the staff's break room along with a box of snacks. At least we won't starve. We have four weapons between the eight of us. Mr. Josh and I each have a bedpost from my room. Keisha holds one from hers. Lucia grips her screwdriver discreetly from within her pocket, keeping it out of Mr. Josh's view. It's not much.

"Okay, everyone, listen carefully," Mr. Josh begins. "First and foremost, it's important that we're all very quiet and stay in the dayroom with the door closed. We need to be calm until help comes." He tells the girls about the sickness and the riots and explains that loud noises will bring back the dead. Hearing him explain it sounds so surreal, but there's no denying it's the truth. For all his assholery, Mr. Josh is a professional. He explains everything in a way even January understands.

When he's finished, Ginger asks the question we all have on our minds. "What are we going to do now?"

CHAPTER 5

I can't believe it's only ten a.m. Our entire world changed over the course of just a few hours, and I have that familiar feeling that things will never be the same. It's the same feeling I had when I realized my adopted parents, Meredith and Daniel, weren't coming back for me. It's the same feeling I had when I arrived here and the doors locked behind me. The change feels heavy and final, and I learned a long time ago that fighting it doesn't help. Only moving forward can do that. So, I promise myself I will.

"We should check the news," Nurse Patrick suggests. Mr. Josh turns on the ancient TV hanging in the corner of the room and flips through the channels, passing by the footage of zombies—no, *carriers*—in city streets until he finds one with actual news anchors. A man in a clean suit explains that the riots first seen in Chicago are spreading rapidly. There are reports of attacks in New York, Los Angeles, and Houston as well as in their neighboring suburbs. The anchor advises everyone to stay in their homes, by order of the governor, and wait for containment, reassuring the masses that everything is under control. I can see his mouth twitch and his eyes shift as he tells the lie. Then, abruptly, the broadcast repeats. Somehow, that's the most unsettling part.

"You heard him. We stay put. Governor's orders," says Mr. Josh.

"How many of those things are lying dead in this building or outside in the streets waiting for the next loud noise to rise up and come for us?"

"Quinn, if we all stay quiet, the police will—"

"Nobody is coming for us. We're on the sixth floor of a residential psychiatric treatment center in Peoria, Illinois, for Christ's sake. We don't have parents. No one is looking for us. No one is coming."

This starts the waterworks, and I realize my mistake when Ginger's hands start to shake.

"I have parents, Quinn! My parents are probably coming to get me right now!" she whines.

"Me too, Quinn. I have parents," January sniffles. Goddammit.

Keisha narrows her eyes and gives me a sharp headshake, letting me know I just messed up big time.

"Of course, Ginger. You're right. I didn't think of that. I'm really sorry. I'm sure they'll probably be here soon," I say quickly. "Yours too, Jan." This placates them, thank god. You can feel everyone in the room breathe a little sigh of relief.

We sit in silence as the anchorman drones on and on, repeating his message. Every few seconds I glance at Cat warily, and I catch Nurse Patrick doing the same.

"We need to make sure the bodies in the other room don't wake up. We need to get rid of them, and fast," Nurse Patrick says, breaking the silence. It's a little strange to hear him refer to Haley, Octavia, Olivia, and Tasha as "the bodies," but besides making sure we have food and water, it's the first helpful thing he's suggested all day.

"And how do we do that?" Mr. Josh asks with an edge of snark in his voice. "I'm not getting in the elevator with the bodies without knowing what will be there when the doors open downstairs, and I'm sure as hell not carrying them down all those stairs and going outside. If we open the window, the alarm will go off throughout the entire building. We'd call every carrier in a five-mile radius right to the lobby."

We sit in silence for a moment, all of us coming to grips with the fact that the next loud noise will mean that a thin particle-board door is all that stands between us and the next attack.

"We could take them to the roof. All of them," Keisha says. "We can't let any of the bodies sit in here with us. Who knows how long we'll be waiting for help? We should get rid of all of them."

"She's right, Josh," Nurse Patrick says. "There's no alarm on the door leading to the roof. I go out there for a smoke sometimes. We'll be safe from whatever is going on outside all the way up there."

By eleven a.m. we have a plan.

Nurse Patrick, Mr. Josh, and I each grip a bedpost and step softly from the safety of the dayroom, quietly closing the door behind us. It bothers me to leave Keisha alone without a weapon and with Cat and her festering bite, but I shake off the feeling, knowing that getting rid of the bodies before they come back to life is most important. If Ms. Michelle taught us anything, it's that a bite on the arm takes about a day to kill you. We have time.

Out in the hallway, everything is still. To our right, Ms. Michelle and Tracy lie in a pool of black muck, their dented skulls ensuring they're harmless. To our left, the empty hallway looks like it could swallow us whole.

When we reach Tasha's doorway, we're relieved to find everyone just as we left them. Diamond's crushed skull makes her our last priority. Tasha, Octavia, Haley, and Olivia lie next to her in odd shapes, their throats ruined. It's like standing next to lit dynamite. I've never seen so much blood in my life, and it's gone sticky under my shoes, making a soft sucking sound each time I shift my weight.

Mr. Josh points to Olivia. Nurse Patrick nods and hands his bedpost to me, while Mr. Josh lays his softly on the bed but still within reach. Carefully, they grab her by her wrists and ankles. I'm ready to swing, just in case movement also brings them back, but she stays still. We breathe a collective sigh of relief. Our sticky shoes are the only sound as we move down the hall toward the back stairwell where Keisha and I escaped just last night. When we get to the end of the hall, I punch in Mr. Josh's security code and pull open the heavy door with a soft click. Mr. Josh's face goes red with anger and embarrassment as he realizes his code has been stolen, but he says nothing.

The stairwell is dark, lit only by the glowing exit signs. I lead the way, and we climb the two flights of stairs in silence. Olivia can't weigh much, but they're both sweating already by the time we reach the door to the roof. I swing the door open as the harsh midday sun nearly blinds us.

We reach the center of the roof, and they gently lower Olivia's body.

"Should we say something?" Nurse Patrick whispers.

"We can do that later. We need to get the others. Who knows how much time we have before some idiot sets off an alarm," Mr. Josh whispers back.

They turn to walk away, but I stay right where I am.

I know our job isn't finished.

"We have to throw her off the roof," I say flatly. They stare at me, wordless, with that horrified look I've grown used to. This time I don't try to fix it.

I whisper, trying to help them understand. "The next gunshot or car horn is going to wake her up. If that happens between now and when we drag the rest of the bodies up here, we're screwed," I explain.

They cringe, but they know I'm right. Sentimentality went out the window hours ago. Gently, they pick her up again and move closer to the edge of the roof.

"On the count of three?" Mr. Josh whispers.

Nurse Patrick nods. They swing Olivia's body back and forth, building momentum, and toss her over the edge. When we hear her body make contact with the concrete below, Nurse Patrick vomits immediately.

I can't help but peer over the edge to see what's left of Olivia, splattered on the Pegasus Center's walkway. She won't be hurting anyone. All of a sudden, the puzzle pieces click together in my mind. I can't believe I didn't think of it before. I'm an idiot.

"We don't have to wait," I say.

"What are you talking about?" Mr. Josh asks over Nurse Patrick's retching.

"I mean, we're idiots. We don't have to wait for them to reanimate to kill them. If we destroy their brain first, they won't get back up. We could have bashed her skull in downstairs and saved ourselves the trouble."

"Idiots," Nurse Patrick sighs, wiping his mouth.

CHAPTER 6

We make our way back downstairs to Tasha's room to finish the job the way we should have all along. I use my bedpost to crush Haley's, Octavia's, and Tasha's skulls so they stay dead while Nurse Patrick and Mr. Josh wait in the hall, looking ill.

The next hour is exhausting. I drag each of the bodies down the hall to the stairwell while Mr. Josh and Nurse Patrick carry them up the stairs and toss them off the roof. It's a messy assembly line that leaves smears of sticky blood and black bile up and down the entire hallway. When the job is finally finished, we're covered in the stuff, and we smell like death, but we're safe.

"We can't go back in the dayroom like this," Nurse Patrick says.

Mr. Josh and I nod in agreement.

"There are extra scrubs in the hall closet," Nurse Patrick says to Mr. Josh. "Quinn, we'll meet you back in the dayroom after you get changed."

Silently, I walk back to my bedroom. When I get inside, I peel off my filthy clothes and roll them into a tight ball, shoving them into the tiny wastebasket under my sink. I turn on my shower, step into the hot water, and the tension in my shoulders melts away.

The roar of the shower allows me to clear my mind and process what just happened. There isn't a sport or gym class that could have prepared me to do what I did today. I've never worked so hard in my life. It occurs to me that this carrier situation is going to demand a lot from me physically, but somehow, I held my own among Mr. Josh and Nurse Patrick. I feel proud and capable, maybe for the first time in my life. Once again, that feeling of readiness rises in my chest, and a sense of peace settles over me. I've always felt like I don't belong, but maybe this is exactly the kind of situation I was made for. When I'm finally clean, I dry off and dress myself in the most practical clothes I can find. It's not like we get to take trips to the mall here, so my choices are limited. Despite it being summer, I choose loose green cargo pants, a soft black T-shirt, and a flannel button-down. You can't go wrong with lots of pockets and layers, and I'd rather not have my skin exposed right now. Not with Cat waiting to die and reanimate in the dayroom. I comb through my hair and pull it back into a short ponytail to keep it out of my face.

In the back of my closet, I dig around for my old backpack. When I first came here, everything I owned fit into that thing. I guess living out of a backpack might have been good practice for the days ahead. I toss extra socks and underwear, spare T-shirts, hair ties, and my comb into the biggest pocket. I tuck a few toiletries into the smaller zipper in front. Finally, I roll up my hospital-issued blanket and pillow, grab my bedpost, and head back to the dayroom.

When I get there, Mr. Josh and Nurse Patrick are already back, clean and wearing fresh hospital scrubs. The only reminder of what happened shows up in little dark red drips on their shoes.

The hours tick by. Keisha and Lucia sit at the corner table, making a house of cards. Ginger stares at the television, lulled by the repetitive message on the screen, while January lies carelessly sprawled out on the couch snoring, her soft belly hanging from a sparkly T-shirt she must have outgrown two years ago.

Nurse Patrick changes Cat's oozing bandage again, while Mr. Josh paces back and forth, worried. I can smell Cat's wound from where I'm sitting. Her arm is already starting to fester, and she's looking rough with red-rimmed eyes and pale lips. It's only a matter of time before she goes gray and turns, but no one seems ready to acknowledge it.

I flop down in a chair and listen to January snore next to me. I almost snap at Ginger, asking her to change the channel so I don't have to hear the anchorman repeat his message yet again, but I think better of it. It's best to keep her calm. But I do need to find a way to get Ginger to let me scan the channels to find some more useful information. *Hmm.*

I nudge January with the tip of my shoe.

She stirs but doesn't wake. I try again, pushing my shoe deep into the flesh of her upper arm. That does the trick. She's awake, but she's not sure why. She blinks slowly and looks around, confused.

"Hi, Jan," I say sweetly.

"I'm tired," she mumbles, turning to go back to sleep.

"Jan, do you want to play a game with me?"

Her eyes fly open. Now she's interested. "Yeah! We can make bracelets! Or we could draw pictures of cats! Or..."

"I have another idea," I say, cutting her off. "Let's see if we can get Ginger to play with us. We can play restaurant."

"Oh, yes! I can be the customer! Ginger, will you play restaurant with me and Quinn?" January practically squeals.

Ginger loves to be loved, and she almost never gets invited to join in with the other girls. Her eyes shift away from the TV, and the trance is broken. Ginger and January dump out the basket of snacks onto the card table and begin sorting through the items, forgetting about me.

Satisfied, I walk over to the TV and start flipping through the channels for something useful. Most channels are playing the same two or three unhelpful clips. Finally, I land on something interesting.

A disheveled woman is broadcasting from a dark studio at the local news station. Her eyes look wild, like a trapped animal, but she's holding it together well enough to maintain her professionalism. I listen carefully as she provides a glimpse into what's happening outside.

I cough, cough, then sneeze. From the corner of my eye, I can see Keisha snap to attention. She needs to see this too.

"This hour, we're learning some disturbing facts about those who become infected with this new and terrifying virus. The carriers are seemingly drawn to the living by sound and attack by biting at the throats of their victims. Those who are bitten typically succumb to their wounds quickly due to rapid blood loss. Those who suffer nonfatal wounds have a typical survival rate of no more than twenty-four hours. Those who are bitten by the carriers will become carriers, regardless of the location of their wounds. Carriers often become stronger than they were prior to infection and are difficult to fight off. Shots or wounds to the chest have proven to be ineffective. Only those receiving blows to the head have been subdued."

This confirms what we already suspected. The anchorwoman shifts awkwardly, and her eyes dart off camera toward the sound of gunshots in the background. She begins talking faster and quieter. I lean toward the screen.

"Once a person succumbs to their wounds, they will appear dead. It is suspected, though unconfirmed, that loud noises will cause them to rise up. Do not fire weapons. Do not shout. Do not make more noise than necessary. Once the new carriers arise, they are very difficult to contain. It is estimated that one in every twenty-five residents of Peoria has been wounded by a carrier or has become a carrier themselves, with that number rising every moment."

The background noise grows louder and makes it difficult to hear the anchorwoman, but she continues dutifully.

"Get out of the cities as fast as you can. We will be overrun. In a matter of days, the power grid will fail. Our water reclamation system will cease. Get out while you have the—"

"Turn that off!" Mr. Josh growls, stepping in front of Cat to shield her from the message. But the broadcast has already cut out. Whatever was happening in that studio just silenced the most honest thing we've heard all day.

I do as Mr. Josh asks and turn off the TV. There's nothing left to hear anyway. Seeing the mood in the room shift, Mr. Josh turns on the soothing music they make us listen to when tensions are high. Usually I'm annoyed by the sound, but the volume is just high enough to allow me to carry on a conversation and not be heard. I sit down next to Keisha, Lucia, and their house of cards and give Keisha the we-need-to-talk look. She gives me a nod, and I begin to tell her what's been on my mind all day.

"We need to get out of here."

"No kidding. This place is a deathtrap," she says, placing two cards in a fragile peak and flitting her eyes toward Cat.

"Cat's going to die before sunrise tomorrow," I say, forgetting Lucia is sitting right next to me. "Oh, sorry, Lucia."

"I get it," she says in the quietest whisper as she tries to put on a brave face.

"Good." I nod at her approvingly. She gives me a small smile in return. Sensing it's safe to speak in front of her, I continue. "We need to take Cat out of the equation, or none of us will be getting any sleep tonight."

"That's kind of harsh, Quinn," Keisha says, but I can tell she agrees. We both know I'm right. Letting this play out naturally isn't an option.

"It doesn't matter if it's harsh. Do you feel like sleeping with one eye open tonight? How do you feel about her taking up resources? Food? Water? Medical supplies? Who knows how long we're going to need to make this stuff last. It's best to just end it," I say firmly.

"I know. I think you're right; I just don't like it," Keisha says, glancing toward Cat again, then looking down at her house of cards. She blows out a deep sigh, sending each carefully placed card fluttering to the floor.

CHAPTER 7

Time passes slowly in the dayroom, and I sit back to take it all in. Nurse Patrick hasn't taken his nervous eyes off Cat. Mr. Josh still can't stop pacing. Every few seconds he glances at the door like a caged animal. January and Ginger are unbothered, keeping each other busy with games and crafts. Keisha has taken on the role of caregiver, occupying Lucia's time with hair braiding and conversation. Keisha is obviously scared, but putting on a brave face for someone seems to help her keep it together.

I stay busy with the library books I got yesterday. I spend an hour or two studying the book on birds of the Midwest and find myself consumed by the birds of prey. Later, from the bottom of the pile, I pull out the US road atlas and find Peoria on the map of Illinois. We're barely a blip on the radar—a small dot next to small, unbolded font, surrounded by even smaller towns with smaller dots. I start to wonder just how many people have become carriers by now and glance at the population information near the atlas's margins. I do the math in my head. There are hundreds of thousands of people within a hundred square miles. If even a small percentage of them have become carriers, we have a big problem. I trace my finger to the larger cities that frame the Midwest. Chicago, Milwaukee, St. Louis, and Indianapolis. I shiver.

There is a very real possibility we'll eventually be surrounded by millions of carriers. Suddenly the dayroom walls feel closer together and the room is much too small. Now I understand why Mr. Josh is pacing. I force myself to think about what I've learned in therapy. I take several deep breaths and try to identify a problem that can be fixed now. That problem is the future carrier in front of us.

Cat.

It's been hours since she was bitten. The sun is getting lower, and her face is getting more ashen by the minute. Her time is running out. I weigh a few possible solutions.

"Mr. Josh, I need to go to the bathroom," January whines, interrupting my thoughts.

He looks at the clock, then shifts his eyes to the dayroom door.

"I've gotta go now!" she says, her temper creeping up.

"Fine, but we all go together. Nobody leaves the group," Mr. Josh says with a sigh.

This is perfect and almost too easy. For once, January's

whining is actually helpful. The spark of an idea forms in my mind. At first, part of me resists, imagining the possible consequences, but those consequences only exist in the Old World. Something in me knows that in this new world the old rules are no longer a factor, and this needs to get done. Excitement thumps in my chest.

"I'll stay here and watch Cat," I volunteer, making sure to keep the excitement out of my voice.

Cat's looking groggy and keeps nodding off on the couch. Keisha gives me a warning look, which I ignore. I arrange the softest, most innocent smile on my face, but Mr. Josh still eyes me with skepticism.

"No. Nurse Patrick will stay," he says dismissively.

Nurse Patrick looks at me. Looks at Cat. Then back at Mr. Josh.

"There should be two of us out there in the hall, Josh. Anybody with a security code could come up the elevator or through the hall doors. We can't trust anybody right now. We should be together. Quinn can handle watching Cat," Nurse Patrick says confidently.

Mr. Josh looks conflicted, but his claustrophobia is winning out. He wants out of this room as badly as January does.

"If anything happens—anything—you come get me first. Have I been clear, Quinn?" Mr. Josh asks.

I nod innocently as Mr. Josh snatches the bedpost from my hand. Nurse Patrick looks at me with what I can only describe as profound sadness. He knows what needs to be done just as well as I do, and he knows me well enough to know what's about to happen. He gives me a nod that I take as permission.

The group leaves the dayroom single-file. Old habits die hard. The girls form a line outside of the staff bathroom down the north hall past the elevator and begin taking turns. I should have about twenty minutes.

Alone with Cat in the dayroom, I move toward the chair where Lucia was sitting just moments ago and pull her screwdriver out of the cushions, right where I saw her tuck it away. This is just carelessness. We'll have to have a talk about her carrying it everywhere she goes.

I shove the screwdriver into the deepest pocket in my cargo pants and get to work.

I nudge Cat on the shoulder of her good arm. "Come on, Cat. We're going to the bathroom too," I chirp, channeling Ms. Michelle.

She groans. "I can't. I'm too tired; I just want to sleep." Her head lolls to the side. She's barely conscious. This might be tougher than I thought.

Ignoring her protests, I put my arm around her waist and pull her to her feet. "Up we go," I groan as we stand.

I half-drag her down the south hall, and she struggles to stay upright. As I pick up the pace, her shoes make a squeaking noise on the linoleum as they drag, and I pause, wincing, waiting to hear Mr. Josh shout from around the corner down the hall. I glance behind me. Somehow, I'm still in the clear.

When we finally get to the stairwell, my legs are burning and I'm barely able to catch my breath. Shakily, I punch in Mr. Josh's code and swing open the door, nearly losing my balance under Cat's dead weight. I know she'll never make it up the stairs, and I'm not strong enough to carry her. This has to be the end of the line.

"Okay, Cat. We made it. Sit down now," I say gently, propping her up next to the stairs.

I look at her slack, hollow face. She's gone downhill so fast. It's hard to believe this is the same girl I've lived with for the last six months. I didn't really bother talking to her much. Her chart wasn't that interesting, so why bother? Like most of us, she was in foster home after foster home before ending up here, but the Pegasus Center seemed to be really good for her. Her new meds evened her out, and she only attempted suicide her first night. Someone forgot to take her shoelaces. Rookie mistake. But Cat settled in and made friends fast. In just six months she was already on her way to graduating into independent housing. But that was before she was bitten. I look at Cat's tired face. Her eyes open, blinking slowly. She looks down at her bitten arm and sighs, defeated.

"I'm just going to rest here, okay?" she whispers.

"Okay," I reply.

Her eyes close again, and she exhales.

My heart beats heavily in my chest, and I can feel the thrill all the way down to my fingertips. I grip Lucia's screwdriver in my hand and trace the contour of Cat's face, carefully choosing a target, taking the potential for mess and efficiency into consideration.

Slowly, I push the tip of the screwdriver into her right eye, through the thin bone of her socket and into her brain. I'm relieved when she doesn't struggle at all. A tiny wince, a sharp inhale, and just a quick flash of fear are all the reactions I see. I push until my fist is flush with her eye, and she goes still. Just to be certain, I move the screwdriver back and forth to destroy as much brain matter as possible. Warm blood drips down my fist. When I'm certain she's gone for good, I stand up, wipe my hand on her jeans, and allow myself to smile.

Cat is gone. She's no longer a threat.

I feel the warmth of excitement. It's a strange feeling, and I try to shake it off, but it itches the back of my brain. Once again, I think back to what I learned in therapy and decide to try to understand where that feeling is coming from.

Do I feel this way because I wanted Cat dead? No. Cat wasn't a bad person. Sure, she was annoying occasionally like everyone else in this place, but killing her wasn't about justice or pleasure; it was just what needed to be done. It wasn't personal, but it did feel good.

Before today I'd never killed anyone. I've always wondered what it would feel like, but I also knew something like that would have consequences. Today, those consequences disappeared. For a moment, I let myself think about all the people who deserve death, and I'm flooded with that warm feeling again, but I need to keep myself under control.

I decide to stop thinking about it. I need to get back to the dayroom, anyway. I leave Cat where she is on the sixth-floor platform. I had hoped to get her all the way up to the roof, but a long day of physical labor has left me exhausted and aching.

I punch in Mr. Josh's code again and quietly push the door open. The hallway is quiet. Before going back to the dayroom, I stop at my bedroom to wash my hands and clean Lucia's screwdriver.

When I'm done, I tuck Lucia's screwdriver into my pocket and carefully arrange the expression on my face, making my eyes as sad as possible. I take a deep breath and walk back.

The others are arriving in the dayroom just as I'm approaching the door. Mr. Josh sees me and grabs me by the arm, pulling me back into the hallway outside of the dayroom.

"Ow! What the hell? Let go of me!" I say, trying to shake off his grip.

"Where the hell have you been? Where is Cat?" Mr. Josh spits, giving my arm a hard shake.

"I took care of it," I answer. "She won't come back. We're safe." I pull my arm out of his grip, and my eyes flash with fury. Mr. Josh's eyes go wide, and he takes a step back.

"You...you killed her!" he stammers accusingly. "We don't know if she would have died from that bite! She could have recovered! You don't know—"

"We both know," I say, cutting him off. "Cat was putting us all at risk. Problem solved," I say firmly, never taking my eyes off his.

"You're out of control! I think you should spend the night in the isolation room and cool off," he suggests frantically.

"Like hell," I say coldly. "This conversation is over." I turn away from Mr. Josh and walk back into the dayroom. In silence, I go to the couch and discreetly tuck Lucia's screwdriver back in its hiding spot. Six sets of wide eyes settle on me.

"Listen up," I say, addressing the room. "While you were gone, Cat died. Just like Ms. Michelle."

I scan the room to see who is buying it. Nurse Patrick looks down at his hands, fidgeting awkwardly. He knew what had to be done. So did Keisha and Lucia. Ginger and January seem to have no suspicion whatsoever. Mr. Josh, of course, fumes behind me.

"You don't have to worry. She won't come back like the others. I took care of it. We're all safe now," I finish.

Silence hangs awkwardly in the room. I wait, looking at each one of them to see if anyone will challenge me, but no one even bothers to meet my eyes. A soft beeping noise breaks the spell.

Nurse Patrick looks down at his watch, then pulls our meds out of the pocket of his scrubs. The bottles rattle in his hands, bringing all of us to attention.

"It's time for meds," he says carefully, still avoiding my stare. "Everybody get a cup of water and line up, please." We all go through the motions. The routine settles the tension that hangs heavy in the room. It occurs to me then that there is a finite supply of meds, but I file it away in the back of my mind. That's a problem for another day.

With evening meds distributed, I can feel the energy of the dayroom begin to slow. The end of the longest day of our lives is coming to a close. My sore muscles complain, and my eyes feel heavy. With Cat gone, I can finally relax.

I find a spot on the floor, curl into my blankets, and stare up at the ceiling. I notice Keisha has made her bed close to mine, and I can't help but feel rewarded. I've spent this last year learning from her, but today, she depended on me. I protected her, and she knows it. Her closeness now is proof. The realization that I could be the one to keep her safe is like a drug, and I want more of it.

CHAPTER 8

The next two days go by at a snail's pace. We mostly stay together in the dayroom, playing games, sleeping, and eating what little prepackaged food we have left. Mr. Josh is finally starting to let us take trips to the bathroom by ourselves, thank god. We're all on edge, snapping at each other for breathing too loudly, but no one is more bothered than Mr. Josh. He's restless, and he hasn't spoken a single word to me since I handled the Cat situation.

As I predicted, no one has come to help us. But we've been lucky, as apocalypses go. Our locked unit hasn't had a single intruder, and the power and water have stayed on so far. None of the alarms have been tripped in the building, and the silence has protected us. The rest of the city hasn't been so fortunate.

From the barred dayroom window, we've watched Peoria fall apart. The street is strewn with bodies and abandoned cars while fires send up smoke throughout the city. The occasional scream, gunshot, or siren sends chills up my spine. Things are bad and getting worse.

It's becoming harder and harder to get updated news from the television. The few broadcasts we were able to get from yesterday repeat, and I'm starting to wonder if anyone is left at the stations. Still, the news from the first day rings in my ear. *We will be overrun. The power grid will fail. We can't stay here.*

I pull Keisha to the back corner of the dayroom for a game of Go Fish. Lucia tags along, and I can't help but roll my eyes. Keisha's new shadow is persistent. I decide to let it slide and allow her to follow us. I deal the first hand, then get down to business, quietly saying the words we all know are true.

"We need a plan to leave. It's just a matter of time before the power and water fail. We can't be stuck here in the middle of the city. Not with thousands of these things roaming around," I say quietly, shifting my eyes to the right to be sure I'm not heard by Mr. Josh.

Behind us, music plays from a small stereo as Ginger argues with January about the human rights of Ken dolls in the Barbie village they're creating together. Mr. Josh appears entertained by their banter, and I can just tell he's wishing he had his electronic chart to document the social and emotional implications of the scene. In the corner, Nurse Patrick reads a thick novel, completely unaware of it all. We're safe to keep talking as long as we're quiet. "There have to be hundreds more bodies waiting to wake up out there," Keisha says with a shiver.

"Probably thousands. But we either face it and find safety or stay here and wait to starve. We have to find someplace with fewer people. And plenty of food and water," I say.

We're quiet for the next few minutes, pretending to play cards and waiting for a solution to appear out of thin air. Then, it does.

"We should go south," Lucia says softly. Keisha and I look at her, surprised, waiting for her to elaborate.

"South of Peoria is all farmland and small towns. There'll be fewer people, like you said. Plus, there are rivers that go south. The Illinois River and the Mississippi. Ms. Rhonda taught us about them in history class a few weeks ago. Rivers have water and food. That's how the Native Americans lived before us," she explains shyly. She's right. I've been staring at that road atlas all day.

I can't believe I didn't think of it.

"That's not a bad idea," I say to Lucia approvingly. Having her around is less annoying with every passing minute.

I walk over to my pile of belongings in the corner of the room and find the road atlas I checked out of the library, turn to the page with the state of Illinois, and carry it back to the card table.

"Look here. Lucia's right," I say, pointing to Peoria and tracing my finger south along a thin blue line. "The Illinois River runs through Peoria and goes south until it meets the Mississippi River here. Then it goes all the way south until it meets the ocean."

"So we follow the river south? That's the whole plan?" Keisha asks skeptically.

"Going south gets us away from the carriers and away from what happens when the lights and water go out. Plus, maybe we'll find help out there," I say, hoping to convince her.

Keisha's forehead wrinkles, and she shifts uncomfortably in her seat. She pulls the atlas toward her and traces her finger along the river. "I guess if this thing lasts until winter, we'll be warmer in the south. Let's do it." She nods a bit more confidently.

"Good. Then we just need an escape plan. Sneaking out isn't an option during the day," I say, thinking aloud. "There's no chance Mr. Josh is going to let the three of us leave the dayroom at the same time, and we're not fast enough to make a run for it."

"What about leaving while everyone is sleeping?" Lucia suggests.

"I don't want to be outside in the dark with those things," Keisha says, wrinkling her nose.

I turn the problem over and over in my mind while we play another few hands of cards.

"I think the best option is to just tell them we're leaving, stay firm, and just walk out. Everything has changed. It's not like they can stop us now. What is Mr. Josh going to do? Tie us up? Ginger would lose her mind. We have rights, you know," I say with a smirk.

"How are we going to get out, though? We have no idea what's happening on the lower floors of the center. Remember, Mr. Josh said there were some outbreaks downstairs on the acute psych units," Keisha reminds us.

"So we won't walk through the building. We'll use the fire escape on the roof," I suggest, avoiding the part about it being ancient and rusty and terrifying.

Lucia looks to Keisha, waiting for her reaction. When Keisha nods, Lucia nods too.

"Both of you need to pack a bag. Pack anything in your room that might be useful on a long trip. And put on clothes you can move around in. I know it's summer, but we need to keep our arms and legs covered out there in case we get attacked. Don't bring your bags in here. Put them next to the door in the south hall. We'll grab them when we leave. First thing in the morning."

"I'll make it happen," Keisha says, nodding.

And I know she will. I sit back and wait, eager to see how she pulls it off. I don't have to wait long.

Keisha whispers something in Lucia's ear, and about an hour later, Lucia walks past Mr. Josh with her thin arms wrapped around herself, shivering just a bit. He notices but doesn't say anything. With Mr. Josh's attention, Lucia walks over to the couch where Keisha is waiting. Keisha then puts her arm around Lucia, rubbing her upper arm briskly, and leads her toward the door of the dayroom. Before they reach the door, Mr. Josh calls out to them.

"Where do you two think you're going?" Mr. Josh demands.

"Oh, sorry! The air-conditioning is freezing, right? Lucia's cold. I'm just going with her to grab a sweater. I have an extra one in the back of my closet," Keisha lies casually.

Mr. Josh buys it, and I feel a flash of envy. He would never let me leave this room alone with Lucia, or any of the other girls for that matter. Keisha moves through the world lying easily, but rarely does she get questioned. Part of it is her preparation. Her lies are believable because she's planted pieces of the lie in people's minds before she ever tells the lie itself. Her lies are patient.

She also has pretty incredible acting skills, but most importantly, people tend to trust her implicitly, including Mr. Josh.

"Be quiet out there. And if you hear anything, you need to come back here immediately. You have five minutes. Go," Mr. Josh says, making a show of checking his watch.

A few minutes later, Keisha and Lucia come back. Lucia is wearing a too-big sweater that I recognize from Keisha's wardrobe. Keisha gives me a small nod to let me know the job is done. Now that we're packed, we just have to wait for morning.

CHAPTER 9

I struggle to fall asleep in my spot on the floor. January's snoring rings in my ears, but knowing that tomorrow we'll be leaving the relative safety of the dayroom weighs on me more. I've lived at the Pegasus Center for the last two years, and every day of those two years I've dreamed about the day I'd get out. I dreamed I would have an apartment waiting for me, or that maybe I'd be going to college. I dreamed I'd get a job to save money to buy a car and get my driver's license. I didn't imagine leaving while running for my life. I have no idea what we'll be met with once we leave.

When the sun comes up, I feel like I haven't slept at all. My nerves are buzzing, and I tap my feet anxiously while waiting in line for the bathroom. Our little routine feels painfully slower today.

We eat a small breakfast from the dwindling pile of tiny cereal boxes and granola bars, and the three of us tuck an extra bar or two into our pockets when the rest of the group isn't looking.

Once we're all clean and fed, I give Keisha the look, making sure we're on the same page.

She nods once. She's ready. Lucia gives a nod as well.

If Keisha's ready, so is she. Here goes nothing.

"I need to talk to you guys," I announce to get the group's attention. "We can't stay here forever. Keisha, Lucia, and I have decided we're leaving. Today. Right now." For a moment Mr. Josh, Nurse Patrick, Ginger, and January say nothing. Finally, Ginger speaks.

"You can't leave, or you'll die; the man on the TV said so," she says matter-of-factly.

"Girls, let's think this through together. It's not safe out there yet," Nurse Patrick says sympathetically.

"We're staying right here. All of us," Mr. Josh commands, his face reddening. "If you take one step out that door you'll lose every privilege you've ever had. We're waiting for help, and that's the end of the discussion. Sit down," he growls with clenched fists.

I shrug on my backpack I had packed earlier, pick up my bedpost, and look Mr. Josh right in his stupid eyes and bare my teeth.

"Like hell we are. Let's go," I snarl.

I turn to leave, knowing Keisha and Lucia are following close behind.

I can hear January beginning to cry, and I walk a little faster.

When fast footsteps come up behind me I wind up, pulling the bedpost back over my shoulder ready to swing, but it's just Nurse Patrick, looking concerned.

"Wait. If I can't convince you to stay, I'm coming with you. Give me two minutes," he says hopefully.

I sigh, annoyed. If it had to be anybody, I guess I'm glad it's him tagging along. He'd better pull his weight, though. I give him a firm nod.

"If you're not on the roof in five minutes, we're leaving without you. Get the other bedpost," I tell him.

He nods and runs quickly down the hall. Keisha and Lucia give me a surprised look, but they don't question the decision.

When we reach the end of the hall, Keisha and Lucia pull their backpacks from their hiding spots. Lucia grips her screwdriver deep in her pocket, and Keisha holds on to her bedpost reluctantly.

Down the hall I can hear both January and Ginger heating up. They're not taking our departure well.

"Here we go." I punch in the door code, and the little light flashes green. When I push the door open, the smell hits me like a brick wall. I almost forgot about that. Cat's body lies still and gray, rotting right where I left her. We startle a colony of flies. Keisha inhales sharply, and a soft whine escapes Lucia's lips.

"Christ, Quinn! You couldn't cover her up? Or at least take her down a flight or two? Anything?" Keisha accuses.

"She was too heavy," I say, shrugging flatly.

"Let's just go," she says, covering her nose and mouth, pushing past me.

I know I'm Keisha's best friend, and I know she cares about me, but sometimes I can tell I'm a little too much for her. That look she's giving me right now? I've seen it before. I've seen it on the faces of disapproving foster parents and disgusted staff and on the faces of kids and teachers at school. I learned pretty early on that I experience emotions differently than most people, and as a therapist once put it, my "*moral threshold is broader than most.*" I don't really feel guilt, but I don't like letting Keisha down. I vow to do better, or at least be more discreet. Despite the smell, we reach the roof in no time at all. The late-June sun beats down on us, and I can feel myself begin to sweat under my layered clothes. It's dead quiet on the streets around us. There are several bodies littering the sidewalks and parking lots that surround our building. From this height it's difficult to tell if they're permanently dead or waiting for the next big noise to rise up. As we reach the rusty fire escape and look down, I realize just how far down we're going to have to climb, and I shiver.

I hear shuffled footsteps and sniffles behind me, and I whip around, reeling back my bedpost again. I don't know which is worse: a carrier waiting to attack or turning around to see Jan's tear-stained cheeks. She's followed by the whole crew, and everyone's carrying a full backpack. Everyone except Mr. Josh.

This is not how things were supposed to go.

"Quinn, Nurse Patrick says we can go with you!" January hiccups.

"It's too hot out here!" Ginger whines, squinting behind her glasses under the bright sun.

This is exactly why I wanted to leave them behind.

"Nobody's going anywhere! This is unbelievable! You are wards of the state of Illinois, and you're under *my* supervision. We stay put. Go back downstairs. Now," Mr. Josh demands, gripping the third bedpost that I told Nurse Patrick to get. So much for that.

"In case you haven't noticed, the state of Illinois is dead," I say, pointing my bedpost toward the street below. "No one's coming for us, and we have to leave before our resources dry up and we die waiting for help. You're welcome to stay here and wait, but you won't stop us. You're not in charge anymore," I say with finality.

Always the peacemaker, Nurse Patrick tries to reason with him gently. "Josh, we really can't stay here. You could just—"

"You shut your mouth, Pat! You have no idea what's out there! What happened to having a united front, huh? She is dangerous, and you know it! You've seen her chart. She can't be out there unchecked," he says, pointing at me. I guess we're no longer being professionally discreet. My blood boils. "And the rest of them need constant supervision. Are you abandoning your post?" Mr. Josh spits accusingly.

The desperation in Mr. Josh's eyes is obvious, and it puts me on edge. Desperate people are dangerous. It doesn't take long for him to prove my point.

In a flash, Mr. Josh grabs a handful of Lucia's brown curls, pulling her in tight against his body and wedging the bedpost under her chin. Lucia gasps for air, her eyes wide and wild.

"Get. Back. Inside," he threatens.

"Let her go, now," I say between clenched teeth. Honestly, I don't care what happens to Lucia. I'd be fine to walk away and leave her behind, but she's important to Keisha, so I stand my ground.

Lucia's tiny fingers claw frantically at the bedpost, and the sound of her fingernails on wood gives me goose bumps, even in the blazing heat.

Nurse Patrick corrals January and Ginger toward the door, backing away slowly.

"Josh, there's no need for this. We'll go back inside. You can let her go," Nurse Patrick says.

Keisha and I stand firm with two bedposts between us. I get into a fighting stance and give him one last warning.

"Do something," Keisha whimpers to me.

"Let her go or I'll end you," I say, baring my teeth and doing my best to stare directly into his soul. I pull my bedpost back threateningly, and I'm a little surprised when Keisha does the same at my side.

"I'm not playing games with you! You think I don't see what

you are, Quinn?" He spits my name as he says it, squeezing the bedpost a little tighter against Lucia's throat. "You're going to get these kids killed out there, and for what? So you can watch them suffer? For the thrill and adrenaline? I've been working with people like you my whole career. All you psychopaths think about is yourself. If anybody knows what's good for them, they'll—"

With his eyes on me, Mr. Josh never sees what's coming next. Lucia stops struggling, reaches deep into her pocket, and pulls out her screwdriver. The sharp metal end glints in the sun, but Mr. Josh is too focused on me to notice. She grits her teeth, squeezes her eyes shut, and then punches the tool deep into Mr. Josh's thigh. She pulls it out just as fast as it went in, and Mr. Josh doubles over in pain, gripping the bedpost in one hand and his fountain of a wound in the other.

Lucia runs into Keisha's arms, shivering, holding on to her for dear life, but I know this isn't over.

There is ice in my veins and fire in my belly. We could easily walk away now and leave him bleeding on this roof, but something in me craves more. I *do* want to watch him suffer, and I *do* want to experience the thrill and adrenaline that would come with ending his life. He may be right about me, but I'm right about him too. Killing Ms. Michelle and the others after they became carriers was about survival. Killing Cat before she turned was just doing what needed to be done. This is different.

I don't have to kill Mr. Josh. I just want to.

Running toward him, I swing my bedpost and send his weapon clattering across the roof. He holds up his empty hand to me like he's backing away from a wild animal. Maybe he is. I press the end of my bedpost to the middle of his chest and smile. I take a step forward, forcing him to limp backward; then I take another.

"I've tolerated you for two years now. I've watched you boss us around with that smug sense of superiority." I take another step. "I see the way you look at us." Another step. "You think *I'm* a loose cannon?" I say, cocking my head to the side. "I think it takes one to know one. I think you're just about to lose control and show us who you really are, Josh. But I guess we'll never know for sure." I take one final step forward.

Before he realizes he's reached the edge of the rooftop, I give him a sharp shove with the end of my bedpost, feeling his chest crack. I stare directly into his wide eyes as he falls backward over the edge. On the way to the concrete below, he lets out an awful scream, then lands with a cracking thud.

I spit over the edge of the roof, satisfied. Free.

CHAPTER 10

I turn around to see five horrified faces, but there's no time to dwell on what I just did or whether it was the right thing to do. All at once, four of the bodies lying still in the parking lot stand and run toward Mr. Josh at a disturbingly fast speed, screeching eerily. "Oh my god, Quinn! You killed him!" Ginger cries out.

Nurse Patrick, Keisha, and I shush her in unison. Anticipating the chorus, I give January a warning look that demands silence.

Nurse Patrick waves us back into the dark stairwell, and we carefully close the door behind us. In the tight space, Lucia trembles beside me, and January is quaking with unshed tears. I swear, if Ginger complains about Mr. Josh's human rights, I'll toss her off the roof too. I feel impatient and frustrated. We'd be halfway to the river by now if these idiots had stayed in the dayroom where they belong.

"Let's give it an hour. If we stay quiet, maybe they'll move on and we can leave then," I suggest.

Silence. Nobody speaks, and nobody meets my eye.

I sigh, annoyed. "Look. He was holding Lucia by the throat. He was out of control. He had to go. You know it as well as I do," I say sharply, looking around the dark stairwell at each face for agreement.

"He has rights, Quinn," Ginger starts. I sigh, annoyed but not surprised.

"What about Lucia's rights! What about ours? Don't tell me that guy didn't give you the creeps! I want to *live*, Ginger! I want to survive this! He was in my way. He was in *your* way. He was in everyone's way! And now he's not. Move on," I demand.

The next hour passes slowly and quietly. The heat outside has turned the stairwell into an oven, and Cat's body downstairs is making this unpleasant situation nearly intolerable. When the wait is finally over, we open the door and breathe deeply, appreciating fresh air like never before.

Nurse Patrick and I walk the perimeter of the roof, scanning the parking lot for carriers. The area seems quiet, but when we pass Mr. Josh's body, one carrier remains by his side, slowly eating what's left of him.

"The fire escape is on the other side of the roof. If we're quiet, maybe we can avoid that one," I say, pointing toward the carrier below.

"And what if it hears us?" Nurse Patrick asks, a bit green in the face.

"Then we take care of it. Quietly. Listen, *you* brought Jan and Ginger with you. That was *your* choice, so now they're *your* responsibility. If one of them screams, I'm leaving them. No exceptions."

"I understand," he says.

"Good. Let's go."

I corral everyone to the fire escape and look down. It's a very long way to the ground, and my vision blurs. I take a deep breath, then speak quickly and quietly to the group, hoping they won't argue.

"I'll go first, just in case the carrier hears us. I've killed the most of these things; I can handle one on my own. Nurse Patrick, you come down right behind me and have that bedpost ready to help me." I give him an almost threatening look. He needs to step up. Now. "Keisha and Lucia, you're next, weapons ready. Ginger and January, you'll be the last ones down. Do *not* make a sound. Do *not* complain. We will leave you behind if you freeze up there." January's bottom lip quivers, and I give her a death stare. Everyone nods mechanically.

I don't waste any more time. I step out onto the fire escape and start my descent. The steel staircase is old, and I cringe with each rusty step, hoping it won't creak too loudly or fall apart completely. When I'm halfway down, I start to relax. I signal for

Nurse Patrick to follow. He hesitates but comes out onto the first set of stairs. The fire escape shifts a bit under his weight, and I freeze, but it holds. I nervously glance down into the quiet street below, searching for movement, but there's nothing. I keep climbing.

Once I reach the end of the fire escape, I use my weight to pull down the last set of spring-loaded stairs to the ground. The scrape of metal on metal pierces the air around me. Again, I freeze, whipping my head back and forth, waiting for a swarm of carriers. My heart pounds, but they don't come.

I climb down and drop the last few feet, landing on my toes with a soft thud. I motion for the others to keep coming. That's when a low growl draws my attention.

The carrier that was making a meal of Mr. Josh rounds the corner and runs head-on in my direction, dripping with Mr. Josh's remains.

Just before it reaches me, I dodge out of its way to the left, swinging my bedpost low, directly in its path. It trips, sliding face-first on the concrete, taking several layers of skin with it. The impact of bone on bedpost vibrates up my arms, and I drop my weapon. The sound echoes through the parking lot, and I scramble to pick up the bedpost before it can bounce again. Dammit. By now, the carrier has almost made it back to its feet. I can't miss my opportunity for the final blow. With the carrier on its hands and knees, I place my right foot onto its back, knocking it down onto the concrete. I lift my bedpost over my head and crack its skull on the way down. Its body goes still under my shoe. I breathe out, relieved.

Above, the rest of the group is frozen on the fire escape, shielded protectively by Nurse Patrick. These cowards didn't even attempt to help me. I kick the carrier at my feet angrily, then motion for them to continue.

I contemplate grabbing Keisha's hand and running away from them all. Except Keisha wouldn't leave Lucia to fend for herself. And anyway, there's no time to think. Clearly they're not interested in helping fight off these things, so I want to get out of here as soon as possible. As they drop to the ground one by one, I scan the horizon, watching for carriers, but thankfully the coast stays clear. "Thanks a lot for the help," I whisper, glaring. I think I see shame flicker across Nurse Patrick's face, but I wave it off. There's no time for this. "We need to head southeast toward the river like Lucia said. We also need to stock up on supplies and weapons. Three bedposts and a screwdriver aren't going to cut it. Nurse Patrick, which way is the river?"

"There," he says, pointing behind us. "We can follow Adams Street all the way south."

"Good." I turn to start walking.

"Wait!" he whispers. "We can drive," he says, pulling a set of keys from his pocket with a grin.

Nurse Patrick may be a passive marshmallow, but I guess he's not completely useless. For just a moment, I'm actually glad he's here, despite him bringing Ginger and January along.

We follow him to the parking lot on tiptoes, ducking low and scanning the area for more carriers. I feel completely exposed as we weave our way through a maze of stalled, empty cars in the parking lot. My nerves are raw, and I listen carefully for footsteps that aren't our own. Eventually we arrive in front of an old blue pickup truck with rust on the fenders, and I cringe. This definitely isn't an electric model, and from the looks of it, it's going to be loud. I guess they aren't paying psychiatric nurses very well.

Silently, I dole out the seating arrangements, pointing Ginger and January toward the cab while Lucia, Keisha, and I climb into the bed. When we're all in, Nurse Patrick slides the center back window panel open.

"Ready?" he asks.

"Ready," I reply.

"I'm thinking we should try to hit the sporting goods store off Interstate 474. We'll grab what we can, then head south following the highway that runs along the river," Nurse Patrick suggests.

"Good plan," I say. And it is. A sporting goods store is exactly what we need. I just hope no one else has had the same idea.

"Then we can go find our parents," Ginger says. My eyes flash toward Nurse Patrick, then to Keisha, silently begging for their help.

"That's right, kiddo. As soon as we can, we'll find your parents." The lie feels strange coming from Nurse Patrick, but his answer seems to satisfy her for now.

Nurse Patrick turns the key to the old blue pickup, and

I swear I almost crack my teeth cringing. The growling of his ancient engine is deafening in the silence of the city. His muffler spews thick smoke, and I stifle a cough.

"Go. Now!" I order through the back window.

CHAPTER 11

Once we start moving, the noise of Nurse Patrick's old truck gets softer, but we're definitely attracting attention. As we pull out of the parking lot, two carriers run toward the truck. Their attempt to catch us is futile, though. I watch as their relentless bodies get smaller and smaller the farther we go. The city is a mess. Stalled cars and permanently dead bodies litter the streets and sidewalks, and Nurse Patrick does his best to maneuver his way around each obstacle. Occasionally though, we have to double back and choose another street. As we pass by the neighborhoods in the heart of the city, I see curtains snap closed and faces peer through blinds as survivors look to find the source of the noise. As we pass one house, I see a man cautiously step out onto his front porch with a shotgun and one angry finger pressed to his lips, warning us to shut the hell up. We keep moving, attracting the occasional carrier, but we have no trouble outrunning them. I look through the glass over Nurse Patrick's shoulder and peek at the gas gauge. One-third of a tank. In a truck like this, that won't get us very far. I decide to worry about that later.

At our slow, careful pace, it takes us forty-five minutes to make it just ten miles south of Peoria. Finally though, we pull into the parking lot of the sporting goods store and find the lot nearly completely empty. I poke my head through the back window of the truck.

"Take a lap around the building. Let's see if anything is lurking out here."

Nurse Patrick nods and makes a wide arc, driving slowly around the building. We're all on watch, peering around every corner, looking for movement, but everything is quiet. Satisfied, Nurse Patrick backs up the truck so the tailgate faces the main entrance, then silences the engine. We file out of the truck, and I look at the reflection of our strange group in the store's sliding glass doors. We're not ready for this. The bedposts in our hands feel ridiculous now that we're outside of the center. I see Lucia is empty-handed, so I give her a nudge.

"Get your screwdriver. Don't let go of it until we're back in this truck or you find a better weapon. Understand?"

She nods and pulls it from her front pocket.

I pause, wondering if Nurse Patrick will take the lead and tell us what to do next. When he looks at me, I sigh and accept that, despite having no idea what I'm doing, I'm going to have to call the shots.

"Okay. We stay together in there, no matter what. We need weapons, food, and water," I say.

"Gas cans too," Nurse Patrick adds. "We can fill up the gas cans when we find a station. And we should each have at least one or two pairs of good hiking boots."

I nod approvingly. "If there are carriers inside, get behind me and Nurse Patrick. If there are people inside, run back to the truck. Got it?" I say mostly to Keisha. Everyone gives a quick nod. "All right. Follow me."

The automatic door slides open as we step closer, and I wonder to myself how much longer conveniences like this will last. The store is lit up as if it were any old day, but the eerie silence is a reminder that nothing about today is normal. We step through the doors carefully, weapons ready, and scan the area for carriers, but the coast seems to be clear.

I decide to work the store counterclockwise. I nod to the right and start walking toward the shoe department as the group follows quietly behind. I scan the displays and quickly find what I'm looking for, a sturdy pair of size 7 hiking boots. I pull two pairs from the shelves, putting one pair on my feet and tucking the second into my backpack, silently urging the rest of the group to do the same. I pull several pairs of thick socks from the racks and stuff them into my pack as well.

I look around to check on the group's progress and see that Keisha has found her size and is helping Lucia try some on. Nurse Patrick wrestles with Jan's feet as she sits helplessly in a heap on the bench. He hasn't even found footwear for himself. I tap my foot, annoyed, but nearby, Keisha flashes numbers with her fingers while giving Nurse Patrick a questioning look. At first, I have no idea what she's doing. Then he flashes a one, followed by a zero. Size 10. Of course Keisha thought of a way to try to help him. She finds two pairs of boots in his size and sets them down gently. He gives her a grateful smile. I set aside my annoyance at the group's slow pace and follow her lead. Ginger is standing idly, staring at a rack of blue shoelaces with yellow stars. I eye her feet and guess a size 9. A pair of pink size 9 hiking boots sits on the sale rack, and when I push them into her hands, her eyes light up and she does a little bounce on her tiptoes. Before she can squeal, I put a finger to my lips and motion for her to try them on. A perfect fit. I pull another set of size 9s from the rack and tie them to the strap on her backpack. Then, I grab the star shoelaces off the rack and hand them to her. She acts like it's the best damn day of her life.

A few feet away, Keisha smiles approvingly and gives me a little nod. I wish it weren't true, but I really do care about what Keisha thinks of me. It wasn't always that way though. When Keisha came to the Pegasus Center a year ago, she was just one more girl on the floor. I looked forward to reading her chart, out of sheer curiosity, but I didn't ever plan on being friends with her. I just wanted to know her weak points and which buttons to push, just in case I needed to pull some strings or use her to get out of a sticky situation. When I read her chart, that changed.

Keisha, like most of us, was a ward of the state. Her mother surrendered her at age eight after a long battle with addiction and multiple interactions with child services. The constant accusations of abuse and neglect must have grown tiresome because she finally quit fighting for her daughter. From ages eight to thirteen, Keisha "failed out" of several foster homes. Between thirteen and sixteen she was kicked out of a few group homes too. As a last resort, they sent her to the Pegasus Residential Treatment Center with a diagnosis of oppositional defiant disorder and a long history of impulsive and "overly sexualized behavior." As it turns out, her dismissal from each and every foster home was a result of that inappropriate sexual behavior. Sometimes it was an older foster brother; other times, a foster father. Her chart says she even had "inappropriate relationships" with both male and female staff in her group homes. What struck me as odd was that they never used the word "abuse" in the chart. Instead, they seemed to blame her—a child—for what was happening. The system can be harsh, but I had rarely seen it twisted like that. After reading her chart, I realized she was not someone to be manipulated; she was someone to learn from.

Keisha can read people just as well as I can, and she doesn't mind manipulating them. In that way, she's a lot like me. The difference between me and her is that she manipulates people to survive. I manipulate people just to see if I can. Just to see what I can gain. Somehow, after everything Keisha has been through, she still has a soft heart.

So, I watched her.

During her first two months at the center, I watched how she interacted with the staff and the other girls. I watched her facial expressions and tried to mirror her body language. I learned a lot of tricks. Then, one day everything changed. Her birthday was coming up, and Ms. Michelle was asking her what kind of cake to order from the cafeteria for the big day. I watched in awe as she negotiated her way from a dry, over-iced cake to a bedroom swap with Haley. The moment Ms. Michelle agreed to allow it—only this once—Keisha locked eyes with me from across the room and gave me the most stunning grin. She'd just become my across-the-hall neighbor, and when she gave me that smile, I was sure she'd done it on purpose. That's when I knew she'd been watching me too. The night she moved in I heard her cough, cough, then sneeze. It sounded so out of place that I got out of bed and went to my doorway. Just as I hoped, she was standing in her room across the hall waiting for me. I knew I'd just made my first best friend. From that day on, we were inseparable. I'd never had a best friend before and never really cared, but Keisha eventually became someone who mattered to me. So, when she nods her approval as I help Ginger, I feel a little warmer.

On the bench to my left, Nurse Patrick ties a double knot in January's new boots and gives me a thumbs-up. We tiptoe down the aisle toward the next department and find the camping gear. We each grab a large canteen and a set of camping utensils.

Sleeping bags, fire starters, and wind-up flashlights are next. There's even a rack of freeze-dried foods, and we pack as much as we can into our bags.

The more gear we collect, the better I feel. We keep moving.

The next department is hunting gear, and my heart swells. I stare at rows and rows of knives behind a locked glass countertop and start to daydream about which one will be mine. I take a few brisk steps around the backside of the counter to look for the keys to the case, but as I turn the sharp corner, I freeze. A carrier. A sleeping carrier. His skin is gray and starting to shrivel, just waiting for a cough or a dropped canteen to awaken. I throw up my hands to get the group's attention and give everyone the signal to freeze. In response to their questioning looks, I mouth the word "carrier" and point down at my feet.

I grip my bedpost and reel back but pause, thinking better of it. Nurse Patrick needs to buck up. He hasn't swung a weapon yet, and he's got more muscle than me and Keisha combined. I wave him over toward the body, inviting him to take a swing.

He gulps audibly and lets out a shaky breath. Across the room, Jan's sniffles start.

"Go!" I mouth.

He grips his bedpost and takes a swing, easily cracking the carrier's skull and spilling his brains onto the tile floor. Then, right on cue, Nurse Patrick heaves his breakfast. For Christ's sake.

I look over the body, curled up in the shelter of the knife display. He grips a large, serrated blade in his cold fist, and I notice a shallow bite on his left hand. He was hiding here. What the hell was he hiding from?

I snap to attention when I realize Nurse Patrick's heaves aren't quiet. The hair on the back of my neck stands up, and I scan the area around me. The other girls do the same, wide-eyed and on edge.

I hear their fast footsteps before I see them. The sound echoes throughout the store, and I whip from left to right trying to guess which aisle the noise is coming from. Finally, two rotting bodies emerge from the aisles and move straight toward us. Lucia lets out the tiniest "yip" of surprise and draws the attention of one of the carriers. The other is still locked in on Nurse Patrick, who, thankfully, has stopped vomiting long enough to pull himself together.

In horror, I watch Keisha step in front of Lucia protectively with her bedpost ready. The carrier is moving too fast and is way too tall for her to reach its head. "Keisha! Trip it!" I shout, hoping she'll react quickly enough. The other carrier charges with its foggy, empty eyes on Nurse Patrick. Unfortunately, I'm directly in its path. I take my own advice and stick my new boot out in front of it. As the carrier spills onto the floor, Nurse Patrick swings at it but only succeeds in breaking its nose. It scrambles toward him on its belly. I punch my bedpost through the glass display case and grab the biggest thing I can find. I aim carefully and swing downward, slicing halfway through the carrier's neck. The carrier goes still, but I take another swing to be sure I've finished the job. I look down and marvel at my new weapon. The way it cut through the air. The way it sliced through the carrier's flesh so easily. The machete in my hands feels like it was made for me, and for a moment I'm in awe. Another yip from Lucia snaps me back to reality, and I run over to her and Keisha to help, but they've already taken care of business. The carrier has a screwdriver in its eye, and I don't have to wonder how it got there.

"I did what you said." Keisha smiles shakily. "I tripped it."

"And I got him in the eye!" Lucia says proudly.

I can't help but smile.

"Good job," I say, meaning it wholeheartedly.

Nurse Patrick is vomiting again. He'd better snap out of this crap fast.

"Where are Jan and Ginger?" I ask. They shrug.

"Jan?" I call out. There's no use being quiet anymore. Any carriers left in the store would have been here by now.

"Jan! Ginger! You can come out now," I say.

They peek around an arrow display and rejoin us cautiously.

"Did anyone get bitten?" Keisha asks.

Everyone shakes their head. But I look them over, just in case.

"Good. Everyone pick a knife," I instruct.

The group walks toward the broken display case, and I see January reach for a hunting knife with a wicked double blade. "Not you, Jan!" I say a little too sharply.

"January can have a knife!" Ginger says, defending her. I can see the tears welling in January's pouty eyes. "Give her a Swiss

Army knife," I say, giving up easily. "The other one." I point to the smaller of the two models.

I hope she won't be able to do too much damage with the two-inch blade. Of all the girls here, January is the most unpredictable. She's also the only one with attempted murder on their record. She's emotional, vindictive, and childishly irrational, and I'm not about to let someone like January carry dangerous weapons.

When Ginger passes her the knife, her tears dry almost as fast as they came. Spoiled brat.

I find a heavy-duty nylon holster for my machete and fasten it around my hips. Fits like a glove. I pick up the hunting knife January reached for too, just in case. Once we've each chosen a knife and a sheath, we move on to the next aisle. The bows look incredibly cool, but none of us know how to use one. We pass up the guns too. One shot would wake up who knows how many sleeping carriers. Unless you have a death wish, using a gun would be completely stupid.

Eventually we make our way to sporting goods. We each grab a wooden bat, and I lay my bedpost on the cold tile floor. It did its job, but it's time to let it go. Nurse Patrick and Keisha lay theirs down next to mine.

"These things saved our lives. It was good thinking, Quinn," Nurse Patrick says warmly.

"It was nothing," I say with a shrug. "Come on. We still need those gas cans."

A few aisles down we find some ten-gallon steel cans, the kind made for riding in the back of off-road vehicles. They're heavier than plastic, but Nurse Patrick assures us this is what we need, so we lug them toward the front of the store.

We've finally made a full circle and end up back at the registers at the front of the store. At the checkout line, a cooler glows, full of sodas, energy drinks, and fancy bottled water. We grab a few baskets from under the closest register and load up as many bottles as we can, then fill another basket full of candy bars.

On a whim, I grab a handful of lighters from the counter. Behind me Jan reaches for one. Without thinking I slap her hand, hard. Too hard.

"*No*," I say with a deep scowl, knocking the lighter from her hand.

The screams erupt instantly.

Nurse Patrick looks at me incredulously, his jaw halfway to his chest. Keisha doesn't miss a beat and swings into action, trying to calm January down.

Ginger starts laying into me, prattling on about January's rights, but I tune her out. I tune them all out. I'm sick of this already. January is going to get us killed. I grab as much gear as I can and stomp toward the door. We need to get out of here, and this little scene is only slowing us down. Nurse Patrick lets Keisha handle the tantrum inside and follows me out with an armload of gear.

Outside, Nurse Patrick and I load the bed of the truck

without speaking. Finally, as we lift the last of the empty gas cans into the back, he breaks the silence.

"You know about January," he says. It's not a question.

"You mean how she set her family on fire? Yeah, I know about Jan. I know about all of them," I admit.

"How?"

I toss my backpack into the back of the truck. "Mr. Josh. His charting password was easy to guess."

He shakes his head. "Then you know about her medication regimen," he says.

"I know she's on a lot of meds."

"And she needs to stay on them. Quinn, if anything happens to me, you have to make sure she takes these." He pulls three bottles out of the pocket of his white coat. The caps are labeled carefully with a *J*.

"Twice daily, with food. Quinn, you can't let her skip a dose."

"I get it," I say, turning to find Keisha and the others.

He touches my arm gently as I start to turn away. I shake it loose, but he has my attention.

"Quinn, I mean it. These two are for Ginger," he says, taking two more bottles out of his pockets.

"What about the rest of us? Did you bring the whole freaking pharmacy?" I ask coldly.

"We both know Keisha never takes hers. I've been monitoring her for months now. She's managing without her medication. She'll be okay. And your ADHD meds won't help you out here.

Lucia needs her meds, though. Her bottle is here too. Everything is labeled, see? Quinn, in a couple of weeks we're going to need to find a pharmacy," he says seriously.

"Okay," I agree with some sincerity.

"I need your word."

"You've got it."

I realize we're not exactly normal teenagers, but it still stings to be reminded with those little orange bottles. Nobody really wants to need medication or therapy or to live in a residential treatment center. But we do. We need those things. I can understand.

I also know ADHD isn't my real diagnosis. Those meds are just supposed to help with my impulsivity during school hours. Technically you can't be diagnosed with antisocial personality disorder until you're eighteen, but the Pegasus medical team has all but made up their mind that that's my fate. My chart says it's incredibly difficult to treat antisocial personality disorder with medication, though. There's no drug that creates the ability to empathize with people and think more altruistically. They tried lots of different medications and therapy during my first year in the center, but the only thing that really seemed to help make me a "better person" was having some structure and a self-serving reason to follow the rules. As much as I hate to admit it, the level system gave me a reason to try to be kind and fit in. Following a few rules and acting like the other girls was a small price to pay for a trip to the movies or a night out bowling—anything to get out into the real world. Everything has changed, though. There are no compliance points to behave for. No demerits. No reason to follow the rules.

With the gear loaded and the medication situation settled, we go back into the store to find that Keisha has January settled down. But Ginger glares at me, hands on her hips.

"Let's go. Everybody back to the truck," I say.

CHAPTER 12

The roar of Nurse Patrick's truck coming back to life makes me cringe again as I sit in the bed of the truck. I whip my head from side to side anxiously, but I don't see any carriers coming for us. I breathe out in relief. Bless the Midwest for sticking these mega stores in the middle of nowhere off the highway.

"Where to?" asks Nurse Patrick through the back window. "You said you wanted to follow the river?"

"Yeah. It was Lucia's idea, actually. That way we always have access to food, water, and isolation. Seems worth a shot."

"Solid plan, Lucia," Nurse Patrick says with his warm smile. "Highway 24 follows the river pretty closely, but we should be on the lookout for a place to stop for fuel. Maybe a farm or a little town," he continues.

"How much gas do we have?" asks Keisha.

"We're almost out. We need to stop somewhere soon," Nurse Patrick says with worry creasing his brow.

"Then let's not waste it," I say, sliding the back window closed and finding a place to sit among our new gear.

We head southeast toward Bartonville on Highway 24. The highway is much easier to navigate than the inner-city blocks. There are far fewer abandoned cars and bodies to navigate, and we move at a much faster clip. But with the extra speed, I imagine the gas in our tank turning to vapors.

My worry lifts a bit when I see a small gas station coming up on our right just outside of Bartonville. Nurse Patrick slows, but my hope sinks quickly and the tiny hairs on the back of my neck stand up, telling me this is not a good idea. Outside of the gas station, six pickup trucks block the entrance and exit, and three men with shotguns stand guard. I slide open the back window.

"Keep moving. This isn't our stop."

"I hear you loud and clear," Nurse Patrick says, speeding up a little.

Keisha, Lucia, and I duck our heads as we pass up the resource we desperately need. This might be more difficult than we thought. The next two towns give similar results. In Mapleton we're followed out of town, our pursuers only turning back once they're sure we're moving on to the next town.

I peer through the window and see our needle dip squarely within the red. If we don't stop at the next station, we'll be walking soon.

I slide open the window. "Pull over," I say.

Nurse Patrick does as I ask and turns off the engine.

"We need a plan," he says.

"My thoughts exactly," I say, but I have nothing to suggest. My best idea is to run our truck over anyone standing in the way of the pumps. Somehow, I doubt Nurse Patrick will go for that. I glance at Keisha, and I can tell her wheels are turning, but she stays quiet. I sigh and try to think through our options aloud.

"The way I see it, we have a few choices," I begin. "We can take what we want by force, try to bargain with them, or convince them that they want to help us. It's that or we start breaking in these new boots," I say.

"We don't have a lot to bargain with, and I'm not confident we could take anything by force. What do you have in mind for option three?" Nurse Patrick asks. Like magic, I see Keisha's eyes light up. She's got something, but that flash of brilliance fades almost as fast as it appears. She's holding back.

"Say it," I push her.

She looks hesitant, but with a little more convincing, she finally spills her idea. It's risky, especially for her, but it could work. It's not like we have a lot of options anyway.

We shuffle our seating arrangements before driving into Kingston Mines. Keisha takes the driver's seat, and I ride shotgun because

I don't know the first thing about driving. Nurse Patrick, Lucia, Ginger, and January lie down in the back of the truck, covering themselves with our gear and one of the plastic tarps from the sporting goods store.

Keisha and I will pretend to be alone.

Keisha is not a great driver. Her jerky movements make me doubt we'll even make it to Kingston Mines in one piece, but after a mile or so she seems to get the hang of it.

Predictably, when we roll into the small town, we see the gas station is guarded, just like the others. Two men in cop uniforms and bulletproof vests stand at attention with their hands on their weapons as we pull up to the pumps.

"Smile, Quinn. It's showtime!" she urges with a little twinkle in her eye as she rolls down the passenger-side window. She's in her element now.

I do as she says, hoping I'm lifting my eyebrows just right so my smile reaches my eyes and comes off as genuine, but somehow I doubt they'll even give me a passing glance. Beside me, Keisha is absolutely magnetic. "Hi there, officers!" Keisha says sweetly, waving timidly, batting her eyelashes just enough.

"Girls, please show us your hands," the tall one says firmly.

We do as he says, but Keisha doesn't miss a beat. "Officers, we're so glad to see you. I'm Keisha, and this is my friend Quinn. We're students up at Bradley University, and it's just a mess up there. We're hoping to find a few gallons of gas to help us get to

Quinn's dad's farm downstate, where we can ride this out. Are you still selling gas?" she says, tilting her head just right with the most innocent smile I've ever seen.

"I'm afraid not, young lady. This pump's for locals only. You'd be wise to move on down the road," the short one says stoically, hand on his weapon.

Young lady. The words grate on my nerves, and I have to breathe deeply to make sure my annoyance doesn't show on my face.

"Officer, I surely understand the need to protect your own. I hope you don't think we'd ever want to take from those in need. We'd happily do a trade," Keisha tries.

"Move along, girls," the tall one says, gripping his weapon tighter.

"Okay, sir," Keisha says, her voice wobbling. "I just... I just don't know how we'll make it is all." She sniffles softly, and two perfect tears drip down her cheeks. She hiccups right on cue and wipes at her tears, seemingly embarrassed. "I'm sorry, sir. I didn't think I'd get this emotional. It's just that we got turned away in Mapleton and Bartonville too. We were so lucky to get out of Peoria alive. I just can't believe our luck has run out like this."

The short cop shifts from his left foot to his right foot uncomfortably and looks down at his shoes. He's wavering. He elbows the tall cop and whispers something in his ear. When the short cop is finished, he sighs. "What do you have to trade?" the tall one asks, annoyed.

"Well, sir, we don't have much. We picked up some candy bars on our way out of town." She holds up a pile of sweets from the sporting goods store. "What will this get us?"

The tall one spits. "That'll get you a liter."

"What about a few bottles of pop and a couple pairs of hiking boots? Sizes 7 and 8?" she asks hopefully, still sniffling a bit with hope in her eyes.

Those were our bargaining chips. We can't afford to give up anything else. If this doesn't work, we'll move on to phase two.

"One gallon," the tall one says. It's not enough. We need more. Without hesitation, Keisha moves on to the next step in the plan.

"Then, officer, why don't you name your price?" She bats her eyelashes a bit, looking down, her cheeks blushing a deep maroon. It's not hard to tell what she's suggesting. This is exactly how Keisha has navigated through life. It's also how she ended up at the Pegasus Center. I knew she'd be able to seduce them. I knew this was coming. I try to stay calm, but inside I'm panicking. I feel an unexpected surge of protectiveness. I don't want these goons to lay a single finger on her. It seemed like a good plan a few minutes ago, but now it tastes sour, and all I want to do is leave.

"Step out of the truck, girls. Let's talk this out," the tall one says, smirking.

I lean toward Keisha to unbuckle my seatbelt and whisper angrily, "This is a bad idea. It's too risky."

She shushes me quickly. We both step out of the truck and stand in front of the officers.

"That's a big knife for such a little girl," the short one says, gesturing at the machete sheathed at my side.

"Can't be too careful these days," I say through my teeth.

His smirk falters a bit. His instincts are telling him I'm dangerous, but my size, age, and gender must convince him I'm not a real threat, because he shifts his focus back to Keisha.

"So, about this trade," the tall one says, licking his lips. I get a sick feeling that nearly makes me double over.

I can't let her do this. This is the part where Keisha is supposed to start making promises. This is the part where I'm supposed to demand that we get what we want first, then drive off before we have to hold up our end of the deal. But something in my gut tells me this isn't going to work, and I can't risk it. I can't risk her.

With their attention on Keisha, I take a subtle step to the right and slowly reach toward my hip for my machete.

The sickening smirk on the tall one's lips makes my stomach turn. As he reaches up to touch Keisha's face, I let my machete fly with a backhanded swing, aiming at the short one's throat. His blood spills quickly, and he stumbles backward, grasping at the wound as if he could stop the flow.

The tall one is stunned stupid, watching his friend bleed out. He snaps back to reality quickly and reaches for his gun, but his moment of hesitation gives me the advantage. I yell for Keisha to stand back and swing my machete upward at his hand before it reaches his weapon. I catch the inside of his wrist, and blood trickles from the wound at a satisfying speed. He backs away, both hands up as if trying to calm a snarling animal.

"Now, sweetheart, there's no need for this!" he says desperately. "You can take the gas. As much as you need." I take two steps toward him, my machete aimed at his belly. I hear the short cop gurgle his last breath behind us.

"You know what? You're right. There was no need for this. You could have helped us. Just two innocent girls trying to get home," I say. "But you wanted to play games."

"Quinn, let's get the gas and go. I think he's scared enough," Keisha says.

"No, I don't think he is, Keisha. I think he'll try this again with the next person who comes through looking for help. Won't you?" I say, moving my machete up toward the soft skin under his chin.

"Your friend is right, girl. You can take what you want. I've learned my less—"

I don't let him finish. I push the machete up slowly into his throat until I feel his spine touch the sharp tip. When I twist the handle, his eyes go wide. I watch until the spark in them goes dim and he slumps to the ground.

"Nurse Patrick!" I shout. "Fill 'er up."

He's shaking as he climbs out of the truck bed. When our eyes meet, I think I see disappointment. He looks away quickly but doesn't waste any time pulling the truck closer to the pump and filling the tank.

When I look at Keisha, she shivers. "You didn't have to do that. The plan would've worked."

"It did work," I say flatly. "We got what we came for." I search her face for any hint of emotion, but she reveals nothing. What is she thinking? Is she angry? Did I do something wrong? The questions are maddening. Adrenaline is still buzzing through my veins. I feel electric. I feel hope that we might actually survive all this. How could she not feel the same way? Before I can ask, she turns to help Nurse Patrick fill the gas cans. I head back to the truck and motion for Ginger and January to climb back into the cab. I get into the truck bed with Lucia and wait for Nurse Patrick and Keisha to finish fueling up. When Nurse Patrick climbs back into the driver's seat, Keisha finds her spot next to me. Lucia curls her small body into Keisha. She gives Lucia a comforting squeeze, then fixes her gaze in the distance, making it obvious she doesn't want to talk. I know I should just let it go, but I can't. I need to know what she's thinking, but asking her directly somehow feels too desperate.

"If we keep sticking together like that, we can survive this," I say, hoping she'll give me even a hint of where her head is.

"That's exactly what I was thinking," she says. But again, her expression is blank.

I sigh and decide to take her words for what they are.

CHAPTER 13

The next few miles pass slowly. Warm country air and the smell of knee-high corn growing in neat rows fill my lungs. Occasionally, we see a carrier wandering along the highway or out in the fields, but we easily leave them behind. I can't help but think of what could have happened if we had been walking along this highway instead.

The sun is sinking lower and lower in the sky, and soon we'll need to find a safe place to sleep. I definitely don't want to sleep in the truck, and clearly these small towns aren't welcoming guests. Lucia must be thinking the same thing because she nudges me and points to a road sign for campgrounds in a little town called Havana just off Highway 24. I give her a nod of approval and tap on the cab window to get Nurse Patrick's attention. He slows the truck, opens the window, and shouts at us over the roar of the engine.

"What's the word, girls?"

"Lucia saw signs for a campground up ahead. What do you think? Could be a good place to stop for the night," I say.

We all agree, and Nurse Patrick pulls off the highway, following the camping signs. We loop through poorly paved roads, bouncing in the back of the truck, keeping our eyes peeled for both carriers and people. Soon, we come to an abandoned camping site.

The lot has space for tents and RVs, each with its own fire pit, all centered around an old, leaning outdoor bathroom structure. The lot is nearly empty, save for a few discarded tent pieces, empty coolers, and deep tire tracks, like someone sped away as fast as they could.

We pull into the clearing, turn off the engine, and climb out of the truck, stretching our sore muscles. I hear birds singing and mosquitoes buzzing. The summer air feels hot and thick as the last few minutes of sun hang in the sky.

We didn't get tents at the sporting goods store, but now I'm wishing we had. At the time, we decided they were too bulky to carry and too weak to protect us, but anything seems better than the thought of sleeping out in the open.

Something beeps softly behind me. "Time for meds," Nurse Patrick says, pressing a small button on the side of his watch. While the other girls line up, Keisha and I walk over to the bathroom structure to see what we're working with. I notice the first problem immediately. The structure has no doors. It's just one long, open hallway split in the middle by a thin plywood wall that delineates the women's side at one end from the men's at the other. Each side has three shower stalls and two toilets. I check the faucet and find that the water is still running through the pipes. I wait for the hot water to kick in, but it never does. Damn.

The structure isn't clean by any means, but it doesn't smell as awful as I had expected. Spiders make their webs in the rafters above us, catching mayflies and tiny gnats, and frogs chirp from somewhere above. The concrete floor doesn't look very inviting, but it seems like we could fit six sleeping bags if we stay close together.

I sigh. "Home sweet home?"

Keisha guffaws. "Hardly!"

"We can make it work," I say, jogging back to the truck for my pack.

Nurse Patrick is carefully placing the cap on the last bottle of medication and tucking it into his pocket when I rejoin the group.

"We can stay in the bathroom structure over there. The water is still running, but it's not hot. One big problem, though," I say with a sigh.

"Well, let's have it," he says, waiting for the bad news.

"There's no door on the building."

"Is that all? I can fix that!" he says with a smile.

We all gather inside the bathroom while Nurse Patrick backs the truck up so the tailgate nearly butts up against the open corridor. I instantly feel safer. Once again, I'm glad to have him around. He jumps into the back of the truck and climbs inside with us.

"Safe and sound!" he says, grinning.

After we each get our brand-new sleeping bags unrolled, Keisha passes around the food we collected. We eat a dinner of candy bars and potato chips. After not eating all day, it doesn't seem so bad. After dinner, Nurse Patrick insists we each brush our teeth before going to bed.

"Trust me. You don't want a cavity in a world without dentists," he says.

His comment gets me thinking about just how different the world is already. It's only been five days since Ms. Michelle was bitten, and everything has changed. Is there anyone left to fix this? Is the government sending the National Guard to fight off the carriers? Are there still safe places? I wonder if I'll ever know for sure.

Exhausted and full of sugar, we climb into our sleeping bags on the concrete floor and try to sleep.

CHAPTER 14

I'm awakened by a crack of lightning. My eyes fly open just as the thunder booms outside, and I can feel it shake my bones through the concrete floor.

I sit up sharply, straining my eyes to see in the dark. The others heard it too, and we all scramble to our feet.

"What was that?" January whines.

"Shh!" we all whisper in concert.

Lightning cracks again, and it feels like it's directly overhead. A boom of thunder rips through the sky in answer as sheets of rain pour down on the roof over our heads. Then I hear something else. Something nature didn't create.

A screech fills the air, then another, and another, until I lose count. I imagine the woods surrounding us, alive with newly awakened carriers, and I shiver.

In the dark, I find my machete and grip it tight. I move my

finger over my lips, hoping the group can see my plea for absolute silence, but I can already hear sniffles coming from Jan's direction. Keisha rubs her arm, attempting to comfort her, but it only makes the sniffles louder. I can only hope the rain muffles the sound.

I begin shoving anything I can find into my pack and rolling up my sleeping bag, silently encouraging the others to follow my lead.

Another crack of lightning screams overhead. This time, the tiny hairs on my arms rise up from the electricity. The next crash is indescribable. Something cracking apart and the scream of twisting metal. The noise is awful, but the realization of what just happened is far worse.

A flash of lightning reveals our truck, pinned under one of the tallest pine trees I've ever seen. Its needles pour through the open doorway, nearly blocking our view to the outside, but another flash reveals just enough of the campground to show we're in big trouble. A mass of carriers races toward us, drawn by the awful sound. I lose count after seven.

My ears are ringing, and it takes me longer than it should to realize January is screaming, wide-eyed and red-faced, her hands over her ears.

"Shut her up or I'll do it myself," I hiss at Nurse Patrick, flashing my machete.

He goes to his bag and pulls out a syringe I didn't know he was carrying. Diazepam. In seconds, January is quiet, slumped against the bank of sinks, crying softly. I don't know what to do.

I wonder if the tree and the truck blocking the open doorway will be enough to keep out the horde outside. I touch the walls around me. Thin plywood. Thin *wet* plywood. I press against the board and feel it give. It won't take much to bring this entire structure down around us. We need to escape.

The horde hits the truck and presses it tightly against the structure. The plywood creaks around us.

"Help! Help us!" Ginger screams wildly.

"Ginger, no!" I whisper harshly. "There's no one to save us. You're giving away our location! You need to be quiet! Get your boots on now! Put your backpack on. We're getting out of here!"

I see the first arm breach the bathroom doorway, coming from underneath the truck. They've already found a way in.

"Keisha! Lucia! Grab your bats. Do not let them in here!"

I eye the back wall. Behind the thin plywood is the other half of the structure. The men's side. It's not barricaded, and I have no idea if the carriers have surrounded us or if they were all drawn to our side. I grip my machete and hope for a miracle.

I swing the machete with everything I have. I can hear the horde growing outside. Ginger sobs uselessly, but there's nothing to be done about it. The others fight off the carriers who breach the barricade one by one.

Soon I've created a hole in the plywood separating the men's and women's bathrooms. I peer through it and see no movement. This might work. I keep hacking through the plywood until there's a hole wide enough to fit through.

"Get your packs! We need to leave! Now!" I yell over a clap of thunder.

I step through the hole and into the other side, then wave the others through. Ginger goes first, followed by Lucia, then Keisha.

"Come on!" I urge. At this pace, it'll be a miracle if we survive the night.

In the dim moonlight I can see Nurse Patrick struggling with the weight of January in his arms. She's like a ragdoll, nothing but dead weight in her medicated state. He nearly drops her several times, but he finally manages to wedge himself and her lifeless frame through the hole in the wall.

We run through the men's corridor, feeling for the exit in the dark, hoping the carriers were all drawn to the other side by the noise.

Above us, we hear the structure begin to give way. The pressure of the carriers and the tree pressing against the walls and roof is too much. The beams tilt and groan.

"Run!" I shout.

As we rush through the doorway, a tiny shriek catches my attention. Behind me, a carrier has Lucia by the ankle.

"Quinn!" In the dark, Lucia's eyes beg me to help. I'm within arm's reach of her, but I hesitate. I can't help it. Every instinct screams at me to keep running.

I look ahead, then back at Lucia. Her tiny arms are locked now, holding the carrier's body just inches above her face. Its snapping jaws drip black bile. When I don't come to help, Keisha whips into action and swings her bat at the carrier's body, but it's no use. Keisha's eyes flash with betrayal and beg me for help. I cave.

I wave Ginger and Nurse Patrick forward silently, pointing to a copse of trees, then run toward Keisha and Lucia as more lightning flashes.

I give the carrier a hard kick to the ribs, and it tumbles to the side. I can feel its ribs crack under the force of my boot. It rolls to the side, disoriented, and I step over Lucia to finish it off. From the ground, the carrier reaches for me, black goo foaming between its snapping, screeching jaws. I throw all my weight into my swing, letting the blade of my machete come down on the soft tissues of its neck. My aim is true, and my swing is enough to separate the carrier's head from its body, but there's no time to celebrate. We've attracted the attention of the horde.

Another flash of lightning reveals what's coming, and my stomach sinks. I grab Keisha's hand and pull her forward, hoping Lucia is following. When we reach the trees, we find Nurse Patrick, Ginger, and a sleeping January crouching behind a pile of fallen branches, stupidly waiting for us when they could have been yards ahead of the horde.

"We have to move. Let's go," I say without stopping. Nurse Patrick picks up January, straining under her weight. We run as fast as we can into the forest with no idea where we're headed. I can hear the wet footsteps of the carriers behind us getting closer. Their screeches grow more and more impatient, and the thick raindrops pour relentlessly into my eyes, making it hard to see. Keisha and Lucia keep pace with me, but when I look back, I see Nurse Patrick struggling to keep up. Ginger runs awkwardly beside them, fighting for each breath.

Another flash of lightning reflects off something shiny ahead. I squint hard. Water. Lots of it. The river ahead of us glistens like a beacon of hope. I force my legs to keep pushing me forward and run faster.

In the next lightning flash, I see a row of canoes bobbing, tied to a small dock. I can taste our salvation. But one glance back tells me our chance of escape is narrowing by the second. The horde is too big and too fast for the others. For Keisha.

An idea forms. For a moment, I worry about what Keisha will think, then shake off the feeling. If I don't do this now, she won't survive.

I double back to Keisha and Lucia, who trail a few yards behind me. "Keisha! Lucia! Get into a canoe. Cut the rope and wait for us. Be ready to go!" I shout, turning back to run toward the others.

As I reach Nurse Patrick, I can see he's barely holding on. January is weighing him down more with every step. The determination in his face is fierce, but the horde is closing in.

"Keep going toward the boats. Do *not* look back," I say sternly. "I can hold off the carriers. Go!"

He nods and pushes forward, shouting over his shoulder in Ginger's direction. "Keep moving, Ginger! We're almost there!"

Ginger hobbles awkwardly just a few steps behind with three screeching carriers on her heels.

I pull out my machete and set my feet. Ginger runs toward me with hopeful eyes. A grateful smile tugs at her lips. When she's just a step away, I let my machete swing downward toward her right leg.

As my blade meets bone, Ginger tumbles to the ground, and I hear the scream I was counting on. I don't waste a single second. I turn and sprint for the canoes, but honestly, I could walk there if I wanted to. I have plenty of time now.

Behind me, Ginger's screams turn to gurgles. Even through the rain and thunder, I can hear them tearing her apart.

I'm the last one to climb into the overcrowded canoe. It bucks wildly as I step inside. I sit down, and it begins to steady. No one speaks.

Lucia uses her new knife to slice through the ropes tethering us to the dock. The river does the rest, and we begin to float downstream, away from the chaos.

As I look back, I try to count the carriers, but they're so tightly packed around Ginger, it's impossible. Thunder booms in the distance. The storm is moving farther away from us now, but the rain keeps coming. Exhausted, we sit in the canoe in silence, shivering as the river moves us south.

CHAPTER 15

When the sun starts to rise, I'm brought out of a daze. Without the rain, the river's current has slowed, and we inch downstream with the sounds of nature all around us.

I've never really been outside like this. City parks, backyards, and trips to the zoo are as close as I've come to really being out in nature. On the river, turtles sit on logs, waiting for the sun. Fish pluck bugs from the surface of the water. Birds start their songs up in the canopy of trees above us. This is what things were like before humans built their cities. Before they made their rules.

In my exhausted state, a moment of clarity takes me by surprise. I realize suddenly I won't miss the world as it was, a world that never planned to accept someone like me. Out here, instinct and survival are the only rules. This is a world that was made for me.

"We should find somewhere to get out and dry off," Nurse Patrick whispers, interrupting my thoughts.

Like me, Keisha and Nurse Patrick haven't slept a wink. They stare forward, red-eyed, taking in the scene around us. On the floor of the canoe, January snores softly in two inches of water, still oblivious. Lucia is curled tightly on Keisha's lap; her even breaths let me know she's sleeping soundly too.

"How far do you think we've gone?" I wonder aloud.

"There's really no telling," Nurse Patrick says. "All I know is we're still headed south. This is the Illinois River. Eventually it pours into the Mississippi, but we're still a long way from that."

I nod. At least we're heading in the direction we planned.

We continue to float in silence. I wonder if anyone will mention what happened to Ginger. I wonder how we'll tell January she's gone. I wonder if they're scared of me.

I don't feel bad about tripping Ginger. She was a liability from day one, and the truth is she wasn't meant for all this. There's nothing fair or just in this new world. There is no order, there are no "*human rights,*" and complaining won't magically make things go your way. I almost smile at the thought of never having to hear her high-pitched whine again. Besides, if we had waited for Ginger to make it to the boat, none of us would have survived. They have to understand that. I hope they do. If Ginger was a liability, then keeping Jan alive is a suicide mission. There is no bigger threat to our group. If I were alone, I'd leave her behind without thinking twice, but the rest of the group would never allow it. I try not to imagine all the risks involved with letting her live.

"The river banks up ahead," Nurse Patrick says, pointing downstream. "See the little beach? We could get out and rest right there."

I see it. A low, grassy riverbank slopes into the water at just the right angle. Nurse Patrick uses one of our paddles to steer us ashore. Keisha begins gathering what little supplies we have left, and when we're close enough, I jump out of the boat to pull us farther onto the bank. Lucia wakes up, takes a quick look around her, and instantly begins finding ways to help. Jan wakes, glances around, then goes right back to sleep. The difference between the two young girls is stark, and I'm again struck by January's uselessness.

When we're completely ashore, we pile out of the boat. We're a sopping wet mess. Nurse Patrick gently shakes January awake, putting his finger to his lips, reminding her to keep quiet.

Jan blinks several times, then sits up. "Where are we?"

"The carriers broke into our shelter last night, remember?" Nurse Patrick explains. "We had to escape. We found this boat and floated away, down the river. We're safe now," he continues, waiting for Jan's inevitable question.

"Where's Ginger?" Jan finally asks.

"Jan, I want you to look around you, okay?" Keisha says, jumping in to help. "Remember, we have to be very, very quiet. The carriers might be out here waiting to wake up and get us, okay?"

"Keisha is right, January. I'm going to tell you what happened to Ginger, but you need to stay calm," Nurse Patrick says.

January's breaths are already quickening, and her face is turning pink. "Is she okay?" Jan asks, her chin wobbling.

"January, the carriers caught up to us, and they bit Ginger. She died. I'm sorry," Nurse Patrick says, delivering the final blow. I appreciate his editing.

January's eyes go wild, and her breathing is so fast I think she might hyperventilate. At least she's not screaming.

"Deep breath, Jan. Watch me," Nurse Patrick says, demonstrating.

It takes several minutes, but her breathing evens out. Finally, the tears come. Her sobs are mournful and far quieter than her tantrum tears. When I'm certain she won't scream, I turn away to walk the perimeter.

I keep my machete ready, but the riverbank and the surrounding area are quiet, save for the birds and the bubble of the river. I decide we're relatively safe and join the others to start unpacking my wet backpack. Anything that isn't in plastic is completely soaked through.

"Quinn, what do you think about starting a fire to dry us off?" Keisha asks quietly as she rubs January's back.

"That's smart. Lucia, come with me. Let's see if we can find some wood. Keep your weapon up."

We start by picking up tiny twigs. Farther inland we find bigger fallen branches. I use my foot to break them into manageable pieces, and we carry them back to the little beach. Soon, we have a pile big enough to start a fire.

From the side pocket of my wet backpack, I pull out one of the lighters I took from the sporting goods store.

I glance at Jan, but she's not watching me. She's still crying softly, hiccuping occasionally, but I think we're out of the woods, so to speak.

I flick the lighter to get the fire started. Nothing. I try again. Nothing. Several more tries yield the same results. It must be waterlogged.

"Give me that," Nurse Patrick says with his hand out. I pass the useless lighter to him. He turns the lighter upside down, giving it a few shakes. Then he presses the lighter's wheel to the rubber on the side of his boot, moving it back and forth quickly.

After a few seconds, he tosses the lighter back to me. I flick it. A flame appears, and I can feel my face light up. "How did you know how to do that?"

"Old smoker's trick," he says, smirking. "Never thought smoking would come in handy in the apocalypse. Here, let me show you how to get that fire started," he says, taking the lighter back.

"Keisha, Lucia, you need to hear this too," he says, waving them over. "Starting fires is tricky. You have to start with tiny pieces, then work your way up to the bigger branches. And remember, fires need to breathe." He uses the smallest bits of wood and a few dried leaves to create a tiny nest. Then he balances a few larger pieces in a peak above the nest and lights it on fire.

January's eyes glow in awe.

"Once the bigger pieces start to catch, you can add more," he says, motioning for me to add more sticks to the fire. "Don't add too much now. Wait for it to catch. Good," he says, smiling proudly. "That'll be a real nice fire." He tosses the lighter back to me.

I catch it in both hands and smile. Once again, I'm almost glad he's here.

The fire grows. Nurse Patrick shows us how to use larger branches to stretch our clothes and hold them close to the fire to dry. Soon, I have something relatively dry to change into.

All this open land makes me anxious, and I find myself gripping my machete every time the leaves rustle. For now, though, nothing comes. So we use the quiet to take inventory of what's left of our supplies.

In the escape, all we held on to were our weapons and backpacks. Luckily each pack had a few bottles of water, some dehydrated food, a mess kit, toiletries, and a spare set of clothing for each of us. Nurse Patrick was also carrying a few pieces of campfire cookware and a few odds and ends. I can also hear the pill bottles shake in his pockets when he moves. We left behind a lot, but it really could have been worse.

We rehydrate some food in a little tin pot and eat. It's tough to choke down, and January whines, asking for candy bars instead.

"Jan, we need to save the candy for when we need quick energy. We have time to cook more nutritious food right now, so we should use this time wisely," Nurse Patrick explains patiently.

Eventually she takes a few bites with her nose turned up. Beside her, Nurse Patrick's watch beeps softly, letting him know it's time to hand out morning meds. He passes Jan a handful of pills, and she swallows them dutifully.

Once we've all eaten as much as we can stand, I realize just how tired I am.

"We need to get some sleep. Maybe we can take shifts?" I ask, yawning.

"Sure. Lucia, why don't you stand watch with me and January, since you both got a few hours of sleep on the boat. We'll let Keisha and Quinn get some rest," Nurse Patrick says, with kindness in his eyes. I nod at him gratefully and carry my almost-dry pack under a big shady tree next to the river. Keisha follows, dragging her feet.

I lay my pack down on the soft grass and use the smooth part as a pillow. I leave a little spot for Keisha next to me. She lies close to me and pulls a big flannel shirt over us. It isn't cold, but somehow it makes me feel safer. Still, I keep my machete gripped in my hand, just in case.

As I'm drifting off, Keisha speaks. "Quinn, you killed Ginger. On purpose."

"I did it to save us."

"What if I had been the slowest one?"

I'm almost too shocked to speak. How could she not know? "I'd never let anything happen to you, Keisha."

"Why?"

I don't know what to say, so I pretend to have fallen asleep, avoiding the question I don't have the courage to answer. Soon, she gives up on waiting for my response. Her breathing becomes rhythmic, and I'm lulled into real sleep by the hypnotic rise and fall of her.

CHAPTER 16

When Nurse Patrick nudges me awake, I'm on my feet in seconds.

"It's okay! It's okay! I'm just waking you for your watch. I'm not sure I can stay awake much longer, and if I'm being honest, I need a break from Jan."

Exhausted as I am, his words send a bubble of laughter through my chest. Most of the staff would never even hint at anger or annoyance while on the job. Especially Nurse Patrick. I always saw him as someone with infinite patience and emotional control, but it turns out January can wear down even the strongest ones.

"Sure. Of course," I say, with a chuckle. "What time is it?"

Nurse Patrick checks his watch. "It's about two in the afternoon. Here." He takes off his watch and hands it to me. "Wake me at six at the very latest."

I nod, fastening the watch around my wrist. It's loose and heavy, and having it on my wrist feels like a big responsibility.

Keisha hasn't moved, and as much as I want someone else to keep an eye on January, I let her rest. Nurse Patrick curls up near her and begins breathing the deep, even breaths of sleep almost instantly.

I walk over to what's left of the fire and find Lucia trying to teach January how to play hopscotch. She's scratched boxes into the hard-packed dirt on the shore of the river.

"Quinn! Do you want to play with me and Lucia?" January begs, her eyes hopeful.

"I'm standing watch, Jan. I need to keep an eye on our camp."

"Oh." She pauses. "Do you think those people will find us?"

"What people?" I ask, not understanding.

"The ones like from yesterday. And like what happened to Ms. Michelle," she explains.

"Oh. The carriers. Jan, those aren't really people anymore." I realize no one has actually had this conversation with January yet. When Mr. Josh explained it he was pretty vague, so I look for the words to explain what's happening in a way that her mind can process.

"Remember what Mr. Josh said? There's something making people sick, Jan. When they get sick, they die, but after they die, they wake up as something different. When they wake up, they're not people anymore."

"That's why it's okay to kill them," she says.

"Yeah. We have to kill them to protect ourselves," I confirm.

"Were Mr. Josh and Ginger sick too?" she asks.

Ugh. I don't want to have this conversation. Lucia stops mid-hop to look up at me, waiting anxiously for my answer.

"No, Jan. Mr. Josh and Ginger weren't sick like the carriers."

January sniffles, and her eyes take on a telltale shine.

"January, don't cry. Mr. Josh needed to die because he turned bad. He was going to hurt Lucia. And Ginger died because she was too slow. If we had waited for her, the carriers would have caught all of us. But when the carriers caught her, she distracted them. That's how we got away. That's why we lived."

"So, Ginger helped us? Like a superhero, sorta?" She sniffles again, but her tears don't fall.

"Sure. Like a superhero."

Lucia continues her hops, and Jan turns to rejoin her. I breathe out, relieved. I don't feel guilty about killing Mr. Josh or Ginger, but I also don't want the others to look at me *that* way. I don't want them to be scared of me. I know I'm not like them. I don't feel the right things.

It's been like this for as long as I can remember. When I was ten, I was placed in a Catholic group home for a few months. One of the older girls stole a pair of my socks—the fuzzy kind I got for Christmas from my last foster parents. I didn't tell on her or even let on that I had noticed. I found them in her drawer. I waited a whole week for her to wear them. When she finally pulled them on, she screamed. A few nights before, while she was sleeping, I had put tiny pushpins from the bulletin board into the bottom of the socks, and the sharp ends sank deep into the pads of her feet. One of the group home staff pulled them out one by one and, after much questioning, figured out what had happened. That night I overheard her whispering to another staff member about me. "God forgot to put a soul in that one," she said. "There's no light behind her eyes." I lost privileges for weeks.

I don't really believe in God or souls, but I can't argue that something in me is missing. I've read about love and intense emotions in books and seen it played out in movies and on TV, but I don't think I've ever felt those things. At least not like *that*. It's not that I've never cared about anyone, but I don't really understand people's need to show emotion or explain themselves to others. I don't need to feel connection like that. I don't need to be cared for. Other people seem to orbit around one another effortlessly. I usually have to force myself to think of anyone but myself, to make the right facial expressions at the right time, and to react the way others do. I've gotten better at it over the years, though. I think being friends with Keisha has helped the most. She makes that stuff feel easier.

As the afternoon wears on, I check Nurse Patrick's watch. Four o'clock. The sun moves across the sky, and the riverbed stays quiet. Keisha finally wakes up around four thirty and joins me near the dead fire. She busies herself with rebuilding it. Why, I don't really know, but it gives her something to do. I keep myself busy watching the surrounding trees for carriers, but nothing comes. I wonder how close we are to a town or a highway, but it's no use wondering. We might as well be on another planet out here.

At six, Nurse Patrick's watch beeps, and I startle out of my daydream. **Meds** flashes across the tiny screen on my wrist. It's time to wake him.

I walk over to the tree where he sleeps and kick his boots.

"Hey. Hey! Six o'clock," I say, forcing him awake.

"Jeez, Quinn, ease up," he complains.

"Here. The meds alarm went off," I say, dropping his watch onto his chest.

He straps the watch back onto his wrist. "Any action while I was out?"

"Not a peep. We must be pretty far from any towns. There doesn't seem to be anything out here."

"We're safe from carriers for now, but we're going to need food and shelter if we want to stay alive."

"Right," I say, kicking at a rock in front of me. "So do you think we should keep going downstream or walk inland and see if we can find a town?"

"We follow the river," Keisha says from behind me. I didn't even realize she was listening. "The river is the safest place for us," she says.

"All right then, we'll stick to the river for a while longer. I'll pass out meds and get some dinner going. We should stay here tonight, but we need to be ready to leave if we have to. Can you two look for more firewood?" Nurse Patrick asks.

I nod. Keisha and I walk the riverbank looking for sticks and large branches. There's not much left. We burned just about everything nearby trying to get dry. We walk deeper into a wooded area and continue the search. The trees grow close together, and high grass comes up to our knees, making us fight for each step. We search in companionable silence. It's something I've always appreciated about Keisha. She's never been one to fill the space with unnecessary chatter. I sneak glances at her, trying to read her thoughts, but she still gives nothing away. Her words from this morning echo back in my mind. *"What if I had been the slowest one?"* She couldn't really believe that I'd sacrifice her, could she?

When our arms can't hold any more, we walk back to camp. Nurse Patrick has packed all the items we aren't using into the boat and has the fire blazing. Lucia and January sit near the base of the fire and wave when they see us. Nurse Patrick smiles at our armloads of firewood. "That'll work! Set those down and come over to the fire. We're learning how to purify water!" he says, slapping his thigh with a goofy grin.

I roll my eyes at his enthusiasm, but I'm eager to learn. He's already filled the small tin pot with river water. He uses his shirt sleeve to grab the handle of the pot, then pushes it into the edge of the fire, right into the hot coals. "Now we wait," he says, rubbing his hands together with a big smile.

"What are we waiting for?" Lucia asks curiously.

"Well, the heat of the fire is going to warm up the water until it starts boiling. When the bubbles are about the size of a quarter, we start counting. When we reach sixty, we can pull the pot out of the fire and let it cool down. Then, *voilà*!" he says with a flourish. "Clean, drinkable water! Never, ever drink water from the river unless you've boiled it first, okay? It could make you very sick."

We all nod. For the millionth time, I'm grateful Nurse Patrick is with us.

As the sun goes down, we work out a watch schedule. Nurse Patrick will take the first watch, then me and Keisha, then Nurse Patrick again. The idea of sleeping in the dark, out in the open without even a sleeping bag, makes my skin crawl. So many bugs. But we don't have much of a choice.

We kill the fire, find a soft spot in the grass, and use our extra clothes as blankets. Jan and Lucia find sleep easily. Their even breaths join the crickets and frogs as the sounds of nature overtake the night. As I wait for sleep, my mind swirls. I reach over and touch Keisha's arm.

"You still awake?" I whisper.

Keisha sighs deeply. "Of course."

I pause, unsure of what to say and how to say it. Finally, I decide to just say exactly what I'm thinking.

"I'm going to make sure we live. You and me. Okay? No matter what."

Keisha is silent. Then, finally, her whisper breaks the tension building in my chest. "I know."

In the dark, her hand finds mine. She gives it a soft squeeze, and the tension melts away.

CHAPTER 17

Nurse Patrick never woke us for our shift. He looks exhausted, but I'm grateful for the rest. We decide not to waste a moment of daylight. We load the rest of our gear into the boat and file in, trying to distribute our weight evenly, but it's crowded and uncomfortable anyway. Nurse Patrick gives the boat a hard shove, and it begins to glide across the muddy bank and into the water. Once we're afloat, he jumps into the seat at the back of the canoe. The boat rocks from side to side, but we stay upright and move into the middle of the river.

The river's current does most of the work for us, but Nurse Patrick uses a paddle to steer and keep us moving at a decent clip. The sun is just barely over the horizon, and I can already tell it's going to be hot today, but the river feels peaceful, and the birds overhead are putting on a show. Hawks cruise the nearby fields, and black birds with red-tipped wings sing from the trees lining the shore. From the corner of my eye, I see a bald eagle fly overhead, and my jaw drops. Bald eagles have always felt mythical, and seeing one in real life out in the wild feels strange. I nudge Keisha and point toward the eagle, and she smiles.

Nurse Patrick sees us and looks up. "Ah, an eagle! Beautiful birds. Used to be pretty rare, but somehow they've been able to survive. They were on the endangered species list for years, but they've been removed just in the last twenty years or so. Got to admire an animal that survives at any cost." He gives me a hesitant smile. At any cost. That's exactly how I feel about all this.

That's why Ginger and Mr. Josh are dead right now. This new world isn't easy, but I was made to survive it, no matter what. I look back over my shoulder at Nurse Patrick. The smile still hangs on his lips.

I try to make myself as comfortable as possible as I watch the world go by. The hours pass slowly though, and soon we're all sunburned, sweat-soaked, and itching from last night's mosquito bites. I vow to find a hat or at least a bottle of sunscreen the next time we stop at a town. As uncomfortable as we are, I'm grateful for the river and the safety it gives us, but we can't stay in the boat forever.

"Nurse Patrick, I have to pee," January says.

"Me too," echoes Lucia.

"We should stop," I agree.

"I'll look for a spot," Nurse Patrick says.

Two days pass like that on the river. We paddle. We take bathroom breaks. We boil water. We sleep in shifts. We even kill the occasional carrier. The river water keeps us hydrated, cool, and relatively clean, but life in a canoe leaves us all aching and longing for a few days of real rest. Not only that, but our food supply is getting disturbingly low.

We pass by a couple of small towns built up along the river, but the sight of roaming carriers and the sounds of distant screams keep us in the boat, moving farther and farther south.

About halfway through our fourth day in the boat, the scenery changes. The river starts to turn, and its edges transform from small cliffs to softer slopes. Downstream, a building appears, just off the water.

"What's that?" I ask, squinting my eyes.

"Hard to say from here. Maybe a grain elevator?" Nurse Patrick wonders aloud. "The Illinois River has lots of barges that haul grain down south. Or it could be the edge of a small town?"

As we move closer, I keep my eyes on the structure and start to feel excitement build. It's the only building I can see from the water. There are no houses and no other buildings in sight. It feels strange that a single building would be standing in the middle of nowhere along the river. Finally, a sign comes into view.

"Boatel," I read aloud. "What's a boatel?"

"I think it's like a riverside hotel. Looks like this one has been turned into some kind of bar or restaurant. We should keep going. There's really no telling what's inside," Nurse Patrick says skeptically.

"No, let's pull over," I insist. "It looks pretty isolated. There's got to be supplies in there. Who knows when we'll find another spot like this? Plus, if we get into trouble, we have a quick getaway with the canoe. If we're lucky, maybe we can even get a good night's sleep here. Let's check it out."

Nurse Patrick is hesitant, but he gives in when Keisha and Lucia agree with me. He steers the canoe toward a tiny wooden dock along the shore. We tie up the boat and walk up to the building cautiously. Nurse Patrick is right; whatever this boatel used to be, it's a restaurant now. Rows of tables and chairs line an outdoor wooden deck. A set of grand doors with a handwritten sign welcomes guests to try the Sunday Special, catfish fritters. From the outside, it looks untouched by the carrier outbreak.

We make a complete loop around the building to check for any signs of people or wandering carriers. In the parking lot, four cars sit undisturbed, but the thin layer of dust on each vehicle's windshield suggests they haven't been moved recently. When we round the east side of the building, a dumpster is heaped with rotting food, making breathing uncomfortable, but nothing seems out of place.

"Let's go inside and check it out," I whisper.

We keep our weapons ready. I reach for the doorknob and turn, but it doesn't budge.

"It's locked?" Jan says a little too loud.

"Shh. Let's try the doors on the patio," Keisha suggests.

We walk around to the side of the building and climb the wooden stairs. The sliding glass door is open just a crack. I push it to the left and peer into a dark dining room.

I breathe in and nearly gag. Jan coughs twice before Nurse Patrick is able to cover her mouth with his sleeve, shushing her. We all go still and silent, waiting, but nothing comes to life.

The dining room is in disarray. Tables lie on their sides. Chairs with broken legs sit at awkward angles. Food rots on plates.

"Can we go to the bathroom?" Jan whispers, squirming. I scan the room for a sign that will lead us to the bathrooms and find one in the shadows to our left. I nod at Jan and point to it with my machete, then give her a stern look with a finger over my lips. She gulps audibly. We tiptoe through the mess toward the bathroom.

When we arrive, I press my ear to the door, listening for any movement. When I hear nothing, I inch it open. The room is nearly pitch dark. I feel for a switch on the wall, but the lights don't come on. Looks like the woman on the news was right. The power grid has failed. I find myself missing the flashlights we lost when we left the truck behind. Instead, I flick the lighter in my pocket. It gives us a tiny cone of light—just enough to see the bathroom is empty.

I wave January and Lucia inside to take the first turn and stand guard with Keisha and Nurse Patrick outside. When they finish, Keisha and I take our turn, followed by Nurse Patrick.

When he comes out, he's carrying a bottle of hand soap, a stack of paper towels, and a few rolls of toilet paper, smiling like he just won a prize. I guess the looting has begun.

Behind the bar, we find a trash bag and toss in the supplies from the bathroom. I throw in a stack of tablecloths and once again mourn the loss of our sleeping bags back at the campground.

When we enter the kitchen, it's even harder to breathe. The air feels thick and hot and the smell is so heavy I can almost taste it. There's smeared blood on the floors, but no sign of a body. It seems like whatever caused the overturned tables in the dining room ended here. The fact that there is no body left behind bothers me, sticking in the back of my mind like an unreachable itch.

Despite the scene, we move forward.

Food rots on every surface. I wonder if we'll even find anything edible. We almost give up, but Lucia grabs my arm and points at a small door that can only be a pantry nearly hidden by stacks of pots and pans all the way at the back of the kitchen.

I wave the others over. Nurse Patrick listens carefully with his ear pressed to the pantry door, hoping for silence on the other side. He nods, satisfied. Slowly, he puts his hand on the doorknob and turns.

"DON'T!" a strange voice calls out desperately from behind us.

I whip around and see a man in head-to-toe camouflage with a hunting knife in hand charging toward us. I pull out my machete, stopping him in his tracks. He puts his hands up in surrender. I pull back my machete, ready to swing, but the man's not even looking at me. He's looking over my shoulder, his face a mask of fear. That's when I realize he isn't the current danger. The biggest threat is behind me.

I hear Nurse Patrick yelling before I'm able to turn back toward the pantry door. What I see makes my heart sink. A blackened claw grips Nurse Patrick's bloody forearm from a gap in the door. Sharp fingernails have carved deep lines in his flesh, and thick black liquid mixes with red blood as it drips to the floor.

Frantically, Keisha and Lucia throw their weight into the door, trying their hardest to push it closed. Even January tries to help. Nurse Patrick works against them, though. As he tries to jerk away from the monster inside, he pulls the carrier forward, and the door inches open. I forget about the stranger behind me and move. I position myself on Nurse Patrick's left, trying to find an angle to wedge my machete into the carrier's head, but it won't stop thrashing for another taste of Nurse Patrick. I've never seen a carrier so frantic. Its jaws chatter as if freezing cold. Its lips are peeled back, turning its mouth into a strange copy of a smile. This carrier looks less human than any other I've seen, and for the first time I feel frightened by the monster in front of me.

Nurse Patrick screams again, bringing me back to my senses. I grab a chair and stand on its seat. From this higher angle I have more control. I stab downward into its eye socket. A sick screech tells me it's not enough. My thick blade sticks in the bones around its eye, but I use my newfound height to my advantage. Pushing downward, I let my weight do the work. Finally, the bone gives way. My machete meets brain, and the carrier falls to the ground, useless.

I look down at the carrier's body lying in a pool of itself. A tiny gold cross hangs from its neck. It's the only thing indicating that this thing used to be human. I shiver.

Nurse Patrick falls to his knees and skitters backward against the wall, holding his arm to his chest. He breathes quickly, eyes darting from side to side. Keisha runs to him, doing her best to calm him down. As my heart starts to slow, I remember we're not alone. I look for the stranger and find him behind a box of rotting lettuce, muttering to himself.

"Hey, jackass! You couldn't give us a warning ten seconds sooner?" I say accusingly, pointing my machete at his chest.

"Look, I was hoping you guys would just leave, okay? It happened so fast!" He starts pacing, raking his fingers through his hair. "Jesus, is he gonna be okay?"

I give him a menacing stare. "Are there more of those things in this building? Tell me now."

"No, I cleared the whole thing last week. It was just her," he says, pointing to the lifeless form on the floor. "It's not what it looks like. I..."

"It looks like you were keeping a carrier as a pet, you moron!" I shout, moving closer.

His hands fly up in self-defense. "It wasn't like that. She was my girlfriend. I thought if I could find a doctor, she might... I thought... I never wanted..."

I back off, dropping my machete, and roll my eyes. It's sentimentality that gets you killed in the apocalypse.

I take another look at the camo-clad man in front of me. He's younger than I initially thought. Maybe twenty-five? He grips a large hunting knife with his tattooed knuckles, but there's no fight in him. Now that he doesn't have a machete pointing at his chest, he stares at the scene unfolding behind me.

I turn back to Nurse Patrick. January and Lucia stare in horror as Keisha wraps his arm in a kitchen towel. She's focused and calm. She may not be much of a fighter, but when she's called to care for others, something takes over her. Too bad it won't help. Nurse Patrick is a goner, and we all know it.

"Hey, G.I. Joe," I say, grabbing the attention of the stranger.

"Name's Ramsey," he says.

"Ramsey, I'm Quinn. That's Keisha, January, and Lucia over there. This is Nur... This is Patrick," I say, avoiding his title. I don't want any questions about who he is to us. "Now, can you please tell us where we can take him to lie down?" I say impatiently.

He stares stupidly for a moment but snaps into action a moment later. "Yeah. Of course. Here, come with me."

Ramsey leads us through the dining room and down a dark hallway. A large staircase remains from when this was a grand hotel. Most of the rooms look like they've been turned into storage space. Old broken chairs and stacks of plastic cups and takeout containers fill the rooms along the hall. At the end of the hall in the last room on the right is a small office littered with bills, napkin math, and an ancient desktop computer. In the corner a sleeping bag lies on top of a stack of broken-down cardboard boxes.

Keisha leads Nurse Patrick to the sleeping bag and lowers him to the ground, fussing over her homemade bandage.

"You've been living here," I say to Ramsey.

"Yeah, I was a bartender. The boss shut this place down after one of those things came in off the beach one night. Everybody panicked. A couple people got bit, and one guy died right down there in the dining room. I never seen anything like it. Anyway, we shut down that night. Then everything went crazy in town, so I came here. I reckoned this would be a good place to ride out the infection. Y'all don't look like you're from around here. Where'd you come in from?"

"North. What happened to your girlfriend?" I ask pointedly, trying to avoid his question.

"I heard it's bad up north. Closer you are to Chicago, worse it is, I reckon. More people and all that."

"We came from Peoria!" January chirps from the corner.

I give her a death stare that shuts her the hell up. This man doesn't need to know where we came from, and the fact that he didn't answer my question about the carrier in the pantry doesn't go unnoticed. I don't get the chance to press him though. Nurse Patrick hisses in pain, and I shift my attention back to him.

"How's the arm?" I ask.

"It burns," he responds through gritted teeth.

"Did you bring any meds for something like that?" I ask.

"There was a first aid kit in the truck, but that's long gone."

"Ramsey, do you have anything for his pain?" Keisha asks, looking up at him through her long eyelashes.

"I'm not sure, but I could take a look," he says, his eyes lingering on her for just a moment too long before he turns to jog down the hall.

I hadn't noticed it before, but Ramsey's not a bad-looking guy. He's tall and muscular and has that bad-boy look that's appealing to some girls. Still, the way he just looked at Keisha makes my skin crawl. When he returns with two ibuprofen and a bottle of water for Nurse Patrick, I decide to let it slide.

Nurse Patrick takes the pills and drinks the water gratefully, then checks his watch and sighs.

We sit in silence, and soon Ramsey leaves the room, giving us privacy. Keisha holds Nurse Patrick's hand. Lucia clings to Keisha. January spins in the office chair behind the desk.

I pick at my nails, wondering how long we're going to just sit here waiting for the sickness to take Nurse Patrick. After what feels like an eternity of awkward silence, he speaks.

"I'm proud of you girls," he says with a warm smile. "You've really held your own out there. You can do this without me."

Keisha's eyes fill with tears. I feel frustrated and completely overwhelmed. This is such a mess. We're still running low on food and supplies. Now we've got some stranger wandering around downstairs thinking god knows what. There seem to be carriers around every corner. January is a living, breathing dinner bell with a dwindling med supply. And now, on top of all of this, I'm going to have to kill one of the only good things we had going for us. It's too much. The office chair squeaks behind me as January does another rotation.

"Cut it out, Jan," I scold her. The chair comes to a halt, and she starts to cry. Goddammit.

"Is there anything we can do to make you more comfortable?" Keisha asks Nurse Patrick, ignoring the fact that I just made things even worse.

"You know, I could use a splint for my arm. Could you go outside and find a couple strong sticks? About a foot long. I think I saw some good ones in the parking lot," he says.

He looks directly at Keisha with the request. It's obvious he's lying. His arm isn't even broken. A splint would be useless. I know it, and when I glance over at Keisha, I can see she knows it too. Sadness flickers across her face, but she plays along.

"Sure. Of course we can do that. Come on, Lu, Jan. Let's go see what we can find," Keisha says. With a newfound purpose, January's tears dry, and she stands up to follow Keisha and Lucia. Even on the brink of death, he's still taking care of her.

"Take Ramsey with you, okay? Have him stand guard," Nurse Patrick says. "Quinn, maybe you can stay back with me?" he says, quietly begging with his eyes.

"Yeah, sure. I'll stay here," I say.

I don't like the idea of Ramsey being alone with the girls, but something tells me Keisha and Lucia can take care of themselves.

"Lu, Jan, go downstairs with Ramsey and wait for me. I'll be right behind you," Keisha says with a soft smile. When they've left the room, she grips Nurse Patrick's uninjured hand. Tears spring to her eyes, and I realize this is the first time I've ever seen her cry real tears.

"Thank you," she whispers to him.

He nods and forces a smile. "You've grown up so much, Keisha. You have a good heart, kid. Listen to it. You'll know what to do."

Keisha lets go of his hand and turns to leave. The interaction is brief, but I can tell it's filled with meaning for both of them. On her way out the door, Keisha's eyes meet mine.

"Don't let him suffer, Quinn," she begs in a whisper.

"I promise."

When the two of us are alone, Nurse Patrick gets down to business.

"We can't wait. I will *not* be a burden to you girls, and I can't become one of them. I need you to end this. Please."

"We have time, though. How long did it take Ms. Michelle to turn? You could have another day to—"

"It has to be now," he says, cutting me off, determined. I'm impressed. I didn't expect him to be so rational about this. I don't want Nurse Patrick to die. I'm pretty sure we owe our survival to him a few times over, and I actually like having him around. The truth is staring me in the face, though. His time is up. He's already turning a pale shade of gray. He's right. We shouldn't wait.

"I get it. I can do it."

He sighs. "Thank you."

He doesn't waste a moment. He pulls several pill bottles from his pocket with his good hand and pushes them toward me.

"Here. You'll need these for January and Lucia. Do you remember what I told you about how to administer them?"

"One of each, twice a day, with food."

"Right. Here, take this," he says, removing his watch. "It'll beep twice a day to remind you. It's waterproof."

I nod and fasten the watch around my wrist. It hangs heavy and loose.

"Most pharmacies will have these meds. You need to find more soon. Quinn, I know what you're thinking about January. Please try to remember that her life has meaning too. She has hopes and dreams just like you. Be patient with her."

"Okay," I say, to appease him.

"Okay. Can we go down to the river? I think the water would be a nice place to rest."

"Okay," I repeat solemnly.

This doesn't feel good. I don't feel that tingle of excitement. I don't want to do this. But if not me, who?

When we step outside, the sun is bright and high in the sky. I can hear January chattering endlessly to her new friend Ramsey. The birds chirp, and the breeze makes the summer weather feel tolerable. It all feels too bright and cheery for what's about to happen.

When we get to the riverbank, Nurse Patrick sits down, pulls off his boots and socks and dips his toes into the water. He looks out at the scene, and a smile touches his lips. "This is okay," he says. "Can you make it fast?"

I nod.

"And you'll make sure I don't come back?"

A strange lump forms in my throat. I nod again.

"Can you make sure they get a chance to say goodbye before you send me downriver?"

"Of course," I say, my eyes on the hard-packed dirt under my feet.

"Okay. I'm ready." He breathes out and closes his eyes.

"Nurse Patrick?"

"Yeah, Quinn?"

"I'm glad you came with us."

"Thanks, kid."

He gives me a final elbow tap, then closes his eyes again, letting the river flow over his feet.

I put down my machete and take the smaller hunting knife from my belt. Its lightness feels shocking after carrying the machete for so long, but somehow it still weighs heavily in my hand.

I walk behind him and get myself into position, placing my left hand on his shoulder to steady myself. He reaches up and touches my hand in a tender gesture. It shocks me, and I almost pull my hand back, but instead, I squeeze his shoulder. He squeezes back.

In my mind, I count to three. One…aim the knife at the base of the skull. Two…place the blade at an upward angle. Three… plunge it in quickly. The blade slides through the soft skin of his neck, then catches on bone before finally finding its way to his brain stem. Just like that, his body goes slack. Nurse Patrick's hand falls from its grip on mine, and he slumps to the hard ground. I move the knife back and forth, making sure there's nothing left of him to return.

Warm blood covers my hand and my knife. I kneel down and let the river wash it away.

I look at Nurse Patrick's crumpled body and the pool of blood near his head. I straighten his legs and place his hands on his chest. I kick fresh dirt over the pool of blood. This is as good as it gets.

For the first time, I wonder how old he is. Was. I guess thirty-five. I glance down at his ring finger and find it empty. For a moment, I wonder if he had any children but quickly decide he didn't. He wouldn't have left Peoria without them. Still, I wish I had asked. He must have dedicated his entire life to working at the Pegasus Center with us. A profound sadness comes over me, and the emotion feels as ill-fitting as the watch hanging from my wrist.

I take one more look at Nurse Patrick's body, then turn and walk toward the parking lot to get the others.

CHAPTER 18

When I reach them in the parking lot, Keisha and Ramsey are talking quietly while January and Lucia add to a growing pile of sticks.

I let my boots scrape the ground so they hear me coming. Keisha and Ramsey startle at the sound, and I see Keisha go for the knife around her waist automatically. She's starting to adapt, and I feel proud of her. When she sees it's me and not a carrier, she drops her hand, but it takes several seconds for her fear to change into relief.

As I approach them, Keisha braces for the news. I can see by the serious look on Ramsey's face that Keisha's filled him in. Lucia also seems to know something's happened, but Jan prattles on about the great sticks she's found with no signs of stopping.

"Jan, cool it. I need to tell you guys something."

She looks slightly hurt but shuts up and gives me her attention. I decide to be frank and to the point.

"You guys all saw that Patrick was bitten by the carrier."

"Where is he? Is he okay? We found him some sticks for a splint! Just like he asked!" January says, oblivious.

"Jan, when people get wounded by the carriers, they get sick. We've talked about this. Patrick knew what was going to happen to him," I explain.

"He's going to turn into one of the monsters?" Jan asks, her chin beginning to wobble.

"He would have, Jan. But he asked me to make sure he didn't hurt any of us. I took care of him. He's dead now, and he won't come back like the others. He didn't feel any pain."

"He's dead too? Like all the rest? Who is gonna take care of us?"

"Me and Keisha will, Jan."

For the first time since I've known her, January is silent. She stares into the distance at nothing, not crying, not screaming. Just...staring. It rattles me more than any tantrum could.

"He...um. His body is down by the river. He wanted me to let you all say goodbye and...you know...pay your respects," I say awkwardly.

I turn to walk back to Nurse Patrick's body, and the others follow me. I hear sniffles, but I don't turn around to see where they're coming from. It doesn't matter. This isn't going to be easy for anyone.

As we approach the riverbank, Nurse Patrick's body comes into view. Jan and Lucia each take one of Keisha's hands. His body is just how I left it. His hands are still folded gently across his chest with only a little blood darkening the dirt near his neck. He looks at peace. Keisha looks at me and gives me an approving nod. I did the best I could. I think she can see that.

Somehow Keisha knows what to do next. She takes a deep breath, steadies her voice, and speaks.

"Patrick was the kind of person who saw the best parts of you and believed that those parts mattered more than anything else. He didn't use your past against you. He didn't take advantage of your weakness even though he could have. He wasn't a snitch." A tear-filled smile brightens her face, and she takes a deep breath, trying to find the right next words.

Ramsey looks on, clearly trying to decipher who Nurse Patrick might have been to us, but thankfully he doesn't ask, and Keisha doesn't give anything away.

"He wanted us to live, and he died trying to make sure it happened. For that, we are forever grateful."

Keisha's words ring true to me. She's right. Nurse Patrick was decent. He didn't wield his power like a weapon. He didn't look at us with pity or fear. He was good. Truly good. And now he's gone.

Keisha's silence lets me know it's time. I grab Nurse Patrick's wrists and attempt to drag him into the water. When he sees me struggling, Ramsey grabs his ankles, and we wade into the water and let Nurse Patrick go.

The current carries him for a moment, then he sinks below the surface. It's done. Behind me, the girls sob. Ramsey comforts Keisha, who comforts Jan and Lucia. I stand in my soggy clothes and watch the spot where he disappeared, hypnotized.

I'm not sure how long we stay there on the edge of the river. I try to be patient and give them the time they need to mourn the loss of Nurse Patrick, but time moves slowly. Soon, I notice the sun has moved behind us and the sweltering summer heat has been quelled by a soft breeze. I let the sound of the leaves blowing in the trees calm me while I wait for the others to be ready to move on.

Lucia's quivering voice rises above the sniffles, breaking me out of a trance. "What is that?" she asks, alarm rising in her voice.

"What is what? I didn't—"

She cuts me off. "*That.*"

Lucia points upstream. Then I see it too.

"Ramsey, what the hell is that?" I say, turning to him for an explanation.

"It's a barge," he says matter-of-factly.

I roll my eyes. "Okay, what the hell is a barge? It looks like a damn floating freight train. Who's on it? What is it doing?" I ask impatiently.

"It *is* kind of like a freight train," he explains. "It's probably full of grain or lumber, heading south toward the Mississippi."

"Okay, but the world is basically over. Why is it still coming?" I ask.

"I'm not sure," he says, never taking his eyes off the barge.

It moves painfully slowly, but the current keeps pulling it toward us. We wait. Soon I think I can see people aboard. I wish for a pair of binoculars to see better.

"Look! Right there! There are survivors on the boat!" Lucia says hopefully. "I bet they're headed toward a shelter, or maybe there aren't even any carriers down south. We could go with them."

I weigh the possibilities in my mind and silently wish Nurse Patrick were here to help make the call. On one hand, if these people really are heading toward someplace safe, hitching a ride feels like the logical thing to do. But another part of me is excited by being out here on my own, fighting through it. There's really no way to know if these are good people. For all we know, teenage girls are already fetching a pretty penny on the brand-new apocalypse black market.

"I don't know, Lu. It's a risk either way," I say, wavering.

"It might be the safest way to move south. And like Lucia said, maybe they're headed toward a shelter. Maybe that barge *is* a shelter," Keisha says with a spark of hope.

"Y'all can always stay here, you know?" Ramsey says, but no one responds. Instead, we watch the barge move closer, and I realize I'm going to have to make the call soon. As it moves toward us, the size of the barge is striking. It's like a floating island, easily as wide as a house. The benefits of living on a mobile object, safe from the carriers and surrounded by an infinite supply of water and fish, finally win me over.

"Okay, let's go get our backpacks from inside. We can see if they'll let us aboard," I say, resigned. Keisha's grateful eyes let me know I've made the right decision. We race inside and up the stairs to where we left our packs. Ramsey follows us, and when I glance over my shoulder, I can see a conflict playing out on his face. I don't have to wait long to find out what he's wrestling with. As we grab our things and turn to run back outside, he speaks.

"I meant what I said. You could stay here. With me," he says, looking intensely at Keisha.

"I..." Keisha begins, conflicted. Her eyes flit to mine as she continues. "This could mean safety for us. Real safety. We can't stay," she finishes.

Ramsey's hope turns to sadness. Unbelievable. We've only been here a few hours, and already Keisha's got this guy pining for a future with her. A beat of silence weighs heavily in the air as Keisha struggles with what to say next.

"We have to go," I say, breaking the tension.

We run back to the river and see that the barge has made steady progress. It's just a few hundred feet away now. We load our gear into the canoe, and then Keisha looks back at Ramsey.

"Do you want to come with us?" Keisha asks.

What the hell? I try to hide my annoyance. He'd better say no.

"Naw, I've got business here," he says. "It sure was nice meetin' you all, and I'm real sorry about your friend. I hope you find some place safe from all this," he says, gesturing at the world in general. "Let me give you a push."

"Thanks, Ramsey," Keisha says. "We're grateful for your help today."

"My pleasure. Safe travels."

He gives the canoe a hard shove out into the middle of the river. Downstream the barge is inching closer. The people on deck move back and forth along the barge.

It's tough to see their faces, but I'm certain they haven't noticed us yet.

"We need to get their attention," Keisha says as I paddle us toward the barge. "Do you think they're close enough to hear us from down here?"

"Only one way to find out," I say. "Let's give it a shot."

"Hey! Down here! Hello!" Keisha shouts.

Lucia and January follow her lead, waving their arms. I join in, amplifying their calls for help. Soon, I can see the people on board make their way toward the front of the barge. They see us. This is it.

As the barge approaches, a ladder comes into view, rising out of the river and bolted all the way up the side of the structure.

"Look! There's a ladder up the side. That's how we get on board! Row toward the barge. We have to catch that ladder," I say.

We row hard with our paddles, aiming for the ladder while January keeps waving wildly at the people on board. I see they're still gathering on the edge. There must be twenty of them, but they're not shouting back at us. They're not waving or trying to communicate. They're not helping.

Goddammit. They're not people.

That's when we hear the moans. The loose flesh of their faces comes into focus. I can see the shape of their hollow eyes, their skin scorched by the sun. I smell the familiar stench of black bile. This ship's been taken by the dead, and we're directly in their path. A deafening screech fills the air, and not even the summer heat can soothe my goose bumps.

The barge comes close enough to block out the sun, casting us in shadow. What must be thirty bodies press against a thin guardrail, reaching for our boat. I stare in horror. They're right on top of us.

"Oh my god," Keisha says.

"We need to move! Now!" I shout.

Our frantic paddling sends the carriers above us into a frenzy. Their screams pierce the air as they reach for us. We paddle hard, but the barge creates its own sucking current, pulling us closer to its side.

"Keep paddling!" I urge the group.

From the shore, Ramsey waves frantically. There's nothing he can do to help us from there. We're on our own.

Then the first carrier falls.

It splashes in front of us, causing a wave that sends our canoe rocking from side to side. The carrier stays afloat by sheer will, waving its arms, trying to get closer to us.

Another carrier tumbles from above. Then another. We

paddle hard and manage to push ourselves a few feet from the barge, nearly escaping its pull. Then everything crumbles.

I watch in horror as a carrier flips over the guardrail directly overhead. I brace for impact, crouching down, covering my head, and squeezing my eyes shut against my will. The impact makes my teeth knock together, and for a moment I lose my center of gravity. The canoe bucks wildly, and I get a sinking feeling that this is the end.

January screams. I force my eyes open. The carrier has landed awkwardly on top of her, the top half of its body flailing in the water. Its legs crush January as she tries desperately to squirm her way out from under it, but she's pinned.

Our boat tips precariously, and carriers keep falling, splashing down all around us.

"Keisha! We have to get out! Swim for the shore! Lucia, come on!"

"We can't leave Jan!" Keisha shouts, her eyes wild.

"We don't have a choice! Let's go!" I urge over January's screams.

Keisha turns away defiantly. She grabs January's hand and pulls. She stands to get more leverage, and the boat rocks harder. Another carrier splashes into the water beside us. Screeches crescendo above. Jan screams louder, and finally, we're out of luck. From the water, a set of decaying hands grips the side of the boat, sending us tumbling into the river.

The shock of the cold water steals my breath, and I sink below the surface. The weight of my machete and wet backpack pull me farther into the dark, muddy river. As I sink, I imagine Nurse Patrick's body below me. I imagine the carriers above. Neither fate feels fair. I shrug off my backpack, letting it sink to the bottom, and swim harder with every ounce of strength I have left.

Finally, I burst through the water's surface, gasping for air, greedily sucking oxygen into my starving lungs. The flood of oxygen brings everything back into focus, and I look desperately for Keisha. But all I see is January, splashing just a few feet in front of me, struggling to stay afloat. She sees me and begins to paddle closer, tears and river water staining her pink cheeks.

"Quinn! Quinn, help!" she cries.

I ignore her and keep looking for Keisha. A few feet behind me, the sounds of splashing, screaming, and snapping jaws is all I can hear. Rotting flesh is all I can smell. Flailing bodies leaking dark, oily ooze into the water is all I can see. To my left, but far beyond my reach, is our upside-down canoe. As I'm frantically scanning the landscape for solutions, something pulls at me from beneath the water. It grips at my arm and squeezes tight, then digs into my ribs, sucking the breath from my lungs. I go under. My heart beats wildly, and I can't seem to find purchase or push myself upward toward the precious air at the surface.

I reach for my belt and feel for the familiar bulge of my hunting knife in its holster next to my machete. I grip the knife as I'm pulled farther and farther down into the dark water. Desperately,

I drive the knife into the thing that's holding me. I know that stabbing a carrier anywhere but their brain won't help, but I can't make sense of the form that's weighing me down. My aching lungs urge me to keep at it. I stab and stab until finally, I feel the weight lift.

I break through the water just as the edges of my vision start to go blurry. I suck air into my burning lungs. Once I've gathered my wits, I see what was pushing me down, surrounded by a halo of muddy red water. The thing I had stabbed relentlessly.

January.

CHAPTER 19

January floats face down in the river, unmoving. The ring of red water surrounding her grows larger as a carrier grabs on to her arm and pulls her soft flesh toward its snapping jaws. I only feel relief. I take in another deep breath, and it soothes my lungs, but I know I'm not safe. Carriers continue to fall from the barge above, and I know it's time to go back to the shore. I swim.

By the time I'm nearing the beach, I'm gasping for air, and my heart feels like it could beat out of my heaving chest. With my knife still in my hand, I drag myself onto the beach to safety, then look over my shoulder, hoping that somehow Keisha is right behind me.

"Are you okay?" Ramsey asks, jogging toward me.

"What happened to Keisha? Did you see her?" I ask him frantically.

"After your boat flipped, it all happened so fast. I saw her go under, but…"

My stomach sinks. I turn back toward the river and wait, hoping that Keisha will emerge from the muddy water, begging God or the universe or even dumb luck that she made it.

The barge keeps inching downstream with the current, still dropping carriers into the water as it moves. They splash awkwardly, continuing the chaotic scene. Their flailing keeps them afloat, but thankfully they're not actually swimming, so we're relatively safe on the shore. In the middle of it all, our canoe bobs upside down in the water, useless. But there's no Keisha.

Then I notice it.

Our upside-down canoe is moving *against* the current. At first, I'm not sure if I'm imagining it, but then it turns toward the shore. The closer it gets, the more I let myself hope.

When I'm sure, I jump back into the river and swim out to meet it. I lift the boat with all my might, trying to flip it over to see who has been steering it toward land. When I look underneath, I can't help but laugh out loud with relief.

Keisha's startles, then smiles back. Behind her, little Lucia holds on to the crossbar in the center of the canoe. They caught the air pocket underneath and used the canoe as a shield. It's brilliant.

"I can't believe… I thought…" I can't even finish a sentence.

"I'm glad you're okay too, Quinn," Keisha says with a warm but tired smile.

For the second time today a lump forms in my throat. I swallow it down and take a deep breath. "Come on, we're almost to shore," I say, turning my face away.

As we swim the last few feet toward the shore, Ramsey meets us halfway and pulls an exhausted Lucia out of the water while Keisha and I drag ourselves and the canoe forward.

When we finally reach the hard-packed dirt of the river's edge, Keisha asks the question I've been dreading.

"Where's Jan?"

Stupidly, I hesitate for a beat too long. "She didn't make it," I say.

I can feel Keisha's eyes study me, and I look away. I don't even try to justify Jan's death, even though I could. In the end, it doesn't matter if I killed her accidentally or on purpose. January wasn't built to survive in a world like this. She was going to die sooner or later. I think we all know that sooner was better for all of us. One less X factor. One less risk. One less loose cannon.

"It's just us then. Like we planned," Keisha says stoically.

I stare at her, trying to decipher her flat expression, but she gives nothing away.

Ramsey steps closer as the three of us turn back toward the river, sopping wet and exhausted from grief and adrenaline. The barge's forward momentum along with the river's current seems to be sweeping the carriers away or pulling them under.

"Do you think any of them will make it to the shore?" Lucia asks, her weak voice quivering.

"No. Look at them," I answer, pointing at the carriers in the river. "They're not really swimming. They're moving enough to keep themselves afloat, but they're not making much progress. Besides, the current is already taking them downstream."

We wait for a few more moments on the shore to make sure I'm right. Finally, the barge disappears downstream, and the last of the carriers is swept underwater.

My wet clothes are cold and heavy. Lucia's teeth begin to chatter as the sun sinks lower. Then some instinct chirps in the back of my mind. It's time for meds. Suddenly my wrist feels uncomfortably light. I look down and see nothing but bare skin. Nurse Patrick's watch is gone. Disappointment kicks me in the gut, but there's nothing I can do. His watch and Lucia's meds are both at the bottom of the river. My eyes flash to Lucia, and I wish like hell I had read her chart. I vaguely remember the name of the drug Nurse Patrick showed me. Something-tine? I just hope she didn't need it that badly.

"Come on. Let's get y'all dried off," Ramsey says, leading us back to the restaurant.

In the dining room, Ramsey lights a fire in the wood-burning fireplace in a corner near the bar. We huddle around it, shivering while Ramsey strips a few nearby tables of their tablecloths.

"Here, it's not much, but it'll do while your clothes dry. Y'all get changed, and I'll get us something to eat," he says.

He turns back toward the kitchen, and we shiver as we peel off our wet clothes and place them beside the fire to dry. For a moment, I mourn the loss of the extra clothes in my backpack, reminded again that, as supplies go, we have almost nothing left.

As I'm wrapping the stiff tablecloth around me, something raises the hair on the back of my neck. Subtly, I glance toward the kitchen. Ramsey is standing in the middle of the doorway. He's watching Keisha.

I clear my throat and his eyes shift toward mine. I give him a look that lets him know he's been caught. Quickly, he looks down at his feet.

He shuffles in the doorway. "Everyone decent?" he asks, as if he doesn't already know.

"We're good," I say with a bit of warning in my tone.

"Then let's eat," he says, bringing over a pile of cans and packaged crackers.

We gather around the fire as Ramsey begins opening the cans. Tuna fish and restaurant crackers feel like a feast after eating candy bars and freeze-dried mush for the last few days. I'm grateful for the food and shelter, but I'm annoyed that Ramsey is here.

I stare at his face, trying to get a read on him. Then, as if he can feel me studying him, he glances up from his work, and his eyes meet mine. Usually, people see me and look away quickly. I'm used to it. I know I'm a little unsettling, but Ramsey doesn't flinch. Instead, he just smiles a big, lopsided grin.

"So, Peoria, huh?" Ramsey muses, filling the void in the conversation. Silently, I curse Jan for not being able to keep her damn mouth shut earlier. Once again, I'm glad she's gone.

"It was a safe bet heading to the river bottoms, seeing as there ain't too many people around here. Looks like it's gonna be a while before things get back to normal. All this farmland'll come in pretty handy once all the canned food runs out. I figure it's just a matter of time before all the folks who survive the city come down this way. Course, people in these parts been training for something like this their whole lives."

"What do you mean?" Keisha asks.

"Well, there ain't a lot going on in the river bottoms. We grow up learning how to hunt and grow food. Way I see it, guns and gardens are the new currency in a world like this, and we've got both. Folks'll be needing a place like this and people like us."

"So, you're a bartender who knows how to hunt *and* farm?" Keisha asks skeptically.

Ramsey gives Keisha a cocky grin, pleased as shit he's got her attention. "I learned how to hunt and tend crops from my dad, but that wasn't what I wanted to do with my life. Actually, I always dreamed of owning this place someday, turning it into something real special," he says, looking around the empty restaurant as if seeing everything it could have been.

"I guess it's yours now," Keisha says, batting her eyelashes.

"I guess it is." He grins, completely hypnotized.

"We should go to bed," I interrupt. "Thanks for dinner, and for letting us stay," I add as an afterthought.

"It's nothin'. Let's get you girls settled then."

We gather our clothes from the edge of the fireplace. They're stiff from the river water but they're dry and relatively clean. Ramsey leads us upstairs and into one of the storage rooms. He uses a utility knife to break down a few of the larger boxes to line the hardwood floor. Then he pulls a stack of tablecloths off a shelf nearby, creating three small beds. Nothing has ever looked so inviting.

"Thanks, Ramsey," Keisha says gratefully. Her eyes look heavy and dazed. We all need rest.

"I'll just be down the hall in my room. Get some rest, and I'll see you in the morning." His eyes linger just a little too long on Keisha.

He turns and closes the door softly behind him, leaving a battery-powered lantern behind. We change into our dry clothes in silence. Lucia pulls her makeshift bed close to Keisha's and snuggles in beside her. Soon, Lucia is fast asleep.

I need to talk to Keisha about Ramsey, but she beats me to the punch with a different topic.

"What are you doing, Quinn?"

"I'm going to sleep," I say, attempting to dodge the conversation.

"You know what I mean. Are you done yet?" she asks quietly.

I know where she's going with this, but I try to avoid the question anyway. "Done? What are you—"

"You can't keep killing off anyone who gets in the way. We're going to need other people to survive." Her voice inches up a whispered octave. The strain in her voice makes my stomach sink.

"We didn't need Jan or Ginger, and you know it. Nurse Patrick was. . ." I try to find the right words, the heavy pause hanging in the air. "I never wanted that," I finish.

"You liked killing them." It's not a question. She doesn't need to ask.

"Not Nurse Patrick," I say quietly. "Look, you and me, we've been thrown away our whole lives. I just spent the last two years in the Pegasus Center following every single rule, playing their game, and being whatever they wanted, and for what, Keisha?" I pause, but she has nothing to say, so I continue. "What were we going to do when they let us out of there? Transition to independent living? Go to college? Get jobs? How much longer were we going to have to try to fit in? We're not the same as other people, Keisha! Out here it's different. We don't have to pretend anymore. We have choices now. We finally have some control over our lives! And if I'm given a choice between living or dying, I'm going to choose to live. Every time. I won't feel sorry for that. I won't feel sorry that they're dead so we can live. You're my best friend, Keisha. At the end of the world, I want to be with you. Doing this." A tear slips down Keisha's cheek as she stares at the floor between us.

"Lucia is scared of you," she whispers.

"I'm not going to hurt her," I say quietly, looking down at my hands, picking at my fingernails.

"Do you promise?"

I look up and Keisha's eyes pierce into mine, challenging me.

"I promise."

"What happened to January, Quinn?" she asks with an edge to her voice.

"She grabbed on to me. I didn't know it was her at first. I thought it was a carrier. But she pulled me under, and I had to make her let go." It's the truth, but does it matter? Could I have found a way to calm January down and get her to shore? Maybe. But I wanted her dead anyway, and it was the perfect outcome. I leave that part out though. "It was an *accident*. I'm not going to hurt Lucia. I promise."

"Okay," she says, holding my gaze. When she's sure I know she's serious, she moves on. "What about tomorrow? We need supplies."

"First we need to talk about Ramsey." I worry that this is going to take some convincing. I take a deep breath and ready myself for the argument.

"We need him," she says with a warning look, cutting off my argument before I can even make it.

"He's not like us, Keisha. We don't even know him. I can tell you like him, but we can't trust him."

"You think I like him?" she says, her smile growing. "Wow. I'm amazing. Oscar-worthy. Too bad Hollywood is gone," she says, throwing her head back dramatically with a quiet giggle.

My mouth hangs open stupidly.

"You know me better than that," she says with a smirk. She's right. I do know her better than that. I'm surprised at the amount of relief I feel realizing that all the eyelash fluttering, cheek blushing, and warm smiling was strategic. I should have given her more credit.

I roll my eyes. "So, if you can see through all that southern gentleman bullshit, then you know we need to get rid of him and keep moving south."

"I get it, we don't know him very well, but he doesn't seem dangerous. Look, we lost almost everything when the canoe tipped. We need clothes, supplies, food—everything, really. Let's see if Ramsey will take us into town tomorrow to scavenge. He knows the area better than we do. We'll use him to help us get what we need, then get back in the boat and head south. Just the three of us. In the meantime, we play *nice*," she says with a warning.

"I'm not flirting with that prick," I say, disgusted.

Keisha stifles a laugh. "HA! Now *that* would be the end of the world!" Her smile is infectious, and I crack a rare smile too.

"I don't want to take any chances with him. We get our supplies, then we leave," I say.

She nods in agreement. "You watch our backs. I'll make sure we get what we need."

"But if he tries anything, it's lights out."

Keisha sighs as she rolls over, snuggling into her stack of tablecloths, but I know there's no real anger behind it. I turn off the lantern, close my eyes, and try to get some sleep.

CHAPTER 20

The empty beds next to me let me know Keisha and Lucia have already started their day. How did I sleep so late? I hate the idea of them alone with that stranger. I quickly pull on my boots and weave my machete and hunting knife through my belt before rushing downstairs.

When I come around the corner, Lucia, Keisha, and Ramsey sit by the fireplace in the dining room, smiling and laughing. The smell of eggs is overwhelming, and I realize I haven't eaten anything that didn't come from a can or a plastic package in days. I'm still annoyed they left me alone upstairs, but the thought of breakfast lifts my mood.

Keisha smiles warmly and hands me a hot mug of tea. The first sip feels like medicine, and I almost start to question our plans for a supply run. It sure would be nice to just stay here and rest for a day. My muscles ache from paddling and sitting for days on end. My skin peels and stings from the sun, and I've practically scratched my mosquito bites into open wounds. Even one day to recover would be nice.

I turn to look out the wide windows overlooking the patio and see the muddy river stretching south out of sight. The current pulls ripples into its surface. As calm as it looks outside, yesterday's events remind me that this place isn't as safe as it seems. No place will ever be safe again.

While the eggs cook and the others talk, I find a pen and a napkin at the bar and begin a list. Backpacks, spare clothes, water bottles, lightweight packaged food, cooking supplies, anything that will start a fire, sunscreen, binoculars, toothbrushes—the list goes on and on.

"Breakfast is served!" Ramsey says, smiling and obviously proud of himself. I watch him carry the hot skillet over to the table and search his expression, looking for signs of danger. All I can see is infatuation. He serves Keisha first and seems to orbit around her. It's off-putting but nonthreatening. I decide to let my guard down for the moment. We sit together and eat scrambled eggs, oranges, and stale bread that is probably just hours away from growing mold, but it's the best breakfast I can remember.

"We really can't thank you enough," Keisha says between bites.

"It's my pleasure. Really. Feels good to not be alone anymore."

"What about the people in town? Naples, I think you called it? Are there any people left?" I ask.

"Well, see, the sickness didn't get to us until a couple days after Chicago fell. We're pretty isolated out here, and a lot of us thought it'd be contained before it ever made its way out here to the river bottoms. It only took one sick guy to blow that theory to bits. Best I can tell, he was coming from the east. Springfield, maybe? Coulda been Jacksonville, but I guess it doesn't really matter. He rolled into town barely alive with a big bite taken out of his leg. Thing is, nobody found him in time to get him in the brain. He died in his truck, parked off Main Street. When the local sheriff came through, he thought the guy was drunk. He knocked on the window, opened the truck door, and shouted at the guy to wake up. Well, as you can imagine, he did. Caught the sheriff right in the throat and then took down a couple guys on his way into town. It's not a big town, mind you. All it took was somebody's car alarm, and the whole fleet of them stood up." Ramsey shakes his head as if trying to shoo away the memory.

"Did you see all this happen?" I ask.

"Naw, one of the new deputies was riding along with the sheriff. Saw the whole thing and lived to tell the tale," he explains. "I'd imagine about a quarter of the town lost their lives in one fell swoop. Another quarter headed to the school a few miles south in the next town over. They set up a shelter there. The rest of us just stayed put." He shrugs his shoulders.

"Do you know who left for the shelter and who stayed in their homes?" I ask.

"I have a pretty good sense, I guess."

"Great. We need to find supplies. Can you take us to the best spots to find these?" I pull my napkin list out of my pocket and hand it to him.

Keisha gives me a look that tells me I'm being too aggressive. I shrug and shift my attention back to Ramsey as he carefully reads the list.

"I'm sure there are families who left behind stuff like this. Though I don't think the people left here in town would take too kindly to strangers scavenging in the houses of their neighbors," he says, sliding my list back to me.

"So we go at night," I say.

Ramsey's mouth twitches, and his eyebrows narrow.

He definitely doesn't want us going into town.

"Why don't you rest up here for a few days? We can worry about supplies later. There's plenty of food and water here."

"Look, if this place gets overrun, we need to be able to leave fast. And I want to leave with more than my weapons and the clothes on my back," I say firmly, my eyes narrowing. "We need the safety of supplies. It's fine; you don't have to help us," I say dismissively. "The three of us have made it this far. We'll go by ourselves." I search his face for a reaction. I see a flicker of panic, and his eyes flash to Keisha.

"Now, now, no need to fuss. I think I know where we might find some of this stuff. I'll take y'all, but we're going to need a day to prepare. Just one day, and then we can go. Keisha, you don't mind waiting one more day, do you?" he says, turning toward her.

Keisha's eyes meet mine. She looks torn. I want her to tell him no, to stand by me and insist that we go today. I can see the conflict on her face. She takes an extra breath, then sides with him.

"That's awfully nice of you, Ramsey," Keisha says, placing her hand on his upper arm gently. I know it's not real affection. She told me so last night. But my stomach still rolls. "I'd feel much better if you were with us. We can spend the day preparing, then go first thing in the morning." Then Keisha coughs. Coughs again. Sneezes.

"G'bless you," Ramsey says affectionately, completely oblivious to the signal Keisha just gave me.

I shut down the argument on my lips. I'm not exactly sure why Keisha would side with this asshole, but obviously her gut is telling her we shouldn't push it, and she found a way to tell me to just go with it. I decide to trust her.

"Well, that's settled then," he says, slapping his thigh and grinning at me, attempting to defuse the building tension.

When we finish eating, Ramsey calls me over toward the bar, where he stands at the frothing, soap-filled sink. "Help me with these dishes, Quinn?" he asks, just a bit too sweetly, scrubbing at a pan. Annoyed, I join him at the bar while Keisha and Lucia clear the rest of the dishes and wipe down the table.

"Here," he says, handing me a dripping plate. "I'll wash, you dry."

I grab a towel and wipe the plate carefully as Keisha brings the mugs from the dining room. As she walks away, Ramsey speaks in a low voice so only I can hear.

"I saw what you did to that little girl in the water." I study his face. Where the hell is he going with this?

"I don't know what you think you saw, but that was an accident," I spit back.

"Guess I'd better be lookin' after you then. Wouldn't want any more accidents to happen to those nice girls over there, now would we?" His chin tilts to the side, challenging me. I glare back at him, and for the first time I realize he can see what I am.

"Stay out of this," I say, baring my teeth.

"Watch yourself, girly." He gives me that stupid lopsided grin, tips an imaginary cowboy hat, and walks back to the dining room.

I follow a few steps behind him, leaving the last few dishes to air dry, trying to make sense of what just happened. I know a few things for sure. He sees me. He thinks I'm a danger to Keisha and Lucia and wants to protect them. We need to get out of this place…and fast. I rearrange my face and my posture and walk into the dining room to join the others.

On one of the dining room tables, Ramsey has laid out a large sheet of paper. As he draws, he explains the layout of the town of Naples, Illinois. It's a crude rendering, but the river behind us helps me to orient myself.

"Now, keep in mind when this whole thing started, Naples didn't even have one hundred fifty people living here. If I had to guess, there are about fifty of us left. The homes in this area are all spread out. There are a few families that I think are still hunkered down here, here, and here," he says, placing a tiny X on the map for every off-limits home. "These families here and here lost everyone," he says, circling a few homes next to the highway that runs parallel to the river. "And I know for sure these four families packed up and went to the high school shelter way over here."

"So, these empty homes are the ones where we scavenge?" I ask, trying to keep my voice neutral as if our little conversation never happened.

"Not quite. We can't just hit empty homes. We need to hit empty homes next to empty homes. We can't have any neighbors seeing what we're up to. Now keep in mind, folks down here don't have much, and if they left for the shelter in town, they woulda brought everything they own right along with them," he explains.

I nod. "So which houses do you suggest we visit?"

Ramsey stares at the map and chews his lip, then circles two houses with a bold stroke. One close to our current location and another farther east near the highway. "Those are your best bets."

"Then that's where we'll go. We sure are lucky we ran into you," Keisha says warmly. "Now it's our turn to pitch in. Since we've got this whole day ahead of us, let us get this dining room and kitchen cleaned up for you. We insist, don't we, girls?" Keisha asks, as if we have a choice.

"It's the least we can do," Lucia nearly whispers right on cue. I roll my eyes.

There's no use arguing with Keisha, and her idea is pretty

brilliant. We need to continue to stay on Ramsey's good side, and this keeps us from seeming like useless freeloaders. So we spend the morning putting the dining room back together, throwing out all the rotting food and stained tablecloths, and getting the kitchen back in working order. We find some cleaning supplies in a closet, and before long you'd never know this restaurant had been touched by the carrier plague.

The only area Ramsey won't let us touch is the kitchen pantry. While we're busy with the dining room, he pulls the body from the pantry himself. I watch out the window as he sends it down the river. Soon, the air inside the restaurant is actually breathable.

Somewhere around lunchtime we finish and eat another round of tuna and crackers; then we spend the rest of the day playing cards with an old deck Ramsey found behind the bar. It isn't exactly the day of rest that I imagined, but it beats another day in the canoe.

When the sun sets and it's time for bed, I'm buzzing with excitement. I can't wait to see what we'll find in those houses, and I'm hoping I can convince Ramsey to take us to more than the two he showed us on his map. We need enough supplies so we can get the hell out of here.

CHAPTER 21

I tiptoe downstairs just as the sun rises to use the bathroom and quickly realize the water is no longer working. Again, I think back to the woman we saw on the news back in the dayroom. *"The power grid will fail. Our water reclamation system will cease."* She was right again. At least we have the river.

I watch the sun finish its ascent from the dining room as I wait for the others to wake up. Soon, they all stumble downstairs half-awake but dressed and ready for the day.

"Water's gone," I say as a greeting.

"Was just a matter of time," Ramsey says, shaking his head and yawning. "Now the fireworks will really start. People'll start flocking out of the cities toward the rivers and lakes. Just wait. It's about to get messy."

"Lucky for us, we have a head start. Let's get going. I want to be ready for anything and we need supplies," I say to Keisha and

Lucia. I toss them a few packs of crackers for breakfast and then turn toward the door.

"Not so fast," Ramsey says. "We really should be waiting 'til dark. Don't wanna chance the locals seeing a bunch of strangers wandering around, do ya?" Ramsey says. It's exactly the opposite of what he said yesterday. He's stalling.

"You're no stranger, Ramsey." I snatch the map he made yesterday from the table and roll it up. "Can't you just toss that charming smile of yours around and introduce us to your friends?" I say, challenging him.

"We should wait," he says, his tone a little darker now.

"I'm not waiting," I say firmly.

"Quinn, maybe we should—" Keisha starts, but I cut her off before she can finish.

"We can't get caught here without an exit strategy. A lot can happen in a day, or have you forgotten our first day here?"

That drives the point home.

"I get it," Keisha concedes. "Ramsey, can't you help us find just a few things today? We'd feel much safer," she says, looking up at him with a hopeful smile.

He sighs. Keisha has that effect. "All right," Ramsey says, shrugging. "But we're going on foot. An engine'll draw those things faster than we can handle. And they sure are fast when they're fresh. Wouldn't want anyone getting hurt, would we?" He looks directly at me as he delivers his final line, but I turn away as if I don't notice that his last words were meant to get under my skin. They didn't.

When we leave the restaurant, the sun is climbing, and humidity thickens the air. For a moment I expect to hear January complain about the heat, and then I remember. A memory flashes of my hunting knife sinking into her soft flesh as the water around me warmed and turned that strange shade of muddy pink. My heart beats double-time in my chest.

I look over at Ramsey and imagine what it would be like to do the same to him. I don't trust him. I don't like the way he looks at Keisha. I know Keisha said she's only flirting with him to get what we need from him, and I believe her, but something about this feels off. I want Ramsey out of my way. I take a few deep breaths and try to shake away the feeling.

We follow a blacktop road that leads us into something resembling a town. The houses are flung across the landscape, each one haphazardly occupying a plot of land surrounded by a thick forest of trees. It looks like a town that sprang up accidentally. There are no blocks or corner stores. There isn't a town square, a park, or even a gas station that I can see. Just homes plopped down wherever their owners saw fit. Most of them are old and falling apart. We walk in silence, each of us straining to listen for extra footsteps. Finally, Ramsey points to a house that backs up against the woods surrounding the little town.

"This house here'll be empty. Let's see what we can find," he says, pointing his knife toward the entrance. I walk carefully through the overgrown lawn and check the front door. Locked. I motion for us to go around to the back door. I try the handle, but it's locked as well. To my right I hear a soft "Psst!" I glance over. Lucia's found a window cracked open an inch or two. She looks back at us with a huge grin. I smile approvingly.

I walk to the window and peek inside. It looks like a child's bedroom. A red race car bed sits in the corner next to a pile of tiny toy cars. The bedroom door is open, and I squint, trying to see into the hallway leading to the rest of the house. I give a low whistle. Nothing moves.

"Hello?" I say quietly. Still nothing. I push the window open wider.

Ramsey, Keisha, and Lucia crowd over my shoulder straining to see inside.

"Hello!" This time I shout. After another beat of silence, I think I hear something move, but I can't be sure if it's just my nerves. Then the small bump turns into something that sounds an awful lot like footsteps.

My heart picks up as the rhythmic footsteps move faster and heavier down the hall toward the open bedroom door. I watch in horror as a tiny boy in blue pajamas charges toward the window. Black ooze bubbles in the corners of his mouth and runs down his tiny chin. Keisha gasps beside me, gripping my arm as a high-pitched moan leaps out of his throat. For a moment I'm frozen. Then the carrier leaps for the window.

On instinct, I sharply pull down on Keisha's shirt with one hand as she throws her body on top of Lucia. The three of us duck below the window and up against the house's brick exterior.

Behind us, the remains of the tiny boy fly through the window and land heavily on top of Ramsey, throwing him to the ground with a thud. I can hear the air being knocked out of his lungs with a deep whoosh. Without air, all Ramsey can do is try to keep the boy at arm's length. He struggles as the boy squirms to get out of his grip. Tiny teeth snap as the boy lunges for Ramsey's throat, and I wait anxiously to hear him scream. A smile creeps toward my lips.

"Quinn, kill it!" Keisha shouts, shaking me by the shoulders.

I sigh.

"Quinn, we still need him!" Keisha's eyes plead with me, and like all the times before, I choose to trust her. Ramsey lies on his back, struggling to keep the boy's gnashing teeth from finding flesh. He flails his impossibly strong limbs wildly as Ramsey struggles to find his grip. Finally, Ramsey finds his center of gravity and presses the boy up and to the side. I see my opportunity and swing my machete down sharply.

A tiny head falls onto Ramsey's chest and its flailing body goes still. Black sludge spills from the wound, quickly soaking through Ramsey's clothes. He pushes the body off him and skitters backward, wiping uselessly at the mess that covers him. Unsatisfied, he rips off his shirt, scrubbing frantically at the skin of his chest with the cleanest parts of the fabric.

When he's wiped the worst of the muck from himself, Ramsey angrily spits onto the ground at my feet. "What the hell was that?" he growls.

"What was that?! *You* took us to a house with a zombie child!" I growl back.

"How the hell was I supposed to know they left their dead kid behind? You let that thing attack me!"

"I saw it coming and ducked. You can't blame me for having better reflexes," I say with a shrug.

Ramsey pulls his knife and walks toward me. "You tried to set me up, just like that little girl in the river!"

I resist the urge to step back and set my feet firmly. With both hands I pull my machete up in front of my body, still dripping with black ooze. His steps stutter.

"Ramsey, hey. There's no need for that. She killed it. We're safe. It was just an accident. That's all," Keisha says, walking toward him slowly with her hands up. She touches his arm softly, pulling his focus toward her with her big brown eyes. "This is nothing more than a big misunderstanding. You're not hurt, are you?" she asks softly.

He winces at her touch but softens when he looks down at her. Keisha's eyes hypnotize him, and once again my stomach drops uncomfortably. I clear my throat, interrupting their moment.

"House is clear," I say. "Let's go inside."

CHAPTER 22

Keisha boosts me through the window, and I stumble onto the carpet below, stepping on a tiny truck. I steady myself and do a quick sweep of the room, then close the bedroom door, just in case. Keisha pushes Lucia through the window next. Finally, Keisha grabs my arm, and I pull her through. Behind us, Ramsey pulls himself up and lands on the floor with a thud.

Once we're all inside, we begin the search. In the boy's bedroom closet we find several practical things that will fit Lucia's tiny frame. We shove T-shirts, sweatshirts, and a raincoat into a backpack decorated with trains. She cringes as she pulls it onto her back but doesn't complain.

When we're ready to move on to the next room, I open the bedroom door a crack and listen. We're met with quiet, so I lead the way down the hall with my machete pointed in front of me. We quickly find what looks like a teenage boy's room. Keisha and I are able to ransack the closet and find a few shirts that will definitely be too big, but they'll be better than wearing wet, dirty clothes. We also find some pants that will work if we trim the legs and use a belt.

Behind us, Ramsey has found a new shirt too. It's comically small, but it allows him to cover his bare chest. Before we go, we grab several pairs of clean socks from a drawer. On our way out, Keisha finds a backpack filled with ruled paper and a chemistry book and dumps the contents onto the floor, filling it with our new wardrobe. We make our way into the master bedroom next. The woman who once owned this home was definitely larger than us, and Keisha and I decide that we're much better off with the teenage boy's clothes. We pick through her closet, though, and find another sturdy backpack for me.

"We're done in here. Let's move to the kitchen," I hear Ramsey call from the bathroom. "Find anything good?" he asks.

"Clothes and junk," I reply.

He scans every corner of my face, looking for a lie. Reluctantly, he turns away. "Let's see if they left any food."

When we walk into the kitchen I'm overwhelmed by the smell of rot. The garbage can spills over with pizza boxes and takeout containers. It buzzes sickeningly with the sound of flies, and I don't dare go near it. We open the cabinets, hoping for food that's easy to prepare. A few half-empty cereal boxes, some canned vegetables, and some just-add-water boxed meals are all we find. In another cabinet I find a bottle of vitamins and two sports-style water bottles, then toss them into a tote bag. We grab a few forks and spoons and a can opener from a drawer and find a small metal pot in a high cabinet. This is not a family that cooks much. We give up and move on.

In the basement near a pile of Christmas decorations, we find a child-sized sleeping bag and roll it up for Lucia, along with a few light blankets. Our final stop is the garage. We lift the large rolling door, and light floods the space. The family car is gone. A tiny bike with training wheels and an old skateboard are the only things we find with wheels. I was hoping for a set of bicycles so we could cut down on walking, but no luck. We open an old rusty refrigerator in the garage, find two bottles of water, and toss them in our bags. I see a few bungee cords and plastic sheets and toss those in as well.

Inside a toolbox I find a small hatchet and hand it to Keisha.

"This looks like it might do more damage than that bat," I say, smiling as I pass it to her. Her eyes shine, and she grips it tight.

"It's perfect!" she practically sings. She gives me the same warm look she's been giving Ramsey all day. I turn away before she can see me blush and grab a lighter and a couple of screwdrivers.

"Whoa!" Lucia says, wide-eyed, as she pulls a tarp off a large cabinet in the back corner. Four fishing poles. I've never been so grateful in my life.

"Good find, Lu! Pack those up. See those little boxes on the bottom shelf? Grab those too," I say, pointing to two tackle boxes. Lucia loads the poles and supplies into a five-gallon bucket for easy carrying.

"I think we've packed everything we can use. Let's move on to the next one," I say to Ramsey.

"No. We're going home," he says firmly.

"No way! You said you'd help us. There's plenty of daylight left, and we still need more supplies," I argue.

"I said I'd help you. I helped you." Ramsey spits on the ground, just missing my boot, and starts walking back the way we came.

Keisha looks over her shoulder at me, and I stare back defiantly, hoping she'll back me up. "Let it go," she mouths.

My fist tightens around the handle of my machete, and my eyes bore into the back of his head. I feel Keisha's fingertips brush my arm, so I shift my eyes back to her. She gives a tiny shake of her head and lets her hand fall back at her side. I think back to what Keisha said when the little boy attacked Ramsey. *"We still need him."* I still can't imagine why. He's basically been useless. I'm the one who's been protecting her. But I take a deep breath and try to calm myself down.

Just as I leave the garage to follow her lead, a loud noise off in the distance freezes me in my tracks. That was definitely a gunshot.

I duck back into the garage, waving for Keisha and Lucia to do the same as the sound of an engine grumbles from the direction of the blast. Ramsey doubles back to us, fear flashing in his eyes. The engine gets louder by the second, and the unmistakable shriek of a carrier rings in my ears. Another shot pierces the air, followed by loud whoops of laughter.

We carefully lower the garage door, leaving a few inches of space between the door and the concrete slab, and wait for these idiots to pass, hoping they don't draw too many carriers out into the open. I pull my machete from its sheath, then lie on my belly, watching the road from the cold floor. It doesn't take long for a huge black pickup truck to come into view in front of the garage. The truck slows. Two men cackle from the cab with the windows down while two more do a victory dance from the bed of the truck, holding their shotguns high in the air like championship fighters.

The driver lays on the horn. "Wake up, you dead bastards!" he shouts over the noise.

It doesn't take long before we hear the shriek of another carrier. This time, it comes from the woods behind the house.

Suddenly the walls surrounding us feel far too fragile, and I itch to make a run for it. Keisha must be able to read my mind, because she grabs my hand, anchoring me to her. I take a deep breath and try to find the patience to let the feeling pass.

Another shriek. Then another.

"Here they come! Call yer shots, boys!" the driver shouts with a twang.

"The blond. Right kneecap!" calls one of the men from the bed of the truck. The blast of a shotgun fills the air, followed by more loud cheering.

"Red T-shirt! Kill shot," shouts the other. Another blast peppers the left side of the garage door and tiny beams of light penetrate the walls around us. Lucia's eyes go wild. She slaps her hand over her mouth and presses herself into Keisha.

"You dumbass." The driver laughs. "He's getting too close. Travis, take the red T-shirt out."

Another blast cuts off the carrier mid-shriek. "Finish the blond while you're at it," he instructs.

Another blast.

"Got 'em!" the passenger shouts. "Looks clear. Let's see what we find."

The roar of the engine goes silent as they get out of the truck and walk up the driveway toward the house we just looted.

Shit. They're coming to look for supplies, and I have no doubt they'll check the garage.

"Who are they?" I whisper to Ramsey.

"Some assholes I went to high school with," he says, gritting his teeth.

"Be. More. Specific," I say sharply.

"The Bowen brothers. Travis and Thomas. And their cousins, Jared and Keith," Ramsey answers, clearly annoyed. "Meatheads. All of 'em took one too many hits on the football field. Not a lick of sense left in any of 'em."

My head swims, trying to think of a way to get out of the garage undetected without losing our new gear.

"Are you on good terms with them?" Keisha asks.

"Naw," Ramsey says, spitting on the dusty garage floor.

"Did anyone see if they took the keys to the truck?" I ask.

"They did. I was watching," Lucia whispers. I sigh impatiently. I'm running out of ideas.

Inside the house, something shatters and loud cheers erupt. Reckless idiots.

"How friendly do you think these guys are going to be when they find us hiding with every useful item from this place?" I ask Ramsey.

"Not very. They'll take everything you got, for sure," he says. "Moral of the story is we need to get out of here fast."

We can't outrun them. We can't hide in the garage. After all the noise, every carrier within a mile is on their way here, so the woods behind the house aren't safe either.

The back door slams. We're out of time. "Check the garage," the driver says.

I scramble to my feet, pulling Keisha up as I go. "Lu, get under the tarp," Keisha whispers, pointing to where we found the fishing poles. Lucia hesitates and clings tighter to Keisha. "Go!" she urges. Lucia obeys, tears already welling in her eyes.

"You too," I say.

"Not a chance," Keisha answers, but it's too late to argue with her. Someone throws open the rolling garage door. The sun temporarily blinds me, and I squint, desperately trying to stay oriented.

"Well, what do we have here?" the driver says, smirking. "Ramsey Johns! We've been looking for you, boy," the driver says with false cheer and a sarcastic smile.

Ramsey cringes, and a flash of panic crosses his face. Confused, I tighten my fingers around the handle of my machete.

"Where's my sister, Ramsey?"

"I don't—"

The driver doesn't let him finish and slaps him hard across the face.

"She left to go check on you more than a week ago. Her car's still sitting outside your house, empty. We thought you two might have run away together, but here you are with these two," he says, casually pointing to us with the end of his shotgun. "So that still begs the question. Where. Is. My. Baby. Sister?"

My mind reels as I try to make sense of what they're saying. Then it hits me. The carrier in the pantry. The one who bit Nurse Patrick. That carrier had once been a woman. Ramsey had said it was his girlfriend.

My heart pounds as I try to decide what to do with this information. Do I rat him out? I'm not sure yet, so I wait.

"WHERE IS SHE?" he yells, startling everyone.

"I never saw her, okay? I haven't even been at my house. She's not with me," he says, panic rising in his voice.

"I don't believe you," the passenger spits.

"What about you girls?" The driver's focus pivots to me and Keisha; the tip of his shotgun follows. "Have you seen my sister while you've been following this asshole around?"

Keisha speaks first, thank god, because I still don't know what to do. "You're the first people we've seen in days, sir."

"What about you?" he says, turning toward me, looking a little more desperate. "Her name's Karla. She has dark hair like mine. She's tall, and she wears a little gold cross necklace."

Keisha stiffens next to me. She knows.

"I've been with her since the start," I say, gesturing to Keisha. "We got here the day before yesterday. I haven't seen anyone but the people in this garage. Aside from the carriers, of course," I say truthfully.

My mind swims as I try to plot an exit. In front of us, four idiots with shotguns block our path to safety. Beside me stands Ramsey, a pain in my ass who's made every attempt to sway Keisha to his side. In the woods, carriers are probably closing in, following the gunshots and loud voices. We're running out of time. I need to take them all out in one fell swoop so we can get back on the river and leave this mess behind. An idea clicks into place. I wish I had time to run it past Keisha, but we don't have that luxury. "Unless…" I say, arranging a horrified look on my face, hoping it's convincing enough.

"Unless what, girl?" the driver says, taking a step toward me. I have his full attention.

"You said a tiny gold cross? Dark hair like yours?" I force more worry into my expression, hoping I'm not overdoing it. Beside me, Keisha widens her eyes as if begging me to stop. Again, I wish I could send my plan to her telepathically. Instead, I just have to hope she trusts me and follows along.

"Ramsey, that wasn't... You wouldn't have... Was that his *sister*?" I say with an accusing tone.

The driver takes a step toward me. "Don't you talk to him. Talk to me! What did you see?" He points his gun at my chest.

"Don't say another word, Quinn! You shut your goddamn mouth!" Ramsey says, spitting with each word. "I didn't hurt her. I would never hurt her!" One of the cousins restrains him as he lunges for me.

It's working. I just have to stick the landing. "Well, when we first got here, we found a carrier locked up in a pantry back at the boatel. It bit our friend, and he died. It's just...the carrier that got him was wearing a gold cross necklace. And she looked a lot like you."

Betrayal flares in Ramsey's eyes. "She's lying!" he screams, trying to break free from the man restraining him. But I'm not lying, and he knows it.

Pure rage colors each of the four faces in front of me. Beside me, Keisha whispers, "What are you *doing*?" Ramsey's desperate words begin tumbling out. "She was already bitten when I found her! I thought I could find a doctor. I thought she might get better. I couldn't kill her. I swear I didn't—"

The passenger fires a warning shot in the air, silencing all of us. "Shut your mouth and drop your weapon, Ramsey. You're coming with us."

Ramsey looks at Keisha. She looks conflicted, glancing from

him, then back to me. When she makes no moves to help him, he places his knife on the ground, defeated, then steps forward to meet his fate. The passenger grabs him by the back of his collar, then slams his fist into his jaw. A chorus of shrieks and moans fills the forest behind us, and everyone freezes.

I can't tell how many footsteps I hear, but it's more than two. And they're moving fast.

The first carrier emerges from behind the garage, running with a strange jerking gait. One of the men fires at the carrier, blasting it in the chest. Its pace slows, but it doesn't stop. It keeps coming, with two more on its heels, screeching as they reach for the source of the noise. More rotting bodies flood out of the woods.

I watch in silence as I lose count. Memories of the campsite come flooding back, and my feet itch to run. Instead, I pull Keisha down to the concrete floor of the garage and whisper just loud enough for her and Lucia to hear. "Stay perfectly still."

Soon, the four men and Ramsey are completely surrounded, their shotguns useless. Two of them drop their guns in favor of knives and begin swinging toward the carriers' skulls, trying to avoid their gnashing teeth and the black bile flinging from their open mouths with every screech.

It doesn't take long. The two men who were shooting from the back of the pickup truck are the first to lose their footing. The carriers lunge for their throats, knocking them off balance and sinking their teeth into the soft flesh under their jaws. Their human screams turn into bubbling gurgles, then go silent as the ground below them turns red.

The passenger and driver of the truck continue the fight as Ramsey ducks behind them. Soon, he sees an opportunity. He picks up one of the discarded shotguns and uses the stock to bash in the skull of the closest carrier, creating some breathing room.

The passenger goes down next when a carrier sinks its teeth into his leg, leaving the driver and Ramsey fighting side by side. Soon, only two carriers remain. I can tell Ramsey is exhausted. He doesn't have much fight left, and he knows it. Finally, he sees his chance. In one swift motion, Ramsey sweeps his leg at the driver's ankles.

The driver falls hard, knocking the air from his chest. Ramsey steps back, and the last two carriers dive onto the driver. They aim their rotting teeth at his neck before he can even regain his breath to scream.

Ramsey looks down at the mess of bodies, exhaustion and rage still coloring his expression. He searches the ground for a knife and finds one next to the passenger, then plunges it into the skulls of the feasting carriers. He takes a deep breath, then pushes the knife into the eye of each dead man, ensuring they'll never awaken.

I stare in awe. I didn't think he had it in him. Ramsey begins rolling the men's bodies over, checking their pockets. The jingle of keys tells me he's found what he's looking for.

Ramsey turns toward us. His new shirt is completely soaked through with dark red blood, thick black ooze, and sweat. His eyes are crazed, and for a moment fear prickles the back of my neck. He wasn't supposed to survive this.

Ramsey holds up the keys to the truck and rings them like a little bell.

"Keisha, Lucia, get in the truck. We're leaving," he says, stone-faced.

We don't move from the shelter of the garage. Keisha looks at me, then back at Ramsey. The tarp crackles as Lucia peeks out from behind it, her big brown eyes still brimming with tears and fear.

"Come on, both of you, get in the truck. More of 'em are probably on the way," he says.

"We're not going with you," I say, answering for all of us.

"Quinn, I..." Keisha starts. Before she can finish, fast footsteps slam into the hard-packed ground coming from the forest. A screech rips through my eardrums. The carrier slams into Ramsey, knocking him to the ground before he can react. It's a familiar scene. He lies on his back and holds the carrier at arm's length, its snapping jaws inching closer and closer to his throat, but this time I don't help.

I walk over and put my boot between the carrier's shoulders and press down slowly.

"Quinn, stop!" Keisha calls out.

Ramsey fights to hold the extra weight of my boot, shaking with effort, but I'm just getting started. I press down just a tiny bit harder. Ramsey gives a rage-filled roar of effort, but he's already exhausted. His arms shake harder as he starts to lose the battle.

"Quinn, please!" Keisha begs, but I don't even look up. My pulse pounds in my ears, and a flood of satisfaction overwhelms each of my senses.

I shift my weight again, putting just enough pressure onto the carrier's back to cause Ramsey's arms to give way. His screams die in his chest as the carrier sinks its teeth deep into his throat. I keep my foot on its back and press its teeth deeper into Ramsey's neck.

When its jaws have done their job, I take a heavy swing at the carrier's spine, sending its head rolling. I wipe my machete on its clothes, then remove my hunting knife from its sheath, driving it into Ramsey's eye socket. He won't follow us now. I spit into his ruined eye.

On the ground, a set of silver keys glistens in the summer sun. I toss them to Keisha.

"We're leaving," I growl.

CHAPTER 23

Keisha drives the short distance back to the boatel in silence. I try to read her mind, but I'm at a loss. For more than a moment, it seemed like she was actually torn between going with Ramsey and staying with me. Did I imagine it? When she cried out for me to stop, was she just being squeamish? Or did she really want him to live?

By the time we get back to the boatel, the summer sun sits low in the sky, painting it shades of pale pink. Night will be coming soon, and I'm absolutely exhausted. It takes the last of our energy to carry all of our new supplies into the boatel before the sun sets and the mosquitoes start buzzing.

"What's the plan?" Keisha asks once we reach the dining room. Her eyes are glazed over, exhausted and emotionless.

While I can't wait to leave this place, getting a good night's sleep behind walls sounds pretty good right now. Looking at all our supplies piled on the floor of the dining room, I feel safer already. Plus, we have access to all the food Ramsey had stockpiled.

"I think we should sleep here tonight, and then tomorrow morning we can pack up and keep heading south in the canoe. What do *you* want to do?" I ask with a little too much accusation in my voice.

"What's that supposed to mean?" she asks, looking hurt.

"Well, back there it looked like you were thinking about going off with Ramsey." I don't even try to hide the anger in my voice.

"Quinn, I already told you. I was only flirting with him so he'd do what we wanted. And yeah, I thought about going with him. He *did* have the keys to the truck. But I was going to make him take you too." She takes one too many breaths between her sentences. Is she lying?

"Could've fooled me," I say sharply.

"I would never have left you behind. Don't be ridiculous!"

"You said we needed him. For what? You tried to keep me from killing him even though you saw for yourself how dangerous he is," I spit back.

"Who's the dangerous one, Quinn?" Accusation and real anger flash in her eyes. "He took us to find supplies. He let us stay here. He probably would have done whatever I asked him to," she argues, her voice louder with each word. Lucia curls in on herself and slinks back to the corner of the room, avoiding the escalating scene.

"*I've* kept us alive! *Me.*" I say, slamming my fist into my chest. "Every single thing I've done is to protect us." I step closer and she winces. I can tell she's scared. I don't care. "Ramsey's dead because *you* couldn't keep him under control. All those melty looks you gave him didn't do shit. He had no interest in helping us. He just wanted to keep you close, and you *let* him," I say, anger dripping from every word.

I expect her to bite back, but instead Keisha cracks a smile, and a giggle escapes from her lips.

"What could possibly be funny, Keisha?" I shout.

She bats her eyelashes and purses her lips dramatically. "Melty looks?"

I wave her playful words away, trying to hold on to my anger. "Stop it. I'm serious. What the hell was going on back there?"

She sighs. "Quinn, listen to me." She takes my hand, and my anger deflates. "It's just us. It was always supposed to be this way. You, me, and Lucia. Now we can keep going south, just like we planned. Ramsey was just a way to get us what we needed so we could keep going." She squeezes my hand, then reaches up to touch the side of my face. I try to look away, but she presses my cheek so I'm facing her. "It's always been us. It's always going to be us. Now can we please eat something? I'm starving," she says, feigning collapse.

And just like that, I melt.

Keisha throws together a meal while I lay out each item we looted, plus as much food as I think we can carry from the boatel's kitchen, trying to find the optimal way to fit it all into our backpacks and, eventually, the canoe. Once everything is rearranged, I set it all next to the sliding glass doors overlooking the patio so we can make a quick getaway if we need to.

I glance over at Lucia. It was her job to start the fire, and she did, but now she's just staring into the flames. She snaps out of it when Keisha calls us to the table. Somehow Keisha's made a decent-looking meal from a can of black beans, jarred salsa, and stale tortilla chips. We eat in silence, but Lucia barely touches her dinner.

"Lucia?" I say, trying to get her attention.

"Hm?"

"Are you okay?"

"I'm just tired," she says with a shrug.

"Why don't you go on upstairs and go to sleep? We can clean up," Keisha suggests with a hint of concern.

"Okay," Lucia replies robotically.

She gets up from the table and walks upstairs. We hear the soft click of our bedroom door echo through the hall.

"She just needs a good night's sleep," Keisha says, mostly to herself. I hope she's right. It's only been two days since her last dose of medication. Surely it's not affecting her already. I shake the thought away.

CHAPTER 24

I wake up feeling rested and hopeful. With Ramsey out of the picture and plenty of supplies, I feel ready to take on the river and whatever it brings. Keisha doesn't look like she slept much, but she wakes easily enough and seems intent on leaving the boatel as fast as possible. It takes multiple attempts to wake Lucia, though. She grumbles when we shake her, begging for another hour of sleep. It's not like her at all. My worries from last night come back. Is she just worn out, or is a third day with no medication starting to affect her? Either way, there's nothing I can do to help her.

We eat crackers and drink purified water as we pack the boat. We can't take nearly as much as we want to. Our packs, the fishing poles, and a few bags full of dry pantry items are all we can squeeze in. By the time we're packed, my shirt is nearly soaked through. It's already hot as hell.

Keisha clears out a tiny nest at the bottom of the canoe and tells Lucia to climb in and get some more rest. She does without hesitation. Then we shove the canoe into the water, jump in, and let the current take us away from the boatel.

We float downstream for hours. We take turns pouring the cool river water onto our skin, but it seems to evaporate before we find any real relief. It doesn't take long for the sun to start to get to me. I silently wish for sunglasses, but some sunblock or a hat sure would be nice too.

"I can feel my skin burning off my body," I complain.

"Sucks to be white," Keisha teases, turning her face toward the sky and reaching her arms over her head like she's actually enjoying the sun. Her deep brown skin hasn't burned at all.

I crack a smile. "Please find me some sunscreen in the next house we loot."

"I have an idea. Here, let me show you." She puts down her paddle and reaches into my bag, taking out a long-sleeved T-shirt. She lets the end of the T-shirt fall onto my back and then uses the empty arms to tie a knot up under my chin. Then she pulls the empty neck of the T-shirt forward over my forehead. She digs around in my backpack again, then pulls out the folded map of Naples that Ramsey made and shoves it between the top of my head and the T-shirt, creating a makeshift hat bill. I laugh out loud when it actually works. I must look ridiculous.

"Keisha, you're a genius," I say, laughing.

Her fingers trace the edge of my cheek. "You look gorgeous!" she teases.

I can feel myself blush and hope my sunburn covers it up.

"Very funny," I say, brushing her off.

A bird caws loudly overhead, and Lucia looks up sleepily from her nest in the bottom of the boat before squeezing her eyes shut again.

"How are you feeling, Lucia?" I ask as I paddle.

"I'm fine. Just tired."

"It's been a while since you had your meds," I say cautiously. I know meds are a touchy subject for a lot of us. Some of the girls back at the center really hated having to take them. I know I did. Some girls tried to hide what they were taking, afraid the rest of us would judge them. Some would brag about who needed the highest dose. Some, like Keisha, flushed theirs down the toilet every day. I didn't even pay attention to Lucia's habits at the Pegasus Center. She had only been there for about a month before everything went upside down. I'm not really sure how she feels about taking her meds or how severe her diagnosis was.

"I know," she says quietly. I wait to see if she'll say more, but she doesn't. I look to Keisha for help.

"Are you feeling any different yet?" Keisha asks. Lucia's eyes shine with just a hint of unshed tears.

"I don't want to talk about it," she says, picking at her fingernails in her lap.

Shit. I don't have to read her chart to know what I'm looking at. Now that it's staring me in the face, I realize I've been seeing it for days now. She's had less energy. She's been sleeping more. She's stopped contributing to our discussions. Shit.

Depression is a tough diagnosis. It's not like it's rare. It was listed in just about everybody's chart, even mine at first, but when depression is bad, it's really bad. I've seen it kick the crap out of some tough people, turning them into lifeless, joyless shells of themselves for no other reason than their brain decided to stop making the right chemicals in the right proportions. I also know that no amount of trying to cheer someone up helps. This is bad. Mentally, I move finding Lucia's meds to the top of my list.

As the afternoon approaches, the sun becomes a little more bearable, but it's too late. The heat and the sun have sucked every ounce of energy and water from our bodies. We have plenty of daylight left, but I feel like I can't paddle another minute. We agree to pull the boat to shore and camp for the night.

We find a low area to pull the boat ashore. With the riverbank at my back, I patrol the trees with my machete, looking for wandering carriers and picking up a few pieces of firewood along the way. The place we chose is dead quiet except for the insects, but I go deeper into the woods that line the river, just to be sure we're alone. I step over dead leaves, snapping branches under my boots, and I cringe at every sound, but nothing moves, so I keep walking deeper. Just beyond the trees, a levee rises up, meant to keep the river from flooding the surrounding fields. It's tall and steep and would be very difficult for a carrier to climb quickly. For us, the giant hill could mean a shelter, keeping us out of immediate reach. I lay the firewood I've been collecting on the ground and climb to the top of the levee, using my hands and my feet to find purchase up the steep hill. When I get to the top, I find cornfields with hip-high plants stretching as far as I can see. In the distance, I think I can see small shapes that could be a farmhouse and a barn, but I'm not sure. I blink hard and squint and once again wish for a pair of binoculars. I give up and shuffle back down the levee toward Keisha, picking up my pile of firewood at the base of the hill.

"I think I found a great spot for us to sleep tonight," I say, dumping the firewood on the ground. "There's a big levee through those trees. I'm pretty sure we'd be safe at the top. Maybe we can all sleep at the same time and skip guard shifts," I suggest.

"Thank god," Keisha says with a groan. "I feel like I got hit by a truck. What do you think, Lu?" Keisha says, trying to keep her engaged in the conversation.

"Sounds good." She tries a little too hard to force energy into her voice.

Keisha flashes a worried look my way, but there's nothing we can do except try to keep her involved. Keisha recruits Lucia to build us a fire, and I haul more water to be boiled. In an hour, we have drinkable water and something resembling a meal. We eat, wash our bowls, and then get to work on setting up our camp. We use our last bits of energy to hide the canoe under long leafy branches and carry our packs up the levee.

The last minutes of sun light up the sky with a purple-pink

hue. I squint again at the little shapes beyond the fields. “Hey, do you think that’s a house?” I ask Keisha.

Her eyes graze across the horizon, and I can see the moment she finds it. “Definitely.”

“I don’t think it would take long for us to walk there. We should check it out. There might be some good supplies. Maybe even some medicine.” I say the last part quietly so Lucia won’t hear.

“It’s risky to be out in the open like that. Those things are so fast. Let’s sleep on it and decide in the morning. I can’t think anymore,” Keisha says with a yawn.

We curl up in our blankets at the top of the levee and sleep until dawn.

CHAPTER 25

I awake with the sunrise at the top of the levee, safe and sound. My muscles burn and my skin feels tight as I sit up, but at least I feel well rested. I expect to see Keisha sleeping soundly next to me, but instead, I find she's already awake, staring off toward the farm we spotted yesterday.

"Morning," I say groggily.

"You're right. The farm is close. I haven't seen a single carrier in hours. And better yet, the farm is completely isolated. We can get there on foot in an hour or so, raid the place, and be back in the canoe before noon. If it's empty, we might even be able to stay there for a few days and get some rest," Keisha says.

"Wow, right down to business. Can I pee first?" I say, rubbing my eyes.

"Be fast," she says, flashing me a wicked smile.

The sight of her smile is a relief, and I can't help but grin back.

Just like that, the Ramsey situation feels like it happened a lifetime ago. This is the Keisha I've always known. I feel excited. Like we're on one of our secret missions back at the Pegasus Center.

Keisha shakes Lucia awake to tell her the plan. She looks limp and lifeless but doesn't argue. Soon, we're packed up, but before we go, Lucia finds a sturdy branch near the river and begins carrying it up the levee.

"What's with the stick?" Keisha asks.

"We need to mark the spot where our canoe is. Everything looks the same out here, and if we need to make a quick getaway, we need to be able to find the canoe fast."

"Smart," I say, giving her a playful shove. She doesn't respond, just hands the branch over to me.

At the top of the levee, I dig the branch into the dirt as deep as I can. To the untrained eye it looks like a little tree. To us, it marks our exit. With that, we head toward the farm.

"We should review the list of things we need and make those our first priority. We might not have time for a room-to-room search if the farm isn't empty. What's on your list? Other than food, of course," I ask.

"If I'm being totally selfish? I'm still wishing for lip balm. Definitely cherry flavored. Sunglasses. A seat cushion for the boat!" Keisha says with a laugh.

"Seat cushions! Brilliant. I'd die for a hat and some sunscreen. We need binoculars too. We need to be able to see farther downriver. And while we're in the kitchen looking for food, we really need another cooking pot or two. And some more water bottles," I add. "Lucia, what's on your list?"

"Chocolate. Anything chocolate," she says, almost smiling.

We keep chattering about what we might find, and soon we come to a weedy dirt road that looks like it will lead us right to the farm. In less than an hour, we're there. Three buildings sit along a gravel path, and my hope grows when I realize there's no one in sight. The building closest to us is a big rusting shed built from slabs of painted sheet metal. Beyond that is a small, white barnlike structure. Then, next to the barn sits a modest gray single-story house with a wide front porch and a brick sidewalk surrounded by an old white picket fence. It looks like something out of a storybook. Parked outside is a red pickup truck that's just starting to rust. So far, the truck is the only sign we might have company.

It's broad daylight, so hiding is a challenge, but a tall line of thick pine trees helps keep us concealed. We try to move swiftly from tree to tree, creeping closer and closer. We peek between branches and watch for movement, trying to get a closer look. When we're only a few feet away from the house, we pause.

"Search the house first?" I ask Keisha.

"Yeah. The sooner we know if anyone's here, the better," she agrees. "I think we should knock on the front door. If there are people in there and we surprise them, they might get hostile. If we knock like we're looking for help, they'll be more likely to open the door. And if no one answers the door, we waltz right in and take what we want."

"Nice," I say with a nod. "Here goes nothing."

I take a step forward, but Keisha reaches out her hand to stop me. "If we find someone, let me take the lead, okay?"

"Please," I say. I know my forced smiles and copied expressions will only fool the most naive. Keisha, on the other hand, will put on a Broadway-worthy performance with barely any effort.

With our plan in place, I shove my machete back into its holster. The three of us step out from the shelter of the tree.

Excitement builds in my chest as we walk slowly up the brick sidewalk toward the front porch. From the large front window, I see the curtains flutter.

"Someone's inside," I say.

"Dead or alive?"

"I can't tell. I guess we're about to find out."

We step up onto the front porch and knock three times on the weathered front door. Immediately, my eardrums are assaulted with the sound of insane barking from behind the door. There's a dog inside. I wait for its human to answer the door. Wait. More barking. More waiting. My nerve endings are on fire. But still, no one comes to answer the door.

I look over at Keisha, and she shrugs her shoulders, so I reach for the doorknob and turn it. Unlocked. Keisha gives me a nod, so I push the door a few inches. A long brown snout peeks out from the gap in the door, sniffing furiously. It gives another short, sharp bark, but when it doesn't snarl and attack, I push the door open a bit farther.

A wagging blur bounces out the front door and nearly knocks me over onto the porch. Keisha practically has hearts coming out of her eyes. If squealing in a whisper is possible, she accomplishes it. The dog melts into her, and she lavishes it with pets and snuggles. Even Lucia smiles and reaches out to pet her.

I look the dog over. She looks well fed. She hasn't been starving alone in there. The hairs on the back of my neck stand on end, telling me I should keep my guard up. I take a single step forward to poke my head into the doorway and peer into the house.

There. In the darkest corner of the living room, in an ancient, worn-out La-Z-Boy, sits an old man in a cloud of cigarette smoke with a shotgun in his lap.

He cocks the shotgun, leaving it lying across his lap, and smiles. Hearing the sound, Keisha freezes next to me, leaving the dog to entertain itself.

"I see you've met Penny," the man says in a gravelly voice. "'Bout the worst guard dog I ever had, as you can see."

"She's so sweet, sir. And awfully cute. We were just out looking for food. We don't mean any harm," Keisha says in her sweetest voice.

"Come inside. All of you," he demands. I try to read him, but it's tough. He doesn't seem angry or hostile, but the clear threat of the shotgun in his lap and the way he doesn't even budge from his chair give him an intimidating confidence that has me on edge.

We do as he says and step inside. His cloud of cigarette smoke hangs heavily in the air. The old man doesn't say a word, just waits as if daring us to make a move.

Keisha breaks the silence first. "We're a little lost out here. Can you tell us where we are? Is there a town nearby?"

"You don't know where you are?" he asks, annoyingly answering a question with a question.

"Well, it's been tough to keep track. There aren't many signs out here, and we're trying to stay off the roads."

"Kids these days can't read a map, I guess," he says with a guffaw, his cigarette bobbing between his lips.

I tap my toe impatiently. "So what's the closest town?" I ask, trying to hide my annoyance.

"Depends on which direction you're headed. Do you even know that much, little girl?"

I open my mouth to respond, but Keisha answers before I can snap back at him. "South, sir."

"Well, there's not much directly south of here until you hit St. Louis. If you're heading southwest though, I reckon the nearest small town will be Winchester or Hillview."

I commit the names of the small towns to memory and cringe at the thought of being so close to St. Louis.

"Have you had many carriers come through here?" Keisha asks, still trying to ease the tension.

"Carriers? You mean the dead ones? We're getting them. Probably rolling in from Jacksonville. Just a few at a time though.

Nothing me and Penny can't handle," he says, nodding at the patient dog sniffing Keisha's hand.

"We heard there are shelters. Why haven't you gone yet? Doesn't it get lonely out here by yourself?" Keisha asks.

"And who says I'm by myself, little girl? I've got no need for one of those deathtraps they call shelters. Anybody who's been paying attention to history knows the worst thing to do in a situation like this is gather in large groups. Which reminds me. The three of you should be going now." His hands casually grip the shotgun in his lap, the subtle warning crystal clear. Keisha moves protectively in front of Lucia.

I'm ready to go back to our canoe, but something on the side table next to him catches my eye. Next to a dirty ashtray and a TV remote control, a pair of heavy-duty binoculars sits next to a book on birds of the Midwest. The same book I had checked out of the school library back at the Pegasus Center, except my copy is hundreds of miles away. I want those binoculars, and I want that book.

"You heard the man, Keisha. Let's go," I say.

"Now that's a wise choice, young lady. Be careful out there now," he says, the threat in his voice thinly veiled.

Keisha pauses to give Penny a kiss on top of her head. "It was nice meeting you, sweet girl," she says in her most sugary-sweet voice.

The farmer clears his throat impatiently.

We let ourselves out, leaving through the front door and

closing it tight behind us. I'm surprised he let us just walk out. Was he unwilling to fire a shot and attract carriers? Did he have a soft spot for us? Or did we convince him we were scared enough to leave and never come back? It wasn't a very smart move, but whatever his reason for letting us go, I'm grateful for it.

We follow the gravel road past the house in silence. I can feel his eyes watching us walk away and make my steps a little quicker. I imagine him picking up the binoculars as we get farther and farther down the road. I already know we have to go back. There's too much valuable stuff in there. When we're finally out of earshot, I open my mouth to tell Keisha, but she beats me to the punch.

"See that bend in the road up ahead? We'll be out of sight there. That's where we wait. When it gets dark, we go back," Keisha says.

I have to admit I'm a little shocked. Since this whole thing started, Keisha has been pretty passive. Very live and let live and all that. She advocated for Ginger and January. She wanted to partner with Ramsey instead of killing him. She even cringed when I killed the men at the gas station and when Ramsey finished off the Bowen brothers back in Naples. She's been soft. I expected her to call this a loss and suggest we move on. Something has changed, though. All day she's been sharper, she's calculating, and she's not waiting for me to tell her what comes next. And there's a slow-burning fire in her eyes. I look at her curiously, trying to imagine what's changed.

"You read my mind," I say. "Did you see the binoculars on the table?"

"I did. Did you get a look at the kitchen when we walked in?"

"No, I was more focused on the shotgun," I say with a dull laugh.

"You had to look at just the right angle to see in, but it was full of food in jars. Not like from the grocery store, though. Remember how we used to go on those summer day trips to the farmers' market on Saturdays back at the Pegasus Center? They were like those jars. He must have a garden somewhere," Keisha says.

My mouth waters at the thought of eating something that didn't come from a box.

"He's not going to give all that up easily," I say, wondering if she's really willing to do what it takes to get what we want. In all likelihood we're going to have to kill this man to take what he has.

"He has what we need to survive," she says coldly.

I steady my face, working hard not to let my shock show through my neutral mask. That sounds like something I would say. What the hell happened? I don't argue with her, though, because I completely agree. It's how I've felt all along.

"Okay then. We're taking the farm," I say. For a moment, I think I see a flash of regret cross her face, but it's gone as quickly as it appeared.

The three of us walk to the curve in the road; then, when we're certain we can't be seen from the farmhouse, we sit under a few shady trees and wait for dark.

CHAPTER 26

The sun finally dips below the tree line along the river, and the mosquitoes start biting. Hours of waiting have left me feeling a little anxious and very hungry, but we have a solid plan, and, to put it mildly, I'm excited. I can practically taste the adrenaline. We leave our hiding place under the shady tree and start to make our way back to the farm. To be on the safe side, we decide to make a wide loop around the farmhouse and come from the opposite side of where the farmer saw us leave. He won't expect us to come from that direction. Soon, the three buildings that make up the farm come into view. The shed, the small white barn, and the gray house.

When we reach the fence surrounding the front yard, we duck behind its white pickets, hiding ourselves from the windows. I shrug off my backpack, unzip the front pouch, and grab one of my lighters. This is our weapon of choice tonight.

Keisha takes a deep breath, then grabs my arm and gives it a squeeze, making my heart jump.

When my eyes meet hers, I can see the excitement in them, and maybe just a hint of fear. I give her a small smile and whisper, "Are you ready?"

"I'm ready," she whispers back, looking a little less bold than she did earlier. "Lucia, are you ready?"

"Yes," she whispers.

"Stay low."

As fast and as quietly as we can, we creep to the back of the little white barn behind the farmer's house. When we reach it, we duck behind another nearby tree and pause. In the quiet of the night, something inside catches my attention. Movement and strange muffled noises come from behind the latched door.

"Are those... Oh my god, I think there are chickens in there," Keisha says.

"I think you're right. This is perfect. There's no way he'll let this place go up in flames. Those chickens are as good as gold."

I lift the latch on the barn's back door, and we slide inside. The chickens startle and make more noise than I'd like. I can't see a thing, so I flick the lighter in my hand. Bags of cracked cornmeal sit next to several piles of dry straw bedding. This place will go up in flames the second I touch my lighter to that straw. It's perfect.

"Maybe we should leave the back door open so the chickens can get out. I don't want them to die," Lucia says a little self-consciously.

"You've got a soft heart for the chickens, but you don't mind us killing the farmer?" I ask, a little annoyed.

"The chickens aren't a threat to anyone," she says sadly.

"I bet if I roasted one over the fire, you'd—"

"I don't want the chickens to die either, Lu," Keisha says, cutting me off, obviously trying to keep her happy.

I sigh. "Fine. Leave the door open if it makes you feel better. Are you ready?"

Keisha gives me a single nod, so I flick the lighter again and hold it to the pile of straw closest to me. It catches instantly, lighting up the entire barn. For a moment I'm mesmerized by the heat and the flicker of the flames. The fire is spreading so fast. I shake my head, breaking the spell.

"Go, go, go!" I say, heading out the back door. As we escape the flaming chicken coop, Keisha leaves the back door wide open. One of the chickens follows us out, clucking wildly as we run.

Sticking to the plan, we sprint back toward the house, crouching low. As we get closer, I pick up a couple of twigs and toss them at the nearest window. Then we race around the side of the house to hide in the front bushes. From inside the house, Penny's bark sounds the alarm. So far, everything is unfolding just as we planned.

In the relative safety of the bushes, we breathe heavily, waiting for what comes next. My heart beats hard, and the excitement of it all sings in my chest. I draw my machete and wait.

It's the middle of the night, but if you didn't know better, you would think the sun was rising. The light from the flaming chicken coop gives off a glow we can see even from the opposite side of the house. I peek around the corner, and the flames flicker with life, crackling louder and louder.

Over the sound of chickens squawking and wings beating the air as they flee, we hear a door slam from the other side of the house. "What on god's green earth!" the farmer grumbles as Penny adds to the noise with a furious bark.

"Now!" From the bushes, we leap onto the front porch toward the door. I turn the knob hopefully. It's still unlocked. We duck into the house, trying to stay in the shadows, but the light from the chicken coop continues to grow. Through the back windows I can see the farmer with a garden hose trying to quell the flames. It's futile, but it's keeping him busy.

With one eye on the farmer, I put my hand on Keisha's shoulder and whisper to her and Lucia, "Stay ready and don't leave my side. Grab as much as you can, but keep your knives out."

Keisha nods, her eyes wide but confident, and Lucia does her best to act brave.

I go for the coffee table next to the empty La-Z-Boy first, snatching the book and the binoculars I'd seen earlier this morning. I scan the bookshelf on the wall and find a pocket atlas. It's not nearly as nice as the one I lost, but I tuck it into my backpack. Next, the kitchen. From under the sink, I pull out a wad of old plastic grocery bags and start piling in as much food as possible. I grab a few cooking pots too, knowing how useful they'll be. Soon, we have way too much to carry.

"We need to stash this outside. Put it in the bushes where we were hiding," Keisha says. It's a smart idea. I grab as many as I can and haul them toward the front porch. We hide them in the bushes, then run back for more.

"Let's try the bedrooms. Stay together. We might not have much—"

The sound of a shotgun cocking cuts me off. I whip around, stepping in front of Keisha instinctively.

"Not a bad plan, girls," the farmer says slowly, his eyes narrowed down the barrel of the shotgun. Penny growls behind him, her jaws dripping.

"We just outran fifty of the dead to get back here; it's probably best not to ring the dinner bell with that thing, sir," Keisha says, delivering the perfect lie to buy us some time.

He hesitates, just for a second, but it's enough for me to make my move.

"Get down!" I shout to Keisha and Lucia as I duck and sweep my machete toward the farmer's legs. I can feel when my blade meets his calf muscle, slicing through it easily. His knees buckle, and a shot goes wild. Plaster rains from the ceiling as he hits the floor with a thud. Penny yelps, then darts out the back door, leaving the farmer on his own.

Keisha kicks the shotgun out of the farmer's grip and stands on his right hand. From the corner of my eye, I can see Lucia cowering in the corner of the kitchen. I raise my machete over my shoulder, preparing to swing at his throat, but he surprises us both when he rolls toward Keisha with way more force than I expected from a skinny old man. Keisha tumbles, freeing his right hand as he rolls onto his feet. He's bleeding badly and has to be in a lot of pain, but he's surprisingly fast. He darts through the kitchen with only a hint of a limp, and I hear a door slam, then a loud clatter.

"What the hell?" Keisha asks. I don't have an answer. I'm just as shocked as she is. We may have really underestimated this guy.

"Don't let him get away," I say, following the trail of blood through the kitchen.

The side door opens into a small garage. I can just barely see the dark, wet stains of the farmer's blood on the concrete floor shining in the moonlight. The big garage door has been rolled up, which explains the noise. My head snaps up as I hear an engine start. The headlights blind me as the tires of the old red truck spin out in the gravel, then tear down the driveway and away from the house.

"He got away," I say, still not believing how quickly the old man moved.

"He could be going for help," Keisha says.

"Or more weapons," I add.

"Then we need to get what we came for and get out of here before he comes back. I'm not fighting this guy again," Keisha says, and I get it. I don't want to mess with him either.

"Let's do a quick sweep of the house, then get the hell out of here," I say, moving to grab more plastic bags from under the sink. I hand a few to Keisha as she heads toward the back of the house.

The house's small size makes it easy to search. Besides the kitchen and living room, there are only two bedrooms and a small bathroom. We sweep the bathroom, hoping for medication, but we come up empty-handed; then we move into the bedroom to the right. It's clearly a child's bedroom, but there's a thin layer of dust on everything, telling me it hasn't been used in a while. The walls are covered in wallpaper with tiny horses. The shelves are filled with small plastic horses as well. In fact, everything is horse-themed: the bedspread, the pictures on the walls, and the books next to the bed.

"Obsessed much?" I say under my breath. Annoyance itches at me. Just a few short years ago I would have killed for a bedroom like this. It's just a reminder that nothing was fair before the apocalypse. Some little girl grew up here with a dad and maybe a mom too. She had this entire room all to herself. She got to play outside and probably got a new toy horse whenever she wanted, while I was trying new meds in a group home and coming up with new ways to keep the older kids from stealing my shit. Now she's gone, and I'm still here. The apocalypse evened the playing field, and now it's the strong who survive, not the nurtured.

"There's nothing here. Let's check the other bedroom," Keisha says, moving with purpose. I follow her into what must be the farmer's bedroom. There are two more shotguns hanging on the wall. I know they'll only draw the carriers to us, so I leave them. On top of the dresser are a few folding knives and another lighter. I sweep them into my bag. Behind me, I hear Keisha rummaging through the closet.

"Anything?" I ask.

"Just clothes and old boots. Oh! Straw hats! I'm taking these," she says. I can hear the smile in her voice. Inside a jar of change I spot a small tube of lip balm. It isn't cherry flavored, but I know Keisha will love it. I tuck it into my pocket to surprise her later.

"Okay, let's get out of here. If the carriers aren't here yet, they will be soon, and this guy could come back any second," I say. "Grab those pillows though," I say, nodding toward the bed. Keisha complies with a big grin, knowing our canoe is about to get a whole lot more comfortable.

Once we're outside, I look at our haul. We have a very big pile of food and supplies, and it's instantly clear that it'll be way too much for us to carry and maybe even too much for the boat. We can't risk two trips, but I don't want to leave any of it behind. The clock in my mind ticks. We're running out of time.

"We're going to need a wagon or a cart or something. Otherwise we'll never get all this back to the river," I say, my anxiety growing with each second we're still here.

We check the garage for anything that will help. It's difficult to see in the dark, but a sliver of moonlight illuminates a shiny red wheelbarrow hanging from a nail on the wall. Lucia spots it first, and we work together to lift it from its nail and set it onto the ground. I steer it back to the bushes at the front of the house and we begin piling our supplies into it. Before we can finish, a screech fills the air like nails on a chalkboard, followed quickly by another, then another. *Shit.* I silently curse the farmer and his shotgun and his obnoxiously loud pickup truck too.

"They're here," I whisper. "Grab the wheelbarrow. Lucia, you help to hold it steady. I'll cover you. Stay close." Keisha nods, and we creep back toward the road. I cringe as the gravel crackles under the weight of the wheelbarrow, but it's no match for the roar of the fire.

Smoke still fills the air as the chicken coop burns. I glance to my right and see the flames reaching toward the night sky. The fire illuminates the entire backyard, and soon I can see the source of the screeching.

Half a dozen carriers run disturbingly fast, screaming toward the chicken coop, throwing themselves against the burning walls, flailing wildly.

"Keisha, look!" I whisper. She pauses and turns to see what I see. The flames have drawn the carriers' full attention, and with no sense of self-preservation, they're burning themselves alive. Relief fills my chest, and I start to hope we might actually get away unscathed.

More and more come, drawn to the flames like a magnet. I can't take my eyes off the scene, and it ends up costing me. I hear the quick footsteps before I see what's coming. My eyes dart away from the bright fire, looking for the source of the footsteps, but my eyes can't adjust quickly enough to search the darkness. I swing my machete on pure instinct, connecting with something I can't yet see. A second later the smell of rot nearly chokes me.

It's a carrier. Which means that swipe of my machete isn't going to slow it down.

"Quinn, watch out!" Keisha yelps from beside me.

My eyes finally begin to adjust, and the shape of a large, decomposing woman with a gaping chest wound comes back toward me with outstretched arms. I duck underneath her limbs, hoping she'll follow me and not the sound of Keisha's voice. Luckily, she keeps her empty eyes on me. When she turns, her face is illuminated by the fire beside us. The sight is horrific.

Her teeth drip with black bile, and the chest wound I gave her oozes with thick congealed blood. The smell nearly chokes me. My body aches to turn and run, but I've seen these things move. I'd never outrun her, even in that condition. I breathe through my mouth and use every ounce of determination I have to move toward her.

I know the only way to gain the advantage is to get the carrier off her feet and onto the ground where I can reach her skull. I use my tried-and-true method, sweeping my leg toward her knees. She tumbles backward, and her head thuds onto the gravel road. I move quickly, standing on her chest, feeling my boot sink into her chest wound. I gag but manage to lift my machete high, then bring it down onto her skull. It splits, and she goes still. I exhale, relieved, then use my boot to pry my machete from bone. When my weapon is free, I turn to check on Keisha and Lucia.

"You okay?" I whisper into the darkness.

Keisha stands firm with her knife up. It drips in the light of the fire, and I look down to see a carrier lying motionless at her feet. Pride fills my chest, and I can't stop the smile that breaks across my face. In all the chaos I had no idea another carrier had arrived. I wish I could have seen it. I wish I could have seen *her*. She did it.

"I'm fine. We're okay. Let's move," she says, smiling back, the thrill of the kill giving her a fresh glow. In that moment I've never seen anything so beautiful.

Lucia is glued to Keisha's side, tears streaming down her face. Lucia is unraveling more quickly than I would like, and, once again, I worry that she's going to become a liability. I shake the thought away. We need to move. Keisha grips the wheelbarrow and pushes as fast as she can. Lucia holds on to the side just in case it begins to wobble. I keep my eyes out for more carriers, listening for the grumble of the farmer's truck as we race back toward the river.

CHAPTER 27

With the glow of the fire and the screeching of the carriers far behind us, we slow our pace, and our breathing starts to even out.

"What happened back there?" I ask Keisha between breaths. I was so consumed with my own fight, I didn't even see another carrier nearby, let alone register that she was fighting one right next to me.

"There were two of them. The carrier that attacked you had another one right behind it. I don't even know what came over me, but I slammed the wheelbarrow into it before it could reach you. It fell, and I just jumped onto it. I had it stabbed through the eye before I even realized what I was doing. It was like I was possessed or something," she says, almost giggling. "I felt..."

"In control," I finish for her. I know the feeling. It's exactly what I felt when I killed my first carrier back at the Pegasus Center.

"In control," she confirms with a wide grin. "Quinn, we really are built for this."

I know what she means. Before the world ended, I didn't realize just how much I was dreading life beyond the Pegasus Center. My choices were slim. I was either going to be flung out into the world to compete with kids who grew up with every advantage or face more confinement. Both choices felt like a death sentence. Keisha would have fared better, though. She has the ability to move through life easily, blending in. She's charming and beautiful and smart. Inside, she may be built differently than most, but she would have made it in the real world. But making it and feeling alive are two completely different things. She's finally understanding.

"It feels pretty great, right?" I say, smiling back at her.

"Where do you think the farmer went?" Lucia wonders aloud.

"Your guess is as good as mine. At least his truck was headed in the opposite direction of the river. I doubt we'll run into him."

"That's good because all of a sudden I'm exhausted," Keisha says.

"Me too," says Lucia.

"Adrenaline crash. Me too. But we got some really great stuff. With those straw hats, I'll finally be able to stay out of the sun. And we've got enough food to last us awhile if we're careful," I say.

"And pillows! Those metal benches in the canoe are about to get a big upgrade," Keisha says with a little smile.

"That's not all. I got something for you," I say, grinning at Keisha.

"For me?" Her eyes light up.

"For you." I pull the lip balm out of my pocket.

She stops pushing the wheelbarrow and drops the handles so she can take the tiny plastic tube and hold it in both hands. She stares at it like it's the most precious thing she's ever seen and does a little hop that makes my smile grow even wider.

"Oh my god, ohmygod, ohmygod!" she squeals.

"Shhh," I whisper, laughing a little at the scene she's making.

"This is the best gift I've ever gotten. Thank you, Quinn." She pops off the top of the tube, wipes the balm on her shirt to remove the top layer, then smooths it onto her lips. "Amazing," she says, closing her eyes, practically groaning.

She puts the cap on, then tucks the tube into her pocket. I'm not expecting what comes next. There, in the dark, she opens her arms, wraps them around my neck, and squeezes her body close to mine until our eyes are perfectly aligned. The heat of her body on mine is like electricity. I place my hands on her hips. Her softened lips graze my cheek slowly until she stops, just to the left of my mouth, and plants a firm kiss at the edge of my lips. She moves away slowly, leaving behind a lip balm print that I feel long after the kiss is over.

From the corner of my eye, I see Lucia turn away from the scene and keep walking.

"You're my best friend, Quinn," she whispers so only I can hear.

"Well, duh" is all I can think to say. I feel awkward. I don't know what comes next. So I let my eyes shift behind us to check for carriers or any sign of the farmer.

"Come on. We've got to keep moving." I reach up and feel the empty space where her lips were and wish for more.

When we reach the base of the levee we're all completely exhausted. After taking my turn pushing the wheelbarrow, my arms and legs feel like lead. Climbing the levee feels impossible, but we're so close, and the sun is already starting to light up the sky and send the temperature soaring.

There's no way we'll be able to push the wheelbarrow up the levee, so we unload the plastic grocery bags, then start the climb up, carrying as many bags as we can. It takes two trips each, but we finally get the job done.

We sit at the top of the levee, surrounded by our hard-earned supplies, and share the last of our water. We smell like smoke, sweat, and dirt, but it was all worth it. This, combined with what we took from the boatel, gives us enough food to last us at least a week, if not more. We also got a few things that will make our lives easier, safer, and a lot more comfortable.

I dig through the bags until I find the binoculars I'd been wanting so badly. They're heavy and obviously very expensive. I hold them up to my eyes, then touch the wheel slightly to bring the world into focus. I scan the horizon, and my mouth hangs open in awe. The farmland seems to go on forever. The corn sways in the breeze in some of the fields, while ankle-high plants I don't recognize grow in the others. In the sky, birds of prey circle the fields looking for a meal.

I can see the farmer's house clearly, and the red pickup truck sits in the driveway again. He came back, who knows when. Thin curls of smoke still rise from the back of the house. My gut churns with anger. I still can't believe he got away. Part of me wants to go back and finish the job, but I know better. We got what we came for, and we're lucky to have escaped with our lives.

I scan farther to the right of the farmhouse and freeze. "Oh god," I mutter under my breath.

"What? What is it? Let me see," Keisha says.

I turn the wheel to refocus the binoculars, but the scene doesn't change. There have to be dozens of them. Carriers of all sizes run swiftly toward the farm, some dragging a leg, some missing arms, all of them dripping in rot. If I didn't know better, I would think I could smell them from here. The memory of the stench sticks with you. I groan and pass the binoculars to Keisha.

She brings them up to her eyes, and I point her in the right direction. A gasp escapes her lips and I know she's found them. She passes the binoculars to Lucia. Lucia puts the binoculars down when she finds them.

"That's the biggest herd we've seen yet," Keisha whispers, even though they could never hear us from here.

"How far away do you think they are?" I ask her.

"At least a mile. Maybe two?" she estimates.

"At the pace they're running, they could be here in ten, maybe twelve minutes," I say.

"They're not coming here. They're headed toward the farm. Looks like we didn't need to finish off the farmer after all. The carriers will take care of him for us," she says. I study her face to see how she feels about that but can't quite read her expression.

"Still, we should get back on the river. If we accidentally draw their attention, there's no way we'd be able to fight all of them off. Stay alert though. Who knows how many of them are still out here."

We search our surroundings for carriers, but nothing moves. The only sounds are us, the breeze, and the birds overhead. We carry each bag down the levee carefully and lay them beside the canoe. When we finally place the last bag in the pile, a new level of exhaustion hits me. "We need water, food, and rest. In that order," I say to Keisha, breathing heavily.

"I'll get a fire going for the water, but do you really think we can afford to sleep right now?"

"No," I admit. "Maybe we can take turns napping in the boat?"

"If you don't mind resting on top of all this stuff," she says, gesturing at the bags.

"I think I could fall asleep anywhere at this point," I answer groggily.

Keisha puts together a fire and sets some water to boil. With our new set of pots, we can boil a whole day's worth of water in one go, saving us precious minutes. I carefully pack the boat, creating neat piles and carving out a narrow space in the front of the boat for sleeping. We'll have to curl up tight to make it work, but it's better than nothing.

Keisha pours the last of the steaming water into our bottles and screws the lids on tight, then hands me a jar of pickles from the farm. It's not a meal, but it'll do. I pass the jar to Lucia, then pile the last of our things into the boat. It's going to be a very tight squeeze.

"Ready?" Keisha asks as she pours river water over the fire.

"I want to check on the herd one more time," I say, grabbing my binoculars and heading toward the levee. "I'll be quick."

When I reach the top, I pull the binoculars up to my eyes and peer toward the farmer's house. There are dozens of them. I try to count the carriers, but I lose track after about thirty. They've surrounded the house completely and it's just a matter of time before they get inside. I sigh, feeling a little disappointed I'm not there to watch it unfold. Something about the scene itches the back of my brain. I can't help but feel like I'm missing something, and then it clicks. Where's the red pickup truck? Could he really have gotten away? I drop the binoculars and scan the area looking for any sign of the truck, but I see nothing. Not even a cloud of dust. I guess we'll never know what happened to him.

I stumble down the levee, then help Keisha shove the boat into the water, jumping in just as the water reaches my ankles. We each grab a paddle and make our way to the center of the wide river, where we'll be safe from the herd and anything else on land.

"You two take the first nap. I'll wake you in an hour or two," I say. I can see they need it more than I do.

"Thanks, Quinn," Keisha says sleepily as she carefully crawls toward the little nest I built at the front of the boat. She practically falls into it, sending the boat rocking, and I crack a little smile. Lucia curls in next to her.

"Here," I say, tossing Keisha one of the farmer's straw hats. "To keep the sun out of your eyes."

"You're the best," she mumbles, already half-asleep.

I sip water and paddle slowly down the river, taking in the early morning sights and sounds. For a brief moment I wonder how far we've come since we left Peoria and exactly where we are now. Then I remember that the farmer gave us a clue.

The current is moving us at a decent clip, so I tuck the paddle back inside the boat and pull out my new pocket atlas. The farmer mentioned two nearby towns, Winchester and Hillview. First I find Peoria on the map, then trace the river south with my finger, looking at the names of the towns to the east and west of the thin blue ribbon. My finger finds Naples, and I shiver, remembering our stay at the boatel. I trace an inch or two farther south and see Winchester, then Hillview just below it. This must be where we are now.

As I look at the map, it's hard to believe the world as we know it ended. I wonder what it's like back in Peoria now. I wonder if anyone in Chicago could have possibly survived. I trace my finger to the lowest tip of the map, then cringe. I wonder what it will be like when we paddle through St. Louis. We'll be there before we know it. If I had to guess, I'd say we'll be there in a little over a week if we don't stop anywhere for too long.

I look down at Keisha and Lucia, curled up in the bottom of the boat, breathing evenly. I crave sleep, but it probably hasn't even been an hour. I put the atlas back in the front pocket of my backpack and keep paddling.

The sun starts to rise overhead, and I'm pretty sure Keisha and Lucia have been sleeping for several hours now. My whole body is begging for rest. I reach down and nudge Keisha awake. She groans and curls up even tighter.

"Keisha, I need to sleep. It's been hours," I say, not even attempting to keep the annoyance out of my voice.

A heavy sigh follows, and Keisha finally sits up, groaning, "How long was I out?"

"I don't know, like four hours," I say impatiently. I nudge Lucia out of the way, a little harder than necessary, then curl into the nest on the floor of the canoe. I place a straw hat over my face and sink into a deep, dreamless sleep.

CHAPTER 28

By late afternoon, my clothes are nearly soaked through with sweat, and my body feels stiff from being scrunched in the bottom of the boat. I sit up and stretch, then gulp down as much water as I can hold. Behind me, Keisha paddles the boat quietly. In front of me, Lucia stares into the water below, letting her fingertips skim the surface of the water.

I glance back at Keisha, giving her a questioning look as if to ask, *Is she okay?* Keisha shakes her head sadly. Lucia's depression has hit her like a train, getting worse and worse with each missed dose of her medication. Again, the only thing I can think to do is distract her.

"Lucia, if you're feeling up to it, maybe you could try to catch some fish. We're going to have to figure it out eventually," I suggest.

"That's a great idea!" Keisha says, just a little too eager.

"Sure, I'll give it a try," Lucia says.

I nudge the tackle box and the bucket of fishing poles we took from the garage in Naples toward her. She picks out a small pole with a rusty hook, then opens the tackle box to see what's inside. There are little metal balls, colored worm-like bits, and elaborate reflective pieces that remind me of earrings. I don't know what to do with any of it. Nurse Patrick would have. I look up at Keisha and shrug as I pick up a paddle.

"Try one of those wormy things," she suggests. "Fish are supposed to like worms."

Lucia ties one of the rubbery fake worms at the top of the hook, then looks at Keisha for approval.

"It could work," Keisha says with an uncertain shrug. Lucia dips her hook into the water so it drags alongside the canoe as we move.

"I think you have to toss it out and get it away from the boat. Does that reel make the string get longer? Or is there a button that releases it?" I ask, with no idea what I'm talking about. I've only seen fishing on TV in the dayroom. It was one of Ginger's favorite things to watch, and it annoyed me to no end.

Lucia pokes around for a bit, looking at the fishing pole from every angle. Finally, she presses a button on the pole with her thumb. The click lets the fishing line go slack, and the weight of the hook and the fake worm allows the end of the line to drag out behind the boat.

"Nice!" Keisha says encouragingly.

"I guess now we wait?" Lucia asks.

"Now we wait," I confirm.

Lucia sits facing us, but she's staring intently at the fishing line dragging behind the canoe. Waiting. Over her shoulder I see the outline of something stretching across the river. I can barely make it out from this distance, but it has to be a bridge.

"Hey, Keisha, look," I say, pointing ahead. "Is that a bridge?"

"Yeah. It's hard to tell from here, but it has to be. Unless it's another barge," she says, shivering.

"Nah, it's too wide. I think it's stretching all the way across. It's got to be a bridge. Hand me those binoculars." Just as I raise the lenses to my eyes, I'm interrupted by Lucia.

"Oh my god!" she nearly shouts. "I think I caught something!"

"Turn the little handle! Reel it in!" Keisha urges.

"I'm trying, I'm trying!" she says, excited, turning the little reel on the pole as fast as she can. For just a moment, the spark in her eyes is back, and the smile on her face is infectious. I can't help but get excited about her catch too. This could mean we have a way to feed ourselves without looting.

The anticipation grows with each turn of the reel. Finally, the end of the line breaks through the water and right there, hanging on the hook, is a tiny fish, about the size of Lucia's hand.

"Oh my god, you did it!" Keisha says, bouncing in her seat, sending the boat wobbling.

"I did it!" Lucia echoes proudly, her smile beaming.

"Well, look at that. Maybe we won't starve out here after all," I say.

Lucia lets the fish rest along the bottom of the canoe. It flops, its tiny mouth opening and closing. Her face falls, her smile disappearing almost as quickly as it appeared.

"It's suffering," Lucia says, the cheer drained from her voice.

"It's nature," I say. "See if you can take the hook out and catch a few more."

"Ew," she says, ripping the hook from the fish's mouth, leaving tiny drops of blood on the bottom of the canoe.

"Ew? Lucia, you stabbed Mr. Josh in the leg with a screwdriver!" I can't help but laugh.

"He deserved it. What did this little guy ever do to anyone?" she says, still looking sad.

"You've been face-to-face with walking, rotting corpses, and *this* grosses you out?" Keisha chimes in, giggling too. I laugh harder, laughing at Keisha. Keisha laughs with me. Soon, Lucia can't help it; she laughs too. Seeing her laugh makes me laugh even harder. Soon, the entire boat is rocking, and the tension of the last few weeks just melts away.

"It's not so bad out here," Keisha says. "It beats school."

"It beats competing for the right to own shoelaces," I add, rolling my eyes.

"It beats therapy," Lucia says.

On the floor of the canoe, Lucia's little fish has stopped fighting. Its eyes stare empty into the sun, and its iridescent scales almost seem to sparkle. My hopes are hanging on this little fish. We need this fish to feed us. We need this fish to give Lucia a sense of hope and purpose. This is how we all survive.

"Does anybody even know how to cook a fish?" Keisha asks.

Another fit of giggles rocks the boat.

Lucia casts her fishing line back into the river, looking just a little lighter than before. Still, I know that the temporary lift in her mood is just that, temporary. I raise the binoculars again to look ahead at the bridge that's getting closer and closer and wonder if it leads to a town where we might find a pharmacy that hasn't already been looted.

"Do you think maybe we should get out near the bridge and see what we can find?" I ask Keisha.

"I could really use a can of Coke. Or peanut butter cups! Lucia, what do you want to look for?" Keisha asks, trying to keep her good mood going. I don't hear Lucia's response, though. My attention is locked on the bridge. We're still pretty far away, but it's starting to come into focus. The bridge is massive and green and reaches across the river in a series of sweeping arches. Several cars sit idle, probably long abandoned. One of the vehicles catches my attention, though. A red pickup truck parked near the center. I remind myself that there have to be hundreds of red pickup trucks in the area. The odds of that being the farmer's rusty pickup truck are incredibly slim. Still, I scan the bridge for movement or any human-shaped shadows. My heart has picked up speed, but I tell myself it's ridiculous to worry.

The farmer couldn't possibly know we were traveling on the river. We didn't give him that much information. We only said we were heading south. But now that I think about it, there's really only one way the three of us could have survived out here, and that's the safety of the river. Could he have put those pieces together? I decide not. And anyway, I cut his leg pretty badly. He couldn't be back on his feet yet. I try to refocus on Keisha and Lucia, chattering on about the snacks and other items they'd like to find at the hypothetical pharmacy, but my eyes keep finding their way back to the bridge.

"Earth to Quinn!" Keisha says. Clearly she's been trying to talk to me for a while now. I snap my attention back to her.

"Yeah. Sorry. What did you say?" I ask, shaking the paranoia away.

"I said, are we stopping at the bridge? If we are, we should probably start steering toward the shore."

"I don't know. Maybe we should pass it. Maybe get a little farther away from that herd before we stop," I say.

"Really? That herd is hours behind us. Do you think—"

A loud boom echoes off the water and through the trees, cutting off whatever Keisha was about to say.

"What the fuck was that?" I ask, craning my neck toward the bridge as we inch closer and closer.

Another boom. This time, a spray of water splashes tiny droplets across my face. I rip off my straw hat and scan the bridge, looking for the source of the shots.

There. In the center. Someone is aiming a shotgun off the side of the bridge. I can't see their face clearly, but I don't have to. It's him.

"Get down! It's the farmer! Get—" I shout uselessly. Another boom.

I cover my head as if it might help and hear something drop into the river. I crack open my eyes, scanning the water for clues as to what just fell. Lucia's fishing pole. I don't want to look up, but I do. There, right in front of me, I watch helplessly as a dark red stain quickly blooms across Lucia's shirt.

Keisha screams. Another boom. Another. Another.

"Get down!" I yell at both of them. We lie flat on the bottom of the boat, making ourselves as small as possible. We're just a few feet from floating underneath the bridge now, but the farmer leans over the railing, ready to shoot again. I chuck an empty pickle jar in his direction and miss. He ducks out of the way, but his chance to shoot at us again has passed.

We're under the bridge now and there's no way he can get another shot off from where he stands. I know Keisha is screaming. Out of the corner of my eye I see her holding on to Lucia, but I tune her out, trying to anticipate where the farmer might appear above me.

Another shot rings out as an inhuman screech echoes off the water. Another shot. Another screech. The carriers are here.

We float in the shadow of the bridge, and time seems to slow. Every nerve ending is alive with the anticipation of what comes next, and I try to force myself to formulate a plan. Finally, daylight hits the tip of the boat where Lucia was sitting. We're out of time. I panic. Keisha is going to be exposed first if I don't do something now. I grip my paddle and row it hard against the river's current to spin us around so I'm the first thing the farmer sees. It takes all my strength, but the boat turns just in time. I set down the paddle and pick up my hunting knife. It feels foolish in my hands, but I'm out of options.

"Get down, Keisha."

"I can't! Quinn, she's...she's..."

I hold the knife tightly, pull my arm back, and wait. The light hits my eyes, blinding me for a moment as we inch out of the shadow of the bridge. I try to focus, squinting against the sun to find my target.

Another screech followed by a deep moan pulls my eyes to the left as something moves on the bridge. I don't think. I just throw. My knife hits the side of the bridge with a loud, heart-sinking clang. From the corner of my eye I see the farmer dart away, but a group of carriers instantly appears at the edge of the bridge, and I realize I've just made a big mistake. Shit. I count the carriers leaning against the edge of the bridge with outstretched hands. Five. One of them wears a snarling expression with a gaping neck wound that's stained its entire T-shirt a dark crimson. My stomach drops as I realize what will inevitably happen next. The carrier's milky eyes find us, and it leaps for our boat.

I can't believe this is happening again.

I grab my paddle and brace for the impact. "They're coming down! Keisha, watch out!" I yell helplessly.

It's like the barge all over again. Bodies splash into the water next to us, blinding me with the spray of water. The waves rock our boat from side to side, slow at first, and then a violent pitch to my right nearly tosses me overboard.

The carrier with the bloodstained T-shirt grips the side of the canoe with white knuckles, reaching for Keisha and Lucia. His eyes are empty. His jaw works back and forth in anticipation of flesh. He tips his head back and screeches. The noise is deafening, and I resist the urge to cover my ears. I drop my paddle and reach for my machete.

The carrier pulls down on the edge of the boat, and it takes everything we have to keep from tipping over. I can hear other carriers splashing nearby. I know they can't really swim, but they're still a threat. We have to get out of here now.

The carrier is just out of reach, and I have to be careful not to tip the boat by shifting my weight too dramatically. Swinging my machete could mean the end of us.

"Give me her knife!" I shout to Keisha. She freezes, looking at me like I've lost my mind. I don't have time for this shit. I rip Lucia out of her arms and grab the knife at her hip, then let Lucia fall to my side. From the corner of my eye I see Keisha's horrified look as she gathers Lucia's limp body back into her arms.

I steady myself, aim carefully, then plunge Lucia's knife into the carrier's eye. I wait for his body to go slack. Except he doesn't stop reaching. I didn't stab deep enough.

I look over at Keisha, holding Lucia in her arms, trying to lean away from the carrier to keep the boat balanced.

"Kick it! Keisha, kick it!"

She knows exactly what I mean. Her foot is a hammer, slamming into the hilt of the knife. The blade sinks deeper into the carrier's skull, finishing the job I started. I see the moment what's left of him dies as his body goes limp and his grip on the boat loosens.

Our boat rocks backward, trying to find its center of gravity, and we shift our weight again to avoid tipping.

Once the boat steadies, I look down into the water and watch the carrier sink into the dark river.

On the bridge, the farmer is standing on top of his rusty red pickup truck, out of reach of the carriers, who screech desperately, trying to get a piece of him. His shotgun must be empty. I search his expression for the fear he must be feeling, but instead he smiles and waves at us as we slip farther away.

A heavy sigh of relief leaves my lungs, but the sound of it is drowned out by the splashing of nearby carriers and Keisha's sobs. She's still holding Lucia in her arms, the red stain on her shirt growing darker and bigger by the second.

I count the splashing carriers. One, two, three, four. Three are far enough away that they're not a concern. One of them seems to be getting closer. Too close for comfort.

I pick up my paddle from the bottom of the canoe and find it's sticky with blood. I ignore it and plunge the paddle deep into the water, pulling with all my strength to move us away from the bridge and the echoing moans. After a few hard rows, I've made enough progress to turn around and check on Keisha and Lucia. Out of the corner of my eye, I see movement along the shoreline, and my heart hitches. A chorus of screams fills the air.

My stomach drops, and every hair on my body stands on end.

The noise of the gunshots and the screeching carriers from the bridge has drawn every monster in the area to the shore, and they're following the only moving object they see. Now, dozens of rotting bodies line the shore.

I whip my head to the other side of the river and find the same horrifying result. I'm suddenly very glad we didn't try to go looking for a pharmacy. It looks like these nearby towns weren't as lucky as Naples.

There have to be at least fifty of them lining both sides of the shore. They screech and moan, fixed on the movement of our boat. They move fast in our direction until the water's too deep for them to find their footing. Then they splash and scream as the current carries them along the river at its own pace.

The river is wide, and we float in the center where the water is at its deepest. I'm not worried about these carriers. I know they can't reach us. We have plenty of time to paddle away. What scares me most is how many of them showed up and how quickly they came after the gunshots. Until this point, I've only seen a few at a time up close. This is different. This is bad. And they're so fast. Suddenly I'm afraid to go back to the shore, and I realize we've been really, really lucky.

Just how bad has it gotten outside of our little bubble on the river? I wish I could tune into the news. There's no going back to the way things were. There's no saving humanity. But I wonder how many people are still alive and how they're outmatching these things. Where are they finding food and water? What will happen in just a few months when winter hits?

There are too many what-ifs. My heart hammers wildly, so I try to center myself in the here and now, just like my therapist taught me back at the Pegasus Center.

I focus on one thing I can see. The handle of my machete strapped to my hip.

One thing I can touch. The weight of the paddle in my hand.

One thing I can hear. Screams of the dead.

One thing I can smell. The stench of the horde hits the breeze, and I gag. Therapists never prepared us for the apocalypse.

I paddle harder, trying to pull us toward fresh air and safety. Behind me, Keisha's sobs have turned into deep hiccups. She's speaking softly to the tiny form lying in her arms, but I can't make out her words over the sounds of chaos around us. I just keep rowing.

CHAPTER 29

When the screeches and moans of the carriers are far enough behind us, I finally set my paddle down and turn around to assess the damage.

Lucia is curled onto Keisha's lap, and Keisha holds her tight in her arms, still whispering in her ear words I'll never hear. Lucia's eyes are closed, her body lifeless, and her clothes soaked in blood. Her curls lie limp against her shoulders. Her tiny mouth hangs open slightly. There's no doubt in my mind. She's gone. Suddenly I feel like I'm intruding on something very private. I don't know what to do or say. I can't leave the boat, so I do the best I can. I look away.

At my feet, a puddle of blood has stained the soles of my boots a deep, dark red. Lucia's tiny fish lies still, eyes wide, mouth open in the pool of blood. I pick it up and angrily throw it into the river with a violent splash, then let my hand glide through the water, washing Lucia's blood from my fingertips and into the muddy water of the river. The silence drags on until I can't stand it any longer.

"Keisha, I'm so… I'm…"

"Shh," she hushes, not taking her eyes off Lucia.

"I should have—"

"SHHH!"

She rocks gently, holding Lucia close, and continues whispering to her. I pick up my paddle and channel my energy into getting us as far away from the bridge as possible.

Hours pass. My skin stings with a fresh sunburn, and my muscles ache from rowing. I'm hungry, thirsty, and utterly exhausted. In just a few hours the sun will set. We need to find a safe place to rest. We also need to figure out what to do with Lucia's body.

"Keisha," I practically whisper. I know she's not ready, but it's been hours, and I can't keep rowing forever. "We need to get off the river. Look up ahead there. What do you think about that spot?" I say, pointing to a low slope in the river's edge.

She sniffs, then nods, but she doesn't look up, so I begin steering us toward the shore. It looks isolated enough, but if I learned anything today, it's that isolation doesn't mean shit. With enough noise, the carriers will find you, wherever you are.

When we reach the shore, I use the strength I have left to pull the canoe out of the water and over the uneven ground.

I hold out my hand to Keisha, offering to help, but she doesn't take it. She tries to stand on her own with Lucia in her arms and nearly loses her balance. I grip her arm and her waist to keep her steady, and she steps out of the boat, laying Lucia down next to the water.

I don't want to be here for this. Luckily I have a great excuse to bolt. I take a lap around our new campsite with my machete to make sure we've picked a safe spot, but I draw out the patrol way longer than necessary. When I finally go back to Keisha's side, I see she's cleaned Lucia's body, washed the blood from her hair, and dressed her in clean clothes. I can't imagine why she would bother, but I know enough to know I shouldn't ask questions. Instead, I build a fire for us.

I busy myself by boiling three pots of water and filling up every bottle we have, then digging around in our packs for something to eat. I find another box of cheesy potatoes and pour the ingredients into the boiling water. When the soggy mess is as good as it's going to get, I walk over to get Keisha.

"Hey," I say quietly. "Let's get something to eat. Then we can say a few words for Lucia together."

"I'm not hungry."

"That's okay. I've got some fresh water too. Come on," I say, holding out my hand. She takes it, interlocking her fingers with mine. She looks over her shoulder at Lucia, then follows me to the fire. We sit in silence. I hand her some water and a bowl of cheesy potatoes, and I'm grateful when she takes a few bites, then a few more, hours of exhaustion and hunger winning out over her grief.

The sun has nearly set by the time we finish eating. I break the silence with the practicalities of our situation. I know I wouldn't say the right thing even if I tried.

"We should sleep here tonight. We could do shifts, just to be safe," I say.

Keisha nods, a new set of tears pooling in her eyes.

When I go to hide our canoe in the tall grass, I notice the pool of dried blood inside. Rather than face Lucia's funeral, I take our supplies out and get to work scrubbing at the stains with water from the river, but soon, the boat is clean, our things are repacked, and the sun is nearly gone. There's nothing left to do. It's time.

I walk over to where Keisha is kneeling next to Lucia's body.

"Are you ready?" I ask, not knowing what else to say.

"No," she whispers.

"How do you… I mean, what should we do with… Do you think Lucia would like what we did for Nurse Patrick?" I ask, trying to find the right words for this.

She nods, and an uncomfortable silence follows. I'm not sure what to do, so I just say what I think Keisha would want to hear.

"Lucia was so small and so quiet. Back at the Pegasus Center, I hardly gave her a second look, but when everything happened, she kept a cool head and had good ideas about what to do next. She pulled her weight. She fought for her life. I'll never forget when she pulled that screwdriver out of her pocket and stabbed Mr. Josh on the roof of the center. That's when I knew she was a fighter. I wish I had thought to ask her where she got that screwdriver from," I say with a chuckle. "I guess I'll never know. But I'm proud of her. And I'm sad it had to end like this. She deserved to live."

I expect Keisha to cry. I expect her to start with a speech of her own. I do not expect her to start laughing. She claps both hands over her mouth, trying to muffle the sound, but it's impossible. She can't stop. What the hell?

"It was Ms. J!" Keisha says, gasping for breath between fits of giggles.

"What?" I ask, worried that maybe we should find Keisha some meds after all.

"The screwdriver. I asked her how she got it when we were back at the Pegasus Center. She took it off Ms. J's cleaning cart the first week she came to the center. She hid it inside her shower curtain rod for months!" A new peal of laughter rings like a bell, and I can't help but join.

"That's brilliant," I say, giggling too.

Smiling now, Keisha starts her speech. "Lucia's creativity kept her alive and helped us find a way to get this far. We wouldn't have thought to follow the river without her. She was a fighter when she had to be, but she was also gentle and kind. Sometimes I worry that only the worst of us will survive all this, but she gave me hope that good could exist at the end of the world. And the world will be worse off without her."

I don't miss Keisha's implication. Pretty soon, all that will be left is a world full of people like me. I can't argue, so I don't try. I just wait. Soon, Keisha looks up at me, her eyes brimming with tears again.

"Will you help me take her to the river? I think that's what she'd want."

"Of course," I say.

We strip off our jeans, boots, and socks and lay them on a fallen tree near the shore. The last thing I want is to go into that river in the dark, but I grit my teeth and do it. As we wade into the river, carrying Lucia, my toes sink into the slimy mud below, and I just hope nothing touches my legs. I control my breathing, and finally, when we're about waist deep, Keisha pauses and lowers Lucia into the water.

"Goodbye, Lucia," Keisha says, pausing to kiss her forehead.

We give the weight of Lucia to the river. The current carries her body above water for a few feet, then swallows her whole.

Keisha grabs my hand and squeezes it tight, then lets go. It's just the two of us now. This is how I wanted it to be all along, but somehow it feels emptier than I thought it would. We wade through the water and back toward the shore. In silence, we dry off, get dressed, and douse the fire to avoid attracting attention.

We lay out our blankets, tuck a pillow under our heads, and lie down.

With each minute that passes, new stars appear, way too many to count. I think back to the night this all started and how excited Keisha was to escape to the roof of the Pegasus Center. She'd marveled at all the stars. That sky couldn't even begin to compare to this one.

As if thinking what I'm thinking, Keisha says, "I've never seen so many stars in my life."

"It's pretty," I say lamely. I want to reach for her hand. I want her to kiss me again. I want her to tell me it's okay that it's just us now. I want her to forget anyone else existed.

"I remember when all I wanted was to be able to go outside and look at the stars whenever I wanted. I still can't believe we got away with sneaking out that night. God, it feels like a lifetime ago," Keisha says with a sigh.

"We had that place wired," I say with a little laugh. "We make a good team, Keisha. We'll be okay out here. Just us."

"I know we will." Her voice hardens. "Whatever it takes, right?"

CHAPTER 30

Our routine continues for days. We paddle, find a place to camp, eat, boil water, sleep, and repeat.

Occasionally we stay an extra day in a spot that feels safe so we can do some laundry, clean the inside of the boat, or bathe in the river, but we try to stay out of the water, knowing that sunken carriers are still a threat. We trade watch duties, but carrier sightings are rare. Once, in the middle of the night, I think I hear people on the river. The sound of soft voices, maybe two women talking, echoes off the river. But the sound passes quickly, leaving me to wonder if it was just a dream.

It's hard to keep your guard up when routine sets in. I know we could face danger at any moment, whether from carriers or people, but after days of relative peace, the need to relax is hard to resist. Still, we try to stay diligent, scanning the horizon with our binoculars, listening for shrieks, and looking for signs of people.

But for six days the river has lulled us into a sense of safety. So when we hear voices ahead of us down the river, I have to scramble to find my machete at the bottom of the canoe under my dirty clothes.

From the front of the boat, Keisha whips around and meets my eyes. We both point toward the voices in a wide-eyed warning to each other. I look down at the water. The current is moving fast today. We won't have much luck trying to backpaddle. I nod toward the opposite side of the river, silently telling Keisha to start rowing to the west, then place my finger on my lips, a plea to paddle as quietly as possible. She understands. We've practiced this. She silently and deeply dips her paddle into the water, then pulls it back, moving the boat toward our destination. I mirror her movements, hoping we don't draw any attention.

By the time we make it to the west side of the river, we're way too close to the mystery group for comfort. I can hear their laughter clearly, and I'm able to distinguish between several voices. We quietly climb out of the canoe and gently drag it ashore. I reach for my binoculars, then search the east bank for the source of the noise.

A gasp escapes my lips, and I instinctively—and stupidly—duck down behind the canoe.

"What? What is it?" Keisha asks, following me behind the canoe.

"They see us," I say.

"What do you mean? How do you know?"

"Because when I looked through my binoculars, I saw another set of binoculars looking right back at us. They know we're here."

"Shit," Keisha sighs.

My feet itch to run and hide, but we can't abandon our stuff, we can't paddle back against the current, and apparently, we can't hide until they leave. Shit.

"Hey, there!" a friendly voice calls from the other side of the river.

We stay low, our backs pressed to the canoe, looking at each other.

"Do we try to outrun them or make friends?" Keisha asks.

"They outnumber us. I saw four people."

"What else did you see?"

"Not much. I saw a pair of binoculars looking back at me and that kind of interrupted things," I say impatiently. "Give me a minute." I pick up the binoculars again.

I peek over the canoe and find the group. The woman with the binoculars sees me and gives a friendly wave. I ignore her. There's another woman at her side and two men sitting in camping chairs, watching our side of the shore. They have a decent amount of camping gear and a wide rowboat docked on the bank. Not a bad setup.

"They've got a lot of good stuff. Might be worth it to check them out," I say, flashing a mischievous smile at Keisha.

She looks hesitant. I can see her turning something over in

her mind. I almost ask her what she's thinking, but then her eyes darken and she sits up just a bit straighter. "We don't really have many good options here. Let's go make friends. How do you want to do this? How long are you planning on playing nice?" she asks cautiously.

"We'll get information from them first. I want to know what they've seen, where they've been, and where they're going. Then I want their stuff. And we can't leave any loose ends this time." I hope she doesn't argue. Surely she understands why we can't leave them alive.

"I can get them talking. But, Quinn, let's not just assume we'll have to kill them, okay? Let's at least consider the possibility that we could take what we want and leave."

I sigh and roll my eyes. "We can't get ourselves into another sticky situation. If we leave them alive, they'll be on our heels just like the farmer."

"Maybe they'll be allies. Sometimes there's safety in numbers. Maybe they actually know what they're doing out here and could help us. Looks like they've made it this far," she says casually. Too casually. Why the hell is she so insistent that we let them live?

Anger heats my chest, but I push it down. There's no time to argue.

"Hello-oo?" the voice calls from across the river.

"Fine, whatever. I'll keep it in mind. Are you ready?"

"Ready."

We get back into our boat and steer it to the east bank of the river and glide onto the shore right next to the strangers' camp. As I pull the boat onto the rocky beach, Keisha gives the strangers her best smile, painted with hints of relief and shyness. It's perfect. I try to mirror her expression, but I let my hair fall into my face, just in case I'm failing miserably.

"We're so glad to run into more people. It's been a while since we've seen anybody. I'm Keisha, and this is Quinn," she says in a very sweet but somehow humble voice.

"Keisha. Quinn," the taller man says as he nods and reaches out his hand. I take it and give it a decent squeeze. "I'm Steven, and this is Grady, Suzanne, and Marcy."

He points to the others as he makes his introductions, and I learn the woman with the binoculars is Marcy. As discreetly as I can, I look them up and down, searching for anything I can use against them. They all look to be in their thirties. They're relatively clean and seem like they haven't missed more than a few meals. They give us genuine smiles and wave us over to their camp.

"Thanks for the warm welcome. It's so hard to know who to trust these days," Keisha says.

"Don't we know it," Marcy says, rolling her eyes, her frizzy brunette hair bouncing as she nods. "Here, why don't you come sit?"

Marcy, Steven, Suzanne, Keisha, and I all take a seat on a blanket in a clearing between the river and the tree line. A few feet away, Grady is busy building a fire. I try to keep an eye on him while I attempt to move the conversation forward.

"Do you all know each other from before?" I ask. I need to know how much they care about each other. People fight harder for people they love. Keisha glares at me, knowing exactly where I'm going with my line of questioning. Oops. They don't seem to flinch at my question, but I decide to let her take the lead from now on.

"Pastor Steven and I have been married for seven blessed years, thank you, Jesus," Marcy says, smiling over her shoulder at her husband. "We ran into Grady and Suzanne a couple weeks ago. They met back at the shelter in Bluffs."

Bluffs. That's the shelter just outside of Naples. The one Ramsey told us about. I wonder if they might know him. I don't dare ask, though.

"Where are you coming from?" Keisha asks.

"We're from Jacksonville. Are you familiar with the area?" Steven asks. Keisha shakes her head, so he continues. "It's a bigger town just northeast of here. We do a lot of camping, so when everything happened, we knew we needed to get out of town and find somewhere less populated, so we piled all our camping gear into the truck and headed to the river," Steven says with a shrug.

"And Grady and I lived in Bluffs," Suzanne adds. "The shelter was getting...out of hand. The evils of this world will always try to dim the light of the Lord, you know. The shelter didn't seem like it was going to hold together much longer, so we walked toward the river for deliverance. We knew we'd have a fresh source of water if we kept to it. That's when we met these two angels in a rowboat," Suzanne says, smiling gratefully at Marcy and Steven.

Jeez. These people are laying it on thick. I'm already annoyed, but I try my best to hide it.

"Wow, that sounds really nice. People helping people, I mean. Have you run into any trouble?" Keisha asks.

"Oh, here and there," Steven says vaguely. "Nothing we couldn't handle." He pats a long, serrated knife on his belt.

"Carriers or people?" I ask him.

"Both," he answers sharply. "There are many evils in this cursed world, girls," he says without elaborating. The entire group's eyes hit the hard-packed ground at their feet.

I look around, trying to take the temperature of the gathering. It got tense fast. Keisha's a professional peacekeeper, though, and I watch in awe as she turns things around.

"Yes, we've seen it," she says, putting her saddest eyes on. "We're from Peoria. We've been on the river since Havana. We started with six, but now it's just us." Somehow, she manufactures a tear that slides down her cheek at the most perfect of moments.

"How old are you two?" Steven asks, raising an eyebrow.

"I'm seventeen," Keisha answers.

"Sixteen," I answer.

"Oh, bless! Just babies!" Marcy says dramatically with her hand on her chest.

I try not to let my annoyance show on my face. Instead, I try to look as sad as I can, mirroring Keisha. In seconds, she's managed to melt away the tension and make them underestimate us. I know it's a good thing, but the pit of my stomach still boils at Marcy's sympathy.

"We've been doing okay," Keisha says through teary eyes and a brave smile. "As long as we stick to the river, the carriers aren't a problem. We only leave the river to boil water, sleep, and look through empty houses for supplies."

"Sounds like us," Marcy says, placing her hand on her chest and smiling her most sympathetic smile at Keisha.

"The river has delivered us from many evils," Suzanne says as she touches an oval pendant hanging from a gold chain around her neck. I'd recognize it anywhere. I saw dozens of them during my time in the Catholic group home. The pendant definitely has some kind of saint stamped onto it. I work hard not to roll my eyes and stare at my boots instead, hoping I look sad.

"Do you think there are many carriers in the area? It's been a while since we've seen them," Keisha asks.

"Oh, we've seen them. In the beginning, you'd just see one or two at a time, but now"—Steven shakes his head as he pauses—"now you'd be lucky to find a nice, neat group of five. They're flocking together. Every day it's getting worse," he finishes.

"Flocking together? What do you mean?" I ask, rejoining the conversation.

"I'm sure you've figured out by now it's loud noises that wake them up?" I nod, and he continues. "So then you know once they're up and walking around, they follow sound and movement. They hear one of their own screaming and come running. Those hear another group screaming, then run to join them, and it keeps going and going until you've got a group of twenty, fifty, or a hundred. After that there isn't a single one of us who stands a chance. Only Jesus himself could save you with the way those things move."

A chill sweeps up my spine.

"You've seen a hundred carriers at once?" I ask in awe.

"The most I've seen is thirty or so. But I've seen the way they buddy up. Imagine Chicago or New York. A flock of a hundred wouldn't take more than a few minutes to gather. We're right where we need to be if we're going to survive this."

Silence sweeps over the group as we all take in Steven's words. We stare at the river until Grady's cheery voice pipes in just over my shoulder. "Fire's alive! Fish should be ready in a bit. Hope you girls are hungry!"

My stomach aches at the thought of protein, and we both smile at him gratefully. While we've been talking, Grady has built a roaring fire. He reaches into a bucket of water filled with live fish, then pulls a short, sharp knife from his belt. I watch, focused on his setup and strategy. We've only caught a few small fish, but figuring out how to make them edible has been tough. They're slimy, scaly, and bony and don't have much meat on them. I decide to take advantage of the opportunity.

"Can you teach me how to do that?" I ask Grady.

He eyes me skeptically, then says, "It ain't pretty, kid. But yeah, I'll show you."

"We can share a jar of green beans," Keisha offers to Marcy, hopping to her feet to pull one of the precious jars we stole from the farmer from our stash in the canoe. "It's our last one, but this feels like a good time to use it."

Everyone's eyes light up at the sight of the jar. Just like that, we've earned their trust.

The next hour passes quickly. Grady is an excellent teacher and walks me through each step of cleaning a fish. It's messy, but way more efficient than the way I was doing it. I pick his brain for tips on catching bigger fish. He tells me the big ones stay toward the bottom of the river and teaches me to use smaller fish as bait and line anchors to sink my hook deeper. The information is like gold.

While I'm learning from Grady, Keisha chats by the fire with Marcy and Suzanne while Steven gathers more firewood behind us. I try to catch bits and pieces of their conversation, but I'm having a hard time hearing them. I can tell their conversation is serious, though. They're hunched over a map with creased brows, pointing to different areas. I hope she's learning as much as I am.

When we finally have twelve neatly sliced fish fillets, Grady lays them on a wire mesh grill and carefully places it over the fire.

"These won't take but a few minutes to cook. You flip 'em once, then they're ready to eat."

"Thanks, Grady. This was really helpful," I say.

"My pleasure, kid," he says with a gentle punch to my shoulder.

I bristle at the word *"kid"* but try not to hold it against him. He reminds me a lot of Nurse Patrick. A little patronizing, but he doesn't seem like a bad guy.

"Can you show me how you keep your knife so sharp?" I ask.

He smiles at me with a look of pride. "It'd be my pleasure."

While I tune up my machete, the fish on the fire start to smell amazing. Keisha puts our jar of green beans into a pot and scoots it into the fire to heat, and soon we have a pretty decent meal.

"Where did you find the green beans, girls?" Marcy asks us as she turns the empty jar over in her hands.

"An empty farmhouse a few miles back. Looks like someone was keeping a garden and had been canning things for years," Keisha says.

Marcy glances at Steven. It's quick, but some knowing glance just passed between them. A prickle of warning flashes in the back of my mind. What was that about?

"Let's eat!" says Grady, interrupting the moment and pulling the wire grill from the fire with a pair of oven gloves. He seems completely oblivious to the exchange between Steven and Marcy.

"Let us pray," Suzanne says, launching into a long-winded prayer.

Everyone bows their head and closes their eyes. I look up and meet eyes with Keisha, glance over at Steven and Marcy, then raise my eyebrows. Keisha knows exactly what I'm trying to ask. She nods once, confirming she saw the exchange too.

Finally, Suzanne finishes her prayer. We divide the food evenly and eat in silence. By the time we finish, there's almost nothing left of the sun, and the mosquitoes have started biting yet again. I wonder how much more my skin can take, but there's nothing I can do about it.

"Guess we'd better turn in," Grady says, slapping his knee.

"Hey now. Dishes? You boys promised," Marcy says with a smirk and a wagging finger.

Grady mimes being stabbed in the heart and falls to his side but smiles and reaches for my empty plate. Steven follows his lead, and the men carry the dishes down to the river to be cleaned, leaving us four women alone at the fire.

"The world ended, and we still argue over the dishes," Marcy says, shaking her head.

Silence hangs in the air. That look between Marcy and Steven has been gnawing at me. Whatever it meant, the mood hasn't been the same since. Sensing the tension, Keisha jumps in again to defuse it.

"Thanks again for the hospitality. It's been so nice talking with you all. I think we can both say we learned a lot. Right, Quinn?" Keisha says with a smile.

"Absolutely!" I say with a little too much enthusiasm. I catch myself though, and dim my smile to show fewer teeth, but Marcy has already taken a subconscious step backward. Dammit. All this time alone with Keisha has made me a little too comfortable, and I'm out of practice.

"Where did you say that farm was? The one with the green beans?" Marcy asks, shifting her eyes like it hardly matters. But I can tell there's something deeper to her question.

"Oh, I'd say about a week behind us, right, Quinn? Just before that big green bridge up north? The place was abandoned, so we helped ourselves."

She should have lied.

Part of why Keisha is so believable is because she weaves lies together with the truth. Her honesty is usually so thick that most people can't find the lie. It almost always works. Almost.

"Funny, we made that pit stop too. Four days ago. We met the man living there and he told us an awful story, didn't he, Suzanne?" Marcy says with a haughty look that starts my stomach simmering.

"Oh yes, that poor man fought the devil! A swarm of carriers flocked to his house after a terrible fire broke out. Attracted every carrier in the area! Such an awful thing. He was saved, though. Survived by the grace of God, no doubt!" Suzanne says with reverence, completely oblivious to the fact that Marcy is grilling us with a purpose.

"Indeed," Marcy says. "Say, Suzanne, do you remember how he said that fire started?" Marcy asks, staring me down in a challenge.

"Oh, he had quite a story. The way he tells it, two strangers came and set his chicken coop on fire and tried to kill him and take his belongings. He almost didn't trust us after going through all that, but it just so happened Grady's daddy went to high school with him! Talk about a small world!" Suzanne says, still not catching on to Marcy's game. My blood is boiling now. She caught us and she knows it. She's watching us squirm.

"Two strangers. Hmm," Marcy says, never taking her eyes off us. "You know, I seem to remember—"

Before she can finish, I pull my newly sharpened machete from my belt and swing it upward toward her throat. A thin red line appears under her chin; then a torrent of blood pours to the ground. A soft gurgle escapes her lips, and she falls to her knees with saucer-sized eyes. The fire in my belly is replaced by a warm, satisfied glow. I allow myself to smile.

My eyes flash toward Keisha. A deep disappointment pulls at her expression. Surely she agrees it had to be done. Marcy knew. I had to do it. But there's no time to try to justify it.

Suzanne screams, clutching her medallion. Behind me dishes clatter, and Steven or Grady shouts behind us asking what happened. I'm not sure who, because I can't turn around. I have to shut Suzanne up. She's cowering on her knees, her necklace in both hands, muttering a prayer between screams.

I swing my machete and make contact with her neck. She doesn't fight, doesn't even try to escape. Pathetic. How did she even survive this long? When she tumbles sideways, I spin around toward Steven and Grady.

Steven falls to his knees at Marcy's side, confused, not even registering yet that the real danger is me.

Behind Steven, Grady stumbles toward the chaos. I can't take them both at the same time. Dammit. I didn't have time to think this through. My heart pounds as I look for a plan of attack, trying to decide who to swing at first. Steven is distracted by Marcy, and Grady is still a few steps away. And I need to protect Keisha. My head swims. I shuffle my feet to move toward Steven, then change my mind and turn my body toward Grady, but Keisha's panicked voice pulls me up short.

"Help! Help me, please! She's gone crazy!" Keisha cries out, running away from me.

Her words stop me cold, and my stomach sinks as betrayal rips my skin into flames, but Grady's focused on her now, giving me the window I need.

Steven watches Keisha too, trying to make sense of her accusation. I swing at him before he sees me coming. He touches his throat, looking at the wet red stain on his fingertips with disbelief. He pulls his shirt up, trying to stanch the bleeding, but in seconds it's soaked through and he's looking pale. He falls to the side, on top of Marcy.

"Grady, do something!" Keisha shouts, ducking behind him. Doubt pulls at me. She has to be acting. *Please* be acting.

Grady pulls out his wicked-looking knife and pushes Keisha behind him. It's the knife he used as he taught me how to sharpen mine. I know exactly how sharp that knife is. I square up, taking my machete in both hands. How the hell am I going to fight a grown man? I start to wonder if I'm in over my head.

Grady stands in front of Keisha protectively, and my anger flares again, hotter than ever. *Please be acting.* I take a step toward Grady.

"Now listen, sweetheart, you can take whatever you want. You don't have to kill us. Just take what you want and go," Grady says, holding his hands in the air in surrender. Slowly, he puts his knife on the ground, then takes a step back, giving up the only weapon he had. Pathetic. He's not even going to fight me.

A smirk grows on my lips. His eyes search mine, and in that moment, he realizes his mistake. As if he's seeing me for the first time, true, animalistic terror distorts his expression.

From behind Grady, Keisha's eyes lock onto mine. It's just a flash of an expression. Only one fraction of a second, but it's enough. For just a moment, I see her mask slip. Panic and fear are written all over her face, and that's when I know. She wasn't acting.

Memories of the last several weeks flash before my eyes, playing in my mind like a movie. A hundred tiny doubts and gut feelings ignored. A thousand red flags overlooked. I trusted her, and she's been using me, manipulating me. Every brush of her hand, every warm smile, that fucking kiss. She wanted my protection, not me. She thought my infatuation with her would keep her alive.

I knew her past. I watched her do this to the men at the gas station and to Ramsey. Why couldn't I see it when it was happening to me? How could I have been such an idiot?

The puzzle pieces click into place. I can see it now. Dammit, she's so good at this. After she tried and failed to align herself with Ramsey, she was like a new person. She became exactly who I needed her to be. A plotting, calculating, cold-hearted villain ready to take over the farm. I forgot about the indiscretion with Ramsey the second she suggested we go to the farm. She's brilliant. And now it's game over.

I wait with my machete aimed at Grady's chest. Keisha's expression steels, and I watch as she effortlessly slips back into character. She whimpers softly behind Grady.

"Stay behind me, sweetheart. I've got—"

He doesn't get to finish his sentence. He crashes to his knees, then tips forward, facedown. The hilt of Keisha's hunting knife glistens with dark red blood, wedged into the base of his skull.

Behind him, Keisha heaves, and her dinner pools at her feet.

CHAPTER 31

"Oh my god." I can't think of anything else to say. I'm shocked. Relief swells in my chest, and I want to run to Keisha, wrap my arms around her, and squeeze her as hard as I can, but she doesn't look up at me. Instead, she wipes her mouth, steps over the sick at her feet, and then walks toward the river and heaves again. My senses come back to me. I force myself not to ignore it this time—force myself to trust what I saw. As much as I want to believe she was going to kill Grady all along, I know the truth.

I follow her without a word. I study her face as she stares into the water. While I stand dumbly searching for the right thing to say, she breaks the silence.

"We need to move. Suzanne's screams probably have a dozen carriers headed our way now," she says, emotionless.

"Right. Okay." I don't know what to do or say, but there's no time for talking. I give her an easy assignment. "Start moving all our stuff from our canoe into their rowboat, and I'll go through their supplies."

Mechanically, she follows my instructions, but I can't help but look over my shoulder as I tear through their campsite, searching for anything valuable. What should be a moment of excitement just feels sour. We just took down four people. *Four!* We get to keep everything they have, including their rowboat. And the best part is, we did it together. This is how the situation with the farmer should have gone. I should feel satisfied. Powerful. Limitless. But I just feel paranoid.

Wait. The farmer. Thinking of him gives me a flash of realization. If they met him four days ago, he must have survived the bridge and made it back to the farm. That old man is like a cockroach. I shake my head in frustration. He almost got us killed yet again.

Behind me, Keisha dumps an armload of our gear into the rowboat while I collect their backpacks and toss them inside. I ransack their tent and roll up their sleeping bags tightly, then set to work trying to disassemble the tent. Its complicated rods and straps are immediately frustrating. The glow of the fire gives us enough light to see our surroundings, but not enough to actually see what I'm doing.

I've just taken down the first panel of the tent when I hear a flock of birds take flight from the nearby trees. Their wings beating the air in the night sky gives me chills, and I know our good luck has run out.

"Leave it. Let's go," Keisha whispers to me.

The first shriek fills the air, and several more follow. The sound seems to bounce around as if coming from multiple directions. I toss the sleeping bags into the rowboat and run back to the bodies.

"What are you doing? We have to go!"

"Push the boat in the water. We need their knives," I whisper back.

I reach Grady's body first. I pull Keisha's knife from the back of his skull, then roll his body over, finding his knife just under his hips. I run for Steven's body next but hear a twig snap a few feet away. They're here.

I hate leaving Steven's knife behind, but I don't have a choice. What's left of the fire shows the campsite filling with carriers. Fast. I take a few steps backward on instinct. The smell is overwhelming, and I have to force myself to breathe through my mouth, though I swear I can taste the rotting bodies when I do.

I turn on my heel and run toward the river, splashing through the shallow water to meet Keisha in the boat. I climb over the edge and practically fall onto the disorganized pile of stuff.

"Let's go! They're right behind us," I say, out of breath, waiting for the boat to move.

"How do these paddles work?" Keisha asks with a note of panic in her voice. "They're fixed to the sides. They're barely moving us!"

Behind us, the sound of water splashing lets me know we're out of time.

"Switch places with me. And take this," I say, handing Grady's knife to Keisha, keeping my eye on her in case she does anything stupid with it.

I grab both paddles and try to mimic what I've seen on TV. The first stroke of the paddles takes us backward. Fuck.

We run right into the first carrier. Keisha expertly stabs it through the eye socket, and it splashes lifelessly into the water.

"Figure it out, Quinn! There are too many!"

I flip myself around in the boat, my back facing our intended direction, and row again. This time, we move forward. I pull the oars again. Then again, finding a rhythm and dipping deeper into the water each time.

"Holy shit," Keisha says under her breath as she looks behind us.

The river and campsite fill with body after body. A few of the carriers stumble through the remains of the fire, lighting up the darkness with their burning clothes. They follow the sound of my oars splashing ineptly into the water and throw themselves into the river, trying to reach our boat. Lucky for us, the current is slow and the river is deep. They sink below the waterline before they have the chance to reach us. I shiver and pull the oars harder until my muscles burn.

"That was too close," Keisha whispers.

I pull the oars again, a wide smile spreads across my face, and I let out a little laugh.

"What on earth could be funny right now, Quinn?" Keisha says sternly.

"Look how fast this thing is. Look how much stuff is in this boat right now. We could both lie down and sleep in this thing and still have room to roll over. We just hit the jackpot, and there's nobody coming after us!"

"Nobody?" she repeats, clearly still annoyed, swinging her arm behind us toward the herd of carriers that nearly killed us.

"Nobody alive." I shrug. "Why are you so upset? We won," I say, challenging her, wondering if she'll finally own up to the game she's been playing.

"I killed that guy. Grady. After he was so nice to us," Keisha says, looking like she's holding back tears. "I wish we could have just taken everything while they slept."

Jesus, she's lying so smoothly, covering her tracks, making me doubt the look I know I saw. I let her lie and play along.

"They would have come after us. Leaving the farmer alive has come back to haunt us twice now."

"How the hell did they know about the farmer anyway? How could they have been ahead of us on the river today but two days behind us when we left the farm? How is that possible?"

"This rowboat is twice as fast as our canoe. Imagine how fast it would be with two men rowing it. They must have passed us while we were sleeping."

In the moonlight, Keisha's face is still scrunched up. She must still be thinking about killing Grady. I row a few strokes in silence. Keisha sighs, then speaks. "You're right. I just don't like doing it."

"I know you don't. But today, you knew when it was time to get your hands dirty. We can keep doing it that way. I'll do all the heavy lifting if you can just watch my back and tie up the loose ends. I can protect you," I say, hoping it reassures her that nothing has changed. I'm not ready for her to know that I know her game. Besides, maybe tonight will make her realize we're the same. We belong together. I scold myself as soon as the thought crosses my mind. Jesus, she's got me in a chokehold.

"You make it sound so simple. Like they aren't people," Keisha says, averting her eyes.

"It *is* simple. If they're not us, they don't matter. If leaving them alive might come back to haunt us, they don't matter. If their lives don't make ours easier? They. Don't. Matter."

Keisha sighs again, then expertly changes the subject. "I learned a few things while you were getting cooking lessons." She raises one eyebrow, and I instantly know it's something good.

"Spill."

"St. Louis," she says, as if it's supposed to mean something to me. I roll my eyes. I know this trick. She's trying to get me curious so I'll get excited and go along with whatever she's about to propose.

"What about St. Louis?" I say, willing to take the bait.

"That's where they were headed. It's only about sixty miles from where we are now."

"Why were they going to a big city? That's the last place anybody should be headed these days."

"Exactly! That's what I said when they told me their plans, but they knew something we didn't." She pauses dramatically.

"What did they know?" I say with a sigh, wishing she'd just get on with it instead of making me ask.

"I'm so glad you asked," she says with a smirk, knowing she's driving me nuts. "There was a ham radio at that shelter Suzanne and Grady were staying at, and they were in contact with some people, even after the power went out. I guess they had it hooked up to a car battery. Anyway, they were talking to a group in St. Louis. Sounds like they rallied what was left of the city to build an enormous wall around over a dozen city blocks and walled in part of the river. They have protection, fresh water, and all the fish you can eat. Sounds pretty tempting, right?"

She's building herself another escape route. This time I see it clearly. I ignore the sinking disappointment and continue my argument.

"Okay, but St. Louis is a pretty decent-sized city. It's got to be full of carriers. And if they have a nice setup like that, it would make St. Louis a target for gangs and assholes. There's nothing there for us."

"That's what I thought. Until they told me about their rover squads."

"What the hell is a rover squad?"

"You're going to love this. The way Suzanne described it,

it's a group of mercenaries wearing riot gear who just roam the surrounding area looking for carriers *and* people to take out. It sounded like the squads were pretty big. Suzanne said they've got the carrier population under control."

I see exactly where she's going with this. I have to admit, if there were a place for me in society in the apocalypse, that would be it. On a rover squad. They probably have beds and decent meals too. Now that I think of it, St. Louis weather wouldn't be too bad either. Nothing too extreme in either winter or summer. I guess if I had to pick a place to be long-term, St. Louis wouldn't be too bad. She's so persuasive.

"Keisha, a lot can happen in a few weeks. The entire city could fall by the time we get there."

"It could," she says with a nod. "But what if it hasn't?"

"If that's how you feel, I guess it doesn't hurt to go check it out. All right. Let's go to St. Louis. But the second things get weird, we're leaving. Together. Okay?"

"Together."

Keisha holds out her hand, palm up. I place my hand over hers and intertwine our fingers, but the electricity is gone, and the promise she just made rings hollow. She's plotting again. Escaping with Ramsey failed. Joining up with Grady and Steven fell flat. Now she wants me to get her to St. Louis. It's fine. Two can play this game.

CHAPTER 32

The days go by slowly, but we move at nearly double the speed once we both get the hang of rowing. The rowboat's not only faster than the canoe, but it also gives us plenty of space for our new gear and for sleeping. That's not to say it's easy. My muscles still ache at the end of every day, and sleeping in the boat isn't exactly comfortable. It's better than sleeping with one eye open on the shore, though. The farther south we go, the more often we hear the screeches of carriers echoing off the river. Who knows how far away they are or who they're chasing? I'm not willing to give up the protection of the river to find out.

At the end of every day before the sun sets, we check the map trying to guess where we are, but most days, it's impossible. There are no clear landmarks, and one mile of river looks pretty identical to the next. All we know is we're still in that long stretch of river between the middle of nowhere and St. Louis. Today, though, the river takes a distinctive sharp turn and nearly doubles in width. We stay close to the shallow edge, and soon we start to see more and more of what used to be populated areas. A highway traces along the left side of the river, and that's when I realize this must be the point where the Illinois River meets the Mississippi River. We're getting very close to St. Louis now. Maybe just a few days away.

I pull out the pocket atlas, trace my finger along the blue line of the river, and immediately know where we are.

"Grafton!" I shout.

Keisha startles and nearly drops the oars mid-row. "Jesus, Quinn, you just about gave me a heart attack. What is it?"

"We made it to Grafton. Look, on the map right here. This has to be it, see?" I say, pointing to the restaurants and shops lining the highway.

Keisha studies the map carefully from under the brim of her straw hat, then looks up at the highway and the shops. "I think you're right. That means we're close now. Probably just a few days away from St. Louis," she says, taking the map to study it more closely. She squints at the tiny letters, a little wrinkle appearing between her eyes. "It looks like between here and St. Louis it'll be pretty populated. Especially once we get here," she says, pointing to a town called Alton. "That means no stopping until we get to St. Louis. How are we doing on supplies?" she asks.

"We could use more water. We're running pretty low on everything that isn't fish. We could use some more packaged food. Now that I think about it, it might give us an advantage to have something to trade once we get to the city. We should probably see what we can find," I say.

We pull the boat onto the shore near the highway and make our way toward the cluster of shops and restaurants. I'm optimistic, but those hopes are dashed the moment I see the first two carriers. They both lie awkwardly in the ditch next to the highway with deep wounds in their foreheads. Someone has been through here already, and I'm guessing this entire stretch of highway has been looted.

Every few yards, another carrier appears, stinking and open-mouthed, lying lifeless on the ground. I'm grateful that somebody saved us the trouble, but I start to worry that we might have to meet that somebody.

"Keisha," I whisper. "How long ago do you think this happened?" I say, gesturing to the corpses at our feet.

"Hard to say. The wounds look dry. I'd guess anywhere from a few hours to a few days," she says with a shrug. It's not a super helpful answer. But at least we know we're not on someone's heels. I keep my machete in my hand, and we walk toward the first shop.

The sign on the door of the closest building says GRAFTON FUDGE AND ICE CREAM SHOP. You can tell it's been a favorite tourist attraction for years. Its front porch welcomes customers to sit in old rocking chairs to enjoy their sweets and watch the river flow by. I can't help but feel a rush of excitement at the possibility of chocolate, and my steps get quicker. As we get closer, I can see the door was left wide open. Again, not a good sign, but I try to hold on to hope. We climb the three steps onto the creaking front porch and peer into the dark shop. Empty wrappers litter the entrance, and my heart sinks. I step through the doorway first, scanning the shop for danger, but nothing moves. The glass display cases are shattered, and what probably used to be ice cream is dried in a sticky paste on the old wood planks of the floor. Every shelf in the place is completely empty. I kick around the trash with my foot, looking for anything that might be left. Keisha looks as disappointed as I feel. We check behind the counter just to be sure, but it's no use. The whole place has been swept clean.

"A peanut butter cup would have made my whole year. Just one," she says, lazily kicking an empty box across the floor. "Or even cherry-flavored gummy bears. I think today might be my eighteenth birthday. Would have been nice."

"Today? Is it the end of July already?"

"I think so. I tried to keep track, but I might be a day or two off. Either way, if we were back at the Pegasus Center, I'd be packing my stuff."

"Happy birthday, Keisha," I say with a warm smile. "I know it's selfish, but I'm glad you're not packing your bags. It would have sucked to say goodbye," I say truthfully.

"I'm glad too. This is way better than getting a job and paying rent," she says with a grin. I can tell she means it.

"Sorry you didn't get a peanut butter cup on your birthday. I promise I'll catch you a big fish for dinner tonight."

"Oh, joy, more fish." She laughs.

"If this place was cleaned out, it's a safe bet that everything else on this strip is gone too," I say, kicking aside more trash.

"Think it's worth it to go farther into town and look through a few houses?"

"I'd rather keep moving. Who knows if whoever looted this place is still out there. Anyway, maybe we'll find something else farther downstream."

Keisha nods. Neither of us is desperate enough to go looking for trouble. Not yet. We turn to walk out of the shop, but something on the floor catches my eye. A cellophane-wrapped lollipop swirled in shades of red and pink. Cherry. I reach down to pick it up, and my smile must be a mile wide. A laugh bubbles in my chest.

"What is it?" Keisha asks.

"Happy birthday," I say, handing over the lollipop with a little curtsey.

Keisha's smile matches mine as she reaches for the sweet, and she does that little hop, like she can't contain her happiness. It's my favorite version of Keisha. The one that does little hops.

"It's even cherry! Thanks, Quinn." She tears off the cellophane wrapper, then uses her teeth to bite off a big chunk of cherry-swirled sugar. She takes the broken piece from her mouth and takes a step toward me. "Open your mouth," she says with a wry smile. My jaw drops dumbly, and she slides the broken piece over my tongue, letting her fingertips linger on my bottom lip. After days of fish and jarred vegetables, the taste is otherworldly.

My eyes close, and I feel dizzy with the sugar rush, so I'm completely unprepared for the feeling of Keisha's lips on mine. "Muah!" she says, with an exaggerated kiss, leaving a sticky feeling on my mouth.

I blush a thousand shades of red.

"Ugh. You're impossible," I grumble, wiping my mouth. I remind myself it's just an act. She's just doing this to make sure I'll do anything to protect her. But even the truth can't dull the smile that takes over my face, and I hate myself for it.

Keisha laughs, puts the rest of the lollipop in her mouth, grabs my hand, and intertwines her fingers with mine. Together, we walk out of the shop back toward the boat. The weight of her hand in mine brings on a million feelings. I never want her to let go of me. I never want the taste of cherry sugar to leave my lips. I want this moment to be real, but it fades just as quickly as the fake cherry flavor.

A carrier's screech echoes somewhere far behind us, interrupting my thoughts. I look over my shoulder instinctively, but I already know the carrier is too far away to matter. Still, the tiny hairs on my arms stand up, and we walk a little faster.

We climb back into the boat, and I volunteer to keep rowing. She knew I would.

Now that the two rivers have merged, it's twice as wide. I

could easily stick to the middle of the river, and it would probably be safer, but I stay close to the river's edge, keeping an eye out for any looting opportunities. The scenery is like something out of a storybook.

Tiny buildings line the riverfront, while little houses dot the hills that rise up to surround the river. Masses of trees paint everything else a deep green. Soon, the little buildings along the river are farther and farther apart, letting me know we're almost past Grafton. Just when I think we've left the town behind, I look up into the hills and see something I don't immediately recognize. Behind a chain link fence, huge colorful tubes snake their way through the hills. A wide parking lot sits nearly empty next to a large building. I think I see a big swimming pool farther back into the hills.

"Is that a water park?" I ask, squinting.

"It has to be. Look at the size of those water slides!" She beams.

"I've never been to a water park. I've only seen them on TV. Have you?"

"Only once, with a group home a few years ago. It was amazing! Oh, I wish we could go!"

"It looks like someone beat us to it. See the sign?" I say, pointing toward the edge of the park.

A message has been painted over the original sign, leaving the name of the park a mystery. In thick black letters, the new sign reads SAFETY. ALL SURVIVORS WELCOME. As we inch closer, I start to see movement behind the chain link fence.

"There are people in there. I bet that's who cleared out the shops along the riverfront," Keisha says as I take my binoculars from my backpack, hoping to see more. I adjust the lenses until my vision is clear. As the fuzzy edges of the scenery come into focus, my heartbeat picks up and my hands start to sweat. Memories of the barge passing the boatel come back into my mind. Those aren't people, and that isn't a shelter.

"It's been taken," I say, passing the binoculars to Keisha and picking up the oars.

I row quicker, even though I know the carriers can't get to us. Seeing so many of them packed together like that reminds me of what Steven told us about the herds that have been accumulating. If that many come at you at once, you're finished.

"Wow. All that food. All those supplies. Wasted," Keisha says, shaking her head. "I bet they have dozens of peanut butter cups."

"I'm not going in there to find out. How many carriers do you think there are?" I ask.

"If I had to guess, I'd say two hundred. Maybe three?"

"I wonder how long it took for that place to fall. Makes you wonder if any shelter could actually be safe. I mean, is St. Louis even going to be standing when we get there?" I say, wishing she'd change her mind and agree to row past St. Louis and keep moving south.

"There's really no sense wondering about it. We'll know when we know," Keisha says.

My insides twist. I've always hated wondering. I've always needed control. For now, I'm comforted by the fact that I have the upper hand. She still needs me to keep her safe out here. I row until the water park disappears.

CHAPTER 33

Another night passes as we take turns rowing toward St. Louis. When the sun rises, Keisha wakes me up with a soft whisper and a hard shove to my ribs. I grumble, still exhausted and feeling like I was robbed of at least a couple of hours of rest.

"There's no way it's eight already," I complain, still half-asleep and blurry-eyed.

"It's not. Look," she says, handing me the binoculars and pointing forward.

I lean up on my elbows and sigh, annoyed. I blink several times, trying to bring the world into focus, then lift the binoculars to see what was so important to Keisha that she'd sacrifice my sleep. Then I see it. Ahead of us, a boat sits idle in the middle of the river. Calling it a boat is really an understatement. This is a ship. And it's huge. Every inch is painted with blocks of bright colors, and tall letters fan out from the top deck of the ship. It looks like the letters are designed to light up, but the bulbs are dark.

"A casino? On a boat?" I ask, lowering the binoculars. "Weird, right? It's just sitting in the middle of the river too. It must be anchored there. The current is strong enough to sweep it away, but it hasn't moved."

I lift the binoculars again and scan every inch of the ship looking for danger.

"I don't see any carriers or people. Did you?" I ask.

"No, nothing. I think we should check it out. Casinos have food, right? This could be our lucky break. Maybe no one's searched it yet."

"Or maybe people are hiding on board, and we're about to meet a bunch of casino pirates," I say.

"Casino pirates? Really, Quinn?" She chuckles.

"The dead are walking the earth, Keisha. At this point, nothing would shock me."

"Okay, point made. But I have a good feeling about this place. Let's just take a quick look."

"Fine," I say with an exaggerated sigh, but I can't help but smile. I'm excited too. If we're right, this ship could be a gold mine.

"Yes! Okay, I'll keep rowing. You watch through the binoculars for anything suspicious. There's got to be a ladder on the side of the ship somewhere, like with the barge. We could use it to climb up and look around. Let me know when you find it," Keisha says with more energy than I've seen since the night we snuck out of the Pegasus Center. It's refreshing, and it makes my heart swell. Keisha has always been one of the most joyful and adventurous people I've ever met, and seeing her like this again makes me feel… There's really only one word for it. I look up at Keisha. Her brown eyes are lit from within. Her hair is wild from the river breeze, but it frames her soft face perfectly. Her strong shoulders row us forward, and her smile makes the pit of my stomach feel like it's bouncing.

I love her, and I hate her for it. I respect the game she's played so well, and I also resent her for making me part of it. I wish she could see it. She's just like me. We both manipulate; we both love the rush of power. We both have to hide who we are. We're the same. Why does she keep trying to run from it when we're so perfectly matched? If she could just accept who we are, we could be untouchable out here.

"What's with your face right now?" Keisha asks, giggling as she rows.

"My face?" I try to rearrange my expression to something neutral.

"I've never seen you look so…happy? Are you actually happy right now?"

I feel caught. The blood rushing to my cheeks is making things worse.

"I'm just excited to see what's in there," I say, pointing to the ship, trying to deflect her curiosity.

She looks into my eyes and smiles. With the Grady incident

now several days behind us, for a second, I could swear she's changed her mind about me. Maybe.

I awkwardly shift my attention back to the floating casino. Silence fills the space between us, and raw hope has me in a chokehold. Hope for our survival. Hope that this ship gives us what we need. Hope that she feels the same way I do.

We're so close to the ship now that I don't even need the binoculars to spot the ladder reaching up the side of the boat.

"There. On the right side, toward the end. We can tie the boat to that ladder and climb up," I say, pointing at our target.

Keisha's brow creases with determination, but the joy on her face still shines through. She rows with purpose and expertly steers us toward the ladder while I keep an eye on the boat's deck above, watching for any movement.

When we reach the ladder, Keisha tosses me the rope, but I hesitate. We need to be sure we're not climbing into a pit of carriers. I look around the boat and find a glass jar. It used to be full of vegetables from the farmer's garden, but now it's just holding clean water. I open the jar, chug what's left, then aim toward the boat's lower deck. Keisha understands what I'm doing and gives me a nod, then crosses her fingers for good luck.

I hurl the empty jar upward, and it shatters on the deck with a loud clatter, breaking upon impact. We wait, frozen in silence, listening for the screech of a carrier or the footsteps of a protective inhabitant. After several tense seconds, we smile at each other. It sounds like we're in the clear.

I tie up the rowboat and grip the ladder, keeping my machete in one hand.

"Cover me," I say to Keisha waiting behind me. "Be ready to cut the rope and go if you need to. I'll give you the signal when it's clear."

She nods, gripping her knife, scanning the length of the boat for trouble. I climb up one step, then another. When I finally reach the top, I carefully peek over the ledge of the ship and into the lower deck. The shattered glass from the jar lies undisturbed next to a row of lounge chairs and empty bar glasses. A handful of coins and poker chips are scattered on the ground.

"Hello?" I say, hoping no one answers. "Hello?" A little louder this time. "Anyone here?" When no one responds, I give Keisha a nod, then climb over the ledge and onto the deck. I hold my machete tightly as she climbs up to join me, waiting for any threat to appear.

Once she's over the edge and by my side, I feel better instantly. I've always worried about her getting hurt, but I remind myself that she's shown over and over again that she can handle herself when things go sideways. She's as lethal as I am when she has to be.

"Let's take a lap around the deck. Once we clear the outside, we'll go into the casino and see what we can find," Keisha whispers.

I follow her lead. We step carefully, making our way around the perimeter of the boat, keeping our weapons ready. We check every inch of the lower deck, but all we find are slimy floorboards and empty lounge chairs. There's nothing dead, alive, or useful down here. On the far side of the boat, we reach a spiral staircase that leads to the upper deck. I point upward and Keisha nods.

I climb the spiral staircase, keeping my eyes focused upward, and it makes me dizzy. By the time we reach the upper deck I have to steady myself against the railing and my machete clanks loudly against the metal bars. I freeze, waiting for the screech of a carrier or the click of a gun. Seconds and heavy heartbeats pass; then I hear Keisha exhale below me. I think we're in the clear.

I step out onto the upper deck and my jaw drops. The upper deck is much smaller than the lower one and has far fewer places for trouble to hide, but it's clear immediately that we're not in danger here. Behind me, a bar is lined with empty stools and littered with half-empty bottles of liquor. Video slot machines sit dark in every corner, some of them knocked on their sides. Shattered glass covers the nearby dance floor and glitters in the sun. Puddles of dried blood let me know this ship wasn't immune to the chaos that unfolded in the rest of the world. Near the edge of the deck, a circle of bodies completes the scene. Six of them, each with one bullet to their forehead. A seventh body lies nearby, shot through the temple. It isn't hard to imagine what happened here. We're looking at a group suicide. Some people weren't meant for this world. At least these people knew it.

"Jesus. I guess we know who anchored the boat," Keisha says solemnly. "Why do you think they gave up?"

"I don't know, but I hope they did it before they finished off their food and supplies. We should check the bodies for weapons. That gun could come in handy, even if it's empty. The more we have to trade in St. Louis, the better," I say, walking toward the bodies.

I head toward the seventh body first. I check his pockets but find nothing. Then I pry the gun out of his dried-up hand. His joints crack with my effort.

Out of the corner of my eye, I see Keisha cringe as she watches. She has that look I hate. The one that's full of judgment, but too cautious to call me out. I ignore her. She'll be glad we did this later.

I don't know anything about guns. Only what I've seen in movies. I fumble around with it and finally find the magazine release. It's empty. I replace the magazine, turn a tiny lever that I'm pretty sure is the safety, and tuck it into my backpack, then look back at Keisha. All evidence of her earlier reaction is gone. She's smiling and warm again, just like before.

"Come on. Let's get this over with," I say. Hesitantly, she joins me to check over the remaining six bodies. We come up with a few wallets and a single Swiss Army knife. It isn't much, but so far this detour has been worth the effort for the gun alone. Nobody would dare use it out here in the wild, but if we end up in St. Louis, I bet a gun would be good as gold. I look back and notice that Keisha is eyeing the bar behind us.

"We should take as much liquor as we can," Keisha says. "For trading," she adds quickly when I raise an eyebrow.

"Good idea."

I grab a big empty designer bag from one of the women in the circle and head to the bar to stock up. We prioritize the unopened bottles and try to get a variety. I'm not really sure what would count as the good stuff. I'm obviously underage, and group homes are monitored too closely to get away with drinking. We definitely couldn't have gotten away with it at the Pegasus Center.

"Have you ever drank before?" I ask Keisha.

"Once."

"What was it like?"

"Awful. It tasted bad, plus we got caught and got in tons of trouble. And to top it off, I felt sick the entire next day. I don't get the appeal, but I'm sure we'll make somebody happy with all this," she says, patting the designer bag full of liquor. "I'm pretty sure alcohol disinfects wounds too. So it could come in handy for just about anyone," she adds.

"We did pretty good here. Should we even risk going inside the boat?" I ask, gesturing to the closed doors next to the bar.

"We still need food, and anything else we can trade. Let's drop the alcohol in the rowboat, then come back for a quick look. We can leave at the first sign of trouble. Deal?"

I nod, grab a few more bottles, then follow her back down the spiral staircase toward the rowboat. Keisha heads down the ladder, and I lower the bottles down to her. Over my shoulder I see a flock of birds land on the upper deck and imagine them pecking at the dried-up flesh of the bodies above us. Even I'm creeped out by that. I'm ready to get out of here, but Keisha's right. We need more.

Keisha climbs back up the ladder and smiles. "Ready to go in?"

I swing my machete in a fast circle and nod. "Of course," I say, even though my gut is still telling me to leave.

"Hey, how far away do you think we are from St. Louis?" Keisha asks, out of nowhere.

"I don't know. A day and a half if we don't stop?"

I watch Keisha carefully as her eyes harden, and I get an uneasy feeling. I'm getting emotional whiplash today, and it's exhausting.

"Good. Here," Keisha says, handing me a few empty grocery bags and two of the battery-powered lanterns we took from Grady's group. "Let's be fast then."

I tuck the grocery bags into my pockets hoping we can fill them quickly. The more time we spend on this boat, the more I feel like we shouldn't be here.

We decide to enter the casino through the lower deck first. We find the main entrance and peek through the glass doors. I use my sleeve to smudge away the layer of dust that's settled on the surface but still have trouble seeing what's inside.

"I can't see a thing," Keisha says, echoing my thoughts. "Let's see if we can draw anything out."

I pick up an empty wineglass from one of the outdoor patio tables, open the door just a crack, then toss the wineglass inside like a live grenade and brace for impact. It shatters loudly, but it's the only sound we hear. We're getting extremely lucky here. Too lucky. How could this entire ship really be safe?

I turn on my lantern, and Keisha does the same. I meet her eyes and place my hand on the door. When she mirrors me, I know she's ready. Together, we push the doors inward and walk into the dark casino.

The little rings of light from our lanterns don't give us much of a view. In the shadows, a hundred slot machines sit dark in tidy rows, leaving way too many places to hide. I inhale deeply and catch a very faint scent of rot.

I point to my nose and look at Keisha. She nods, letting me know she smells it too. I tell myself it could just be another dead body or a rotting meal and keep walking. Between the rows of slot machines, round tables carpeted in green felt are stacked with neat piles of playing cards. Each table is surrounded by an arc of empty chairs. It looks like the casino has closed for the night, not that there has been an apocalypse. Everything remains in place, undisturbed. Almost. Out of the corner of my eye I see a jagged piece of cardboard propped up on one of the card tables. I squint to read the messy black marker handwriting in the dark.

THIS WAY TERRY COME AND GET IT

I nudge Keisha, then point to the sign. She studies it and shrugs. Clearly she's just as confused as me, so we keep walking.

The farther in we go, the stronger the smell gets. I tell myself again that it could be nothing, but after everything we've been through, I've learned that the smell of a carrier is distinctly different from food rot. If you're close enough, it's acid in your nose and coats your lungs in a film of unshakable filth. Now I'm certain there is at least one carrier in this ship. The burn in my nose makes me sure of it.

I tighten the grip on my machete and step as gently as possible toward the back of the ship. In my other hand I push the lantern out in front of me, squinting to see what's ahead.

A glint of light nearly makes my heart stop, and Keisha inhales sharply behind me. I raise my machete, and the shine of metal and a haggard face appear several yards ahead. It takes a few erratic heartbeats, but soon, I realize I'm seeing myself in a mirror. The wild girl reflecting back at me makes me pause. I look older, harder. Muscles I've never had before stretch down my arms. My hair looks filthy, and my skin is a quilt of pink sunburn, peeling skin, dirt, and dark freckles.

I see Keisha staring back at herself too. I wonder if she's as shocked as I am. I've seen her every moment of every day, so I've seen the change happen gradually, but the change in her appearance must feel pretty stark to her fresh eyes. Her shoulders are broader from the strain of a million rows, and she's lost the soft curves she once had. Her hair no longer sits in neat, tidy braids but is pulled up into a messy puff that sits on top of her head like a crown. Her skin, which was once a light shade of soft brown, has grown darker with the sun and looks like velvet. My fingertips ache to reach out and touch her to ease the shock that has made her stare wide-eyed in the mirror.

"Couple of badasses, right?" I whisper with a smirk, trying to bring her back.

A soft puff of humorless laughter escapes her lips. She shifts her eyes back to me, gives me a forced smile, then nods ahead, letting me know she's ready to get moving. We creep farther into the darkness, anticipating what lies ahead four feet at a time in the dim lantern light.

When we finally reach the back wall, I start looking for a door that could lead to the kitchen.

Keisha pats my arm gently and points just as I see it. Two swinging doors, each with a circular window at the top, come into view out of the darkness. That has to be the kitchen. With every step toward the doors, my nose burns a little more, but I push forward, adjusting the grip on my machete.

I place my hand on the kitchen door, then glance back at Keisha. Her worried expression mirrors the feeling in the pit of my stomach. I shift my focus back to the kitchen and slowly push the swinging doors open.

The smell hits me first. I nearly jump backward, trying my best to avoid the acrid stench burning all the way to the back of my throat. When nothing lunges at us, I take a few steps forward, letting the door swing closed behind us. Where is that smell coming from? Our lantern light reflects off the shiny metal surfaces. Like the rest of the ship, the kitchen looks like it's just closed for the night. Everything is in its place, and the surfaces would be perfectly clean if it weren't for a fine layer of dust. Unfortunately, there's no food on the shelves. It must be in storage somewhere.

We keep walking, moving as slowly as we can to keep our footsteps quiet. A soft, but high-pitched squeak breaks the silence, and I hear tiny claws clicking across the floor. Against my own will, I let out a quiet "Yip!" and jump backward and into Keisha. A few feet in front of me, a rat skitters across the floor. I bite my lip and look back at Keisha apologetically as I strain to hear more movement, but thankfully we're met with quiet.

I release my breath and point ahead to let Keisha know I've collected myself and am ready to keep going. We step carefully toward the back of the kitchen, and soon we arrive at a corner leading to a wide, darkened hallway. The moment we turn the corner I'm hit with a wave of nausea that nearly knocks me over. The burn reaches my lungs, and I almost run, but I'm glued to the sight in front of us. Shock wins out over fear and disgust, and I can't help but stare.

I count them first. One, two, three, four, five, six, seven, eight. Eight carriers, each sitting quietly on its own dining room chair, blocking the entire hallway as well as the door to what I can only assume is the food storage room we've been looking for. In each carrier's lap is a hastily torn chunk of cardboard spelling out a message written in thick black marker.

GOOD LUCK TERRY YOU THIEVING PIECE OF SHIT

I take a step forward to get a closer look and notice that

each sleeping body is handcuffed to the next, just waiting for a loud noise to wake them up. I shine the light on the first set of handcuffs. Something is dangling from them but I can't quite tell what it is. I take another step forward, and Keisha grabs my hand. I squeeze her hand back, hoping she understands what it means. I'll be careful. I'll be quiet. I continue forward and lean toward the mystery object, holding my lantern out in front of me. Freaking jingle bells?

I squeeze Keisha's hand a little harder and take a few careful steps backward, pulling her toward the kitchen. We round the corner of the hallway and step a little quicker until we're finally out of the kitchen and back on the casino floor.

"What the hell was that?" I say breathlessly.

"Boobytraps set by the pirates of the zombie apocalypse," Keisha deadpans.

I can't help it. I start to laugh and have to slap my own hand over my mouth to muffle the sound. There is absolutely nothing funny about this, and yet the whole thing is pretty hilarious. It's also brilliant, and part of me wants to meet whoever did this. It's elaborate, it's spiteful, and it's going to make it almost impossible to get to the pantry. The puzzle itches at me and I feel overwhelmed with the need to solve it.

"Sorry," Keisha whispers, waving her hand as if to wipe away her joke. "Look, whoever did this might still be here. Or they may have gone back to the shore and they're coming back any second."

"Or they're one of the bodies on the upper deck," I suggest.

"Whoever did this isn't coming back. Who would willingly step foot on a boat with that monstrosity waiting for them."

Keisha sighs. "Either way, we need to decide whether it's worth it to fight off eight of those things to get to whatever is in that pantry."

"Did you see the bells on the handcuffs?" I ask her.

"Yeah. Do you think they would be loud enough to wake up the carriers?"

"Yes, I do. And if the bells aren't enough, the sound of a body hitting the floor definitely would. This isn't going to be easy, but I need to know what's behind that door. We'll need a pretty good plan though," I say, hoping she has one.

I can see the wheels turning in her mind. She traces the air with her pointer finger, drawing something in midair. Her brow crinkles in frustration and she sighs. "I need a pen. I can't visualize this well enough," she grumbles, scrubbing at her eyes.

"There's got to be one at the bar. Hold on," I say.

I jog as fast as I can in the dim lantern light and slide behind the bar. In a cup by the register, I find several pens and a stack of cocktail napkins and grab them. When I get back to Keisha, she's mumbling under her breath. I shove the pens and napkins into her hands and she takes them to a nearby table. I don't dare interrupt her, but I do look over her shoulder. A series of lines and circles spread across the napkins. When she's finished, there are eight circles and sixteen lines drawn in a careful pattern. Then she begins ripping up tiny shreds of napkin and covering some of the lines with the pieces. She removes the pieces and repositions them several times. Minutes pass. Just as I'm about to ask her what the hell she's doing, her head snaps up.

"There," she says, puffing out her chest.

"There what? What are you doing?" I ask, bordering on annoyed.

"There," she says, pointing at her napkin art, "is the most efficient way to take down the eight carriers." I look at it again, trying to decipher the pattern and make it make sense. She must see my blank stare. "I'll show you. Here are our first two kills. This one is mine. This one is yours," she says, pointing at the third carrier from the end on each side.

"Okay. Why those carriers in particular?" I ask, still confused.

"Because once they're dead, they'll weigh down the entire line and disable eight arms and two mouths all at once," she explains.

I look at her drawing with fresh eyes, and I see exactly what she's done.

"You're a genius! So then we kill these two next?" I say, pointing to the two carriers on the ends of the chain.

"Exactly. That's what I was thinking too. And because they're handcuffed, that leaves the next two without the use of their arms. They'll be weighed down by dead bodies on either side of them. After that we should tackle the ones in the middle. Then go back and kill the two that are left," she says, concentrating on her drawing.

"This is going to work," I say, feeling confident.

"It sounds simple, but it only works if we can do it quickly. If we miss a target or hesitate, this could get out of control fast," she says.

"Then we'll be accurate and quick. We need those supplies."

"And if the person who made this trap comes back?" she asks.

"I still think it's unlikely, but if they do, we'll handle them like we've handled everything else. We've got this," I say, trying to reassure her even though the thought of taking on eight carriers at once makes me want to run screaming. I take in a deep, confident breath. "Let's do this, then."

"Remember. Third from the end, last, middle, second from the end. If things get out of control, turn and run for the rowboat," Keisha says seriously.

I nod, letting her know I understand, then head back toward the hallway.

CHAPTER 34

The carriers sit perfectly still in their chairs, chained together, rigged to wake one another up at the slightest misstep.

We carefully set our lanterns down at the edge of the hall, giving us just enough light to see what we're doing. Keisha reaches out and takes my hand, gives it a squeeze, and locks eyes with me. My stomach does a dozen somersaults, but I squeeze back. We step in front of our assigned carriers, and I grip my machete with both hands.

"Go," Keisha breathes in the tiniest whisper.

I make my first move immediately, swinging downward and at an angle, cleanly taking my carrier's head off its shoulders. I don't stop to check if Keisha's first stab with her knife was successful. If it wasn't, she'll be depending on me to keep going as fast as I can.

The sound of jingle bells is deafening in the echoing hallway, and the thud of the carrier's head hitting the floor adds to the cacophony. Out of the corner of my eye I see a carrier to my right twitch. My heart thuds, and every instinct tells me to focus on the carrier that's waking up, but I stick to the plan. I move to the end of the line of carriers and sweep my machete across the neck of my second target. It takes two swings, but what's left of the carrier slumps in its seat. Two down, two to go.

My last two carriers are now fully awake, and the one in the middle lets out a grotesque screech that makes me desperate to drop my machete and cover my ears, but just like Keisha promised, their arms are weighed down by the heavy, useless carriers handcuffed to their sides. They can't reach for me. I step toward my third target and aim at its throat. Another screech causes me to flinch as I swing. I miss and my machete gets lodged in its shoulder bone.

"Shit," I mutter under my breath as I work the blade out of the bone. When it finally springs free, I stumble backward, nearly losing my footing. I take one breath to steady myself, then take another swing. The carrier goes down mid-scream. One more to go on my side.

I glance to my right to see how Keisha is doing. She's just finished off her second target and is heading toward her third. I'm one kill ahead of her, but she's holding her own. To my left, the final carrier screams from its chair, but it's rendered useless. With both arms pinned down, all it can do is lunge forward, snap its jaws, and scream to be fed. I'm exhausted, but the last swing is easy work. One clean swipe of my machete ends its screeching.

I turn toward Keisha just as she's standing in front of her final target. Its arms are pinned down too, but somehow it rises out of its chair. That's when I notice the size of this thing. Its arms are the size of legs, and its legs are the size of a torso, and it has to be at least six foot five. How did we miss this?

As it rises, the handcuffs dig into its rotten skin and muscle tissue, peeling flesh from bone. I can't help it. I gag. The giant's focus is locked on Keisha. That's when I notice she doesn't have her knife. In one hand is the hatchet I gave to her back in Naples; in her other, she's holding the severed head of one of the carriers I killed. I watch in horror as she brings the hatchet down on the carrier's left wrist. How could she have aimed so poorly? I stare dumbly, trying to imagine what she could possibly be doing. This wasn't on the napkin. This wasn't part of the plan.

The final carrier swings its stump at her as the remaining handcuff strains against the carrier's wrist, peeling rotting skin from bone. I start to worry that it might not hold. The line of dead carriers drags behind the massive monster in front of us as it reaches for Keisha.

With an eerie calmness, she waves the head in front of the carrier as if she's actually trying to get its attention. *What the hell is she doing?*

I grip my machete, ready to come to her rescue. I take the

first step, but Keisha's voice pulls me up short. "Quinn!" There's a coldness in her eyes I've never seen. She swings the head again, and I'm completely unprepared for what comes next.

"Catch," Keisha shouts. Before I can react, she tosses the severed head across the hall and into my chest. The enormous carrier follows the head, shifting his focus to me. My stomach sinks as its hand, stripped down to the bone, slips through the cuff.

No. No. This isn't happening.

The carrier barrels across the hallway, and I scramble backward until I'm trapped in the corner. I don't have enough room to swing my machete. I can't run. I don't think. I just drop my weapon and dive for its legs, putting my entire weight into knocking it off its feet. It's like running headfirst into a tree. I fall backward onto a broken chair, and something scrapes across my left calf, sending a sharp pain shooting up my leg.

Not like this. I can't die like this.

He reaches for me as I try to stand, pinning me against the wall, forcing my chin to the sky with his rotting stump.

Anything but this.

The air is pressed from my lungs, but I can't feel it. I only feel the burn of betrayal deep in my gut. Everything slows, and the last seconds of my life stretch out in front of me. I was expecting her to try to leave me behind in St. Louis. I was not expecting this.

Rage fills me, and I use it. I tuck my knee up and leverage every muscle in my left leg to push the carrier away, creating just enough space to breathe. I gasp for air and reach down to my belt for my knife. The one I took off Grady's body. A scream rips from my throat as I reach high on my tiptoes to shove the knife into the carrier's eye socket, barely out of reach of his snapping jaws.

I'm breathless as he falls at my feet. Then Keisha's wide eyes meet mine. She may be smart. She may have crafted a near perfect plan, but she wasn't counting on this.

She's as much of a liability as Ginger and January ever were; I just couldn't see it. Until now.

I stalk forward, leaning down to sweep my machete from the floor where I left it. She puts her hands up and walks backward. She begs for forgiveness. She tells me it was an accident. She tells me I need her. She tells me she loves me. Her words are just noise though. I barely hear them. I'm numb.

Her back hits the wall. A perfect tear slides down her face. Whether it's real or manufactured, I'll never know. I know better than to ask. I'll never get an honest answer, and besides, if I hesitate now, I'll lose my nerve.

"Quinn, I'm sorry. I was just so scared." There it is. There's the truth.

"I guess you were right to be."

I go for her heart. Aiming the sharp tip of my machete just below her clavicle, I press it as deep as I can and hold her there, caught on the tip of my blade.

She coughs. A tiny drop of blood drips down her chin and a sob shakes her shoulders. I look deep into her eyes and wait for her to take her last breath.

"I really did love you, Keisha."

"You shouldn't have," she whispers.

When she finally slumps to the floor, I pull my blade from her chest and my vision blurs.

I scrub my eyes, and I'm surprised when my hands come away wet. Tears. They feel completely foreign on my cheeks. I step away from the scene until my back hits the wall, and I let myself slide down to the floor. I shake and breathe in and out over and over again, letting the adrenaline drain from my body.

It takes several minutes, but soon, my head clears and my breathing evens out. I look down and see a small pool of blood collecting under my boot. I lift up the cuff of my pant leg over my calf to reveal a nasty cut. I barely remember how it happened. I pull a T-shirt out of my backpack, tear it into strips, and bandage the wound. It's good enough. Besides, it's time to get what we came for.

I step over the bodies, toward the door they were there to protect, and swing it open. It's full of everything we hoped for. I know I should feel relief or joy or excitement, but I don't feel much of anything.

Mechanically, I pull boxes of dried goods and cans off the seemingly endless shelves. I stuff the supplies into bags and carry them back and forth to the boat until it's so full that I don't have to think about the empty space in the seat across from mine.

In the boat, I grip the oars. It's time to go now. I take another deep breath and row, pouring every ounce of anger and grief into each pull. There was only one thing anchoring me to the way things used to be, and now she's gone. With each row, the weight of my sadness is transformed into the lightness of possibility.

KEEP READING FOR A SNEAK PEEK AT BOOK TWO IN THE DEAD WEIGHT SERIES, *IF WE SURVIVE WHAT SAVED US*.

CHAPTER 1

I give up on sleep. The sun will be up soon anyway, and the thick, sticky air makes it impossible to get comfortable in my sleeping bag. Besides, I'm not safe here. Even tucked into the thick brush along the river, it's hard to let your guard down on dry land. Especially now that I'm alone. Now that she's not here.

I need to get back on the river and move on.

I climb out of my sleeping bag as carefully as I can, but the moment I get to my feet, a sharp stab steals my breath. My calf. I was hoping it would be better today. I try to ignore the pain while I pack up my stuff, but it throbs, keeping time with my heartbeat. Goddammit.

The first hints of daylight rise behind the forest along the river, but it's still too dark to see clearly. I turn on one of my battery-powered lanterns and take a deep breath as I roll up the left leg of my cargo pants. Time to assess the damage.

The jagged gash has completely soaked through the scrap of T-shirt I tied around it yesterday. Right after it happened. Right after everything I thought I knew got flipped on its ass forever. I sigh and accept it. It's not going to stop bleeding on its own. I need to take care of this. And I have everything I need to get the job done, unfortunately.

I eye the tackle box with dread. It has plenty of hooks and fishing line. I don't want to do this myself. I wish…

No. Remember what she did.

Maybe this is what it'll always be like without her. Just moving through life, feeling like an open wound. Like someone climbed inside my skin, then tried to claw their way out. Left ruined and raw. I can't let myself think about it.

I pick the thinnest hook with the smallest barb, then dig through my supplies to find one of the bottles of liquor we stole from the casino yesterday. The cap twists off easily and I'm overwhelmed by the sharp smell. Wrinkling my nose, I tip the bottle, gulp, and nearly heave. The clear liquid burns my throat and makes my eyes water. This is a bad idea.

I take another drink.

After several deep breaths, I steel myself and pour a steady stream of liquor over my calf. It burns like hell, but I clench my jaw and let it hurt, telling myself the searing sting is a good sign. That's what our group therapists back at the Pegasus Center always said. Sometimes you have to let something hurt before it can heal. Another drink.

My fingers shake a little, but I manage to tie the fishing line to the end of the hook, then dip the whole thing into the bottle, hoping it kills any germs. My bravery is waning every second.

"Get it done," I say to myself through gritted teeth.

I dig the hook into my leg. My vision blurs and my stomach rolls. I force myself to breathe and pull the fishing line through my flesh. Another drink. The next stitch is easier. By the end of the third, I get into a rhythm and soon there's a jagged row of nine stitches and a half-empty bottle of vodka. The stitches are ugly. They'll scar. But maybe they'll stop the bleeding and keep out infection.

It's okay. It'll heal. I'll be fine.

Dizzy, I fumble through my backpack for a fresh strip of T-shirt and tie it around my stitches. Then I try to tend to my hair. It's a gnarled mess after weeks of open air, sweat, and filthy water. I wince as I work the knots free with my fingers, then part it down the middle and manage a short, sun-bleached ponytail that rests on the back of my neck.

See? It's fine. I don't need anyone. Everything is going to be fine.

A wave of exhaustion comes next. I hardly slept last night. But the sun is up now, and what else am I going to do? Sit on the shore and pout? I pack everything into my boat, push into the middle of the river, and start rowing.

Maybe it's the lull of the river and the birds chirping in the trees. Maybe it's the alcohol. But I can't help it when the memories of yesterday come rushing back.

I still can't believe I didn't see it coming. The most dangerous thing in these woods had been staring me in the face the whole time. A parasite. A con artist. A goddamn liar. Still, she was the partner you'd want at the end of the world. Endlessly creative and just as cutthroat as me, when she had to be. Plus, Keisha had a way of making you feel important. The only problem is she made everyone feel that way. It doesn't make you special. It didn't mean you were safe.

My heart thuds as my last memory of her flashes behind my eyes. The moment my machete pierced her chest. I can feel the bile rising in my throat. Before I can stop it, the burn of vodka creeps back up and I hurl into the water.

That's probably for the best. I rinse my mouth and chug as much water as I can hold, then nibble on a few crackers to settle my stomach.

ACKNOWLEDGMENTS

This book arrived in your hands through a series of wildly unlikely events and support from loved ones and strangers alike. Originally self-published, *If We Survive the Night* was written over the span of three years, mostly between the hours of 4:00 and 6:00 a.m., simply because the act of writing it was the most fun I'd ever had doing anything...ever.

To the readers who loved this book first, thank you for cheering me on. All your messages and reviews gave me the confidence to keep going. This book became an entire series because *you* kept asking for more. This series' transition to a traditional publisher meant that you had to wait longer than expected for book three. I appreciate your patience more than you know. To my new readers, thank you for taking a chance on a new author. I hope you'll stick with me. There's so much more to Quinn's story, and I can't wait for you to see the rest of her world unfold in books two and three.

When I told my mom, sister, and dad that I was writing a

zombie book, they didn't laugh or criticize. They just let me be me and started every conversation with "How's the book going?" Thank you for letting me be a little strange and loving me anyway.

Putting a novel out into the world for all to see is pretty scary. I wanted it to be perfect, and, unfortunately, I'm not a trained writer. Before this book existed, I had never written fiction before. Luckily, I had excellent editors who were excited about this story and took the time to teach me as they made suggestions. Lillian Boyd, my manuscript reviewer, was the first person to ever read this book. Without her encouragement, I may never have had the guts to let anyone else read it. Kay Daly took the reins next, providing line editing and teaching me about locked phrases and the power of using an active voice. Finally, Lisa Gilliam provided proofreading, making sure every comma and quotation mark was precisely placed. With all of my little heart, thank you, Lillian, Kay, and Lisa.

When the self-published version of this book hit the virtual shelves, I was in awe of the love it received. To *The Zombie Book Club* podcast, thank you for creating such an amazing community of people who love this stuff. Your support, friendship, and encouragement have meant the world to me. Thank you for sharing this book with our people. It changed everything. To the *Wicked Words* podcast, thank you for making this book one of your top three indie books of 2025 and telling your listeners about Quinn and the girls. To all of the incredible creators on BookTok and Bookstagram...holy smokes. I still can't comprehend all of the love and support you've given this book. The reviews, the recommendations, the likes, shares, and reposts... You are the reason this book got noticed, and I'll never stop being grateful. In particular, thank you, Kyla Grant. One little invitation to your book club changed the entire trajectory of my life. I don't know what I did to earn your unending support, but I sure am grateful for it. To Matt, thank you for stopping at my table that day.

To my editor, Gabbi Calabrese at Sourcebooks, thank you for seeing this book and believing in its potential. More importantly, thank you for believing in me as an author. Working with you and the Sourcebooks team has been a dream. I am beyond grateful for your willingness to hear my thoughts and collaborate with me. I feel so lucky to be part of the Sourcebooks family.

To my agents at Spencerhill Associates, Renee Runge and Ali Herring, thank you for being there to help me navigate one of the most exciting and important moments of my life. I am incredibly fortunate to have agents who are so communicative, reassuring, and fun to brainstorm with. I feel like I won the agent lottery...twice.

Most importantly, I want to thank my husband. Uli, you have been infinitely supportive and made sure I never felt like I was doing this alone. You have an endless supply of patience and positivity, and I'm so lucky to have had you beside me through every single moment of this. We did it.

ABOUT THE AUTHOR

Jo Salazar grew up in the river bottoms of west central Illinois. Today, she lives in Chicago with her husband, Uli, and their dog, Data. Her fascination with zombies started after she watched *Night of the Living Dead* at a friend's house as a little girl, then refused to sleep alone for weeks.